Zeke began walking. Directly ahead of him, he could make out the figure of a man approaching.

At first, he appeared like a mirage, a shifting, wavy, shimmering form, like heat rising off a hot surface..

"Good morning, Zeke," the man said, his feet planted firmly and squarely, his arms resting at his sides. "What is it that you want?"

To his complete surprise, Zeke answered the man quickly, not even realizing he had a question to ask.

"How do I destroy it?"

The words escaped like a sharp exhale. Zeke had no chance to retrieve them; he was shocked by the sound they made as he uttered them. He had no idea what "it" was. He had no idea what needed destroying.

"Very well," the man said, apparently unfazed by Zeke's response. "But you must follow me. There is an entity in your midst that desires to have you, Zeke."

"An entity?" Zeke asked, his voice sounding strained and awkward. "What entity? What do you mean?"

"Darkness," the man answered simply. "The entity is darkness, chaos, and fear. Moreover, it wants you, Zeke. It wants to destroy you and make you pay for killing its daughter. Trust no one, at least not yet." Then the man turned and began walking, his pace quick and even.

Praise for Brad Cameron's
The Serpent's Ship

I read the latest book in the Zeke Proper Chronicles: The
Serpent's Ship, at one sitting - I couldn't put it down! As a high
school librarian I read a lot of YA fiction and this fantasy has it
all: Adventure, mystery, and murder! You won't believe what is
happening this time in Alder Cove! 5 stars for The Serpent's
Ship!

- Ann Sindelar-Trahin, MS EdML
Beaverton School District Libraries Coordinator

An unforgettable adventure! Brad Cameron has included spine-
chilling action delivering bravery in the face of impossible odds,
enchantment, and shear satisfaction. I can't wait for Book
Three! I gotta see what happens next.

- Loni Thompson, MS. CCC-SLP
Speech Language Pathologist and Reading Coach

Praise for Brad Cameron's
Odin's Light

I finished it virtually overnight! Praise for Odin's Light, Book
One of the Zeke Proper Chronicles. As the mystery unfolds, we
are introduced to fabulous characters. My favorite: Taylre. She
is spunky, enthusiastic, and totally geeky. I immediately wanted
to reach my arms into the novel and give her a giant hug.

Moreover, the climax had me biting my lip in anticipation,
almost yelling at the characters to, "Hurry up!" The book is
addicting. I am excited for the sequel.

- Golda Lobello
High School English Teacher

Did you grow up on Nancy Drew and The Hardy Boys or (insert name of favorite kid detective here)? Then you gotta get a load of Zeke, Devon, and Taylre! The town of Alder Cove has some major supernatural secrets and these kids are out to solve the mystery! Little do they know how deep into the Norse pantheon those secrets delve. Look out Alder Cove! Here comes The Three Investigators for the next generation!

- Tonya Macalino
Author of Faces in the Water

More reviews for **Odin's Light** from Amazon readers:

I would have to say that Taylre is my favorite character in Brad Cameron's debut novel, Odin's Light. She's spunky with a lot of life and enthusiasm. Cameron's writing is very descriptive and easy to follow. He weaves a story that is both fun and exciting.

As a high school librarian, I read a lot of YA fiction and this fantasy has it all: adventure, mystery and murder! I can't wait for the sequel!

Cameron is a great storyteller and a master of description. He really brings all his characters to life and knows how to keep you wanting more. I can't wait for the next book.

Through a complex series of connections and realizations the reader is led on a grand, funny, and at times frightening adventure. As a teacher I am always looking for well-written, high interest stories that my students can make connections to.

Odin's Light is one of those great books that makes you feel as though you are taking part in the story, not just reading it. By the end of the first chapter, I was eagerly reading to see what adventure was in store for the young trio. It's a fantastic combination of adventure, mystery, and mythology. I can't wait for the next one!

The Zeke Proper Chronicles

Book One: Odin's Light

Book Two: The Serpent's Ship

don't miss
The Zeke Proper Chronicles: Book Three
The Gates of Asgard

coming Summer 2013.

Serpent's Ship

The Zeke Proper Chronicles: Book Two

WORLD TREE
FANTASY

THE SERPENT'S SHIP

For information, address World Tree Fantasy, PO Box 264 Hillsboro, OR 97123

ISBN: 978-0-9852417-3-5

Printed in the United States of America

To Laurie
whose quiet strength and support make writing possible.

To Tonya,
a builder of books.

And to Corey,
whose sketch pad brings imagination to life.

CHAPTER ONE
Not Again

Devon was dreaming again.

Heavy fog settled on the deserted main street of Alder Cove. The pavement was wet. Devon peered around in all directions, tasting the damp salt air that clung to his moistened lips. He looked down at his hands and brought them up in front of his face. Using the back of his right hand he wiped away the accumulated dampness that dripped from his forehead. He marveled that he could actually feel his hand dragging across his face, making him realize that this "dream" might not, in fact, be a dream at all. The pavement below his feet felt hard and substantial. The air was thick about his face, and as he exhaled, he could see and feel the puffs of breath that hung in the gray air before him.

He stood at the north end of Main Street where the road took a gentle rise toward the foot of Odin's Pass. To his right, Devon could barely make out the sidewalk; the fog's mist settled on the ground, giving the landscape an eerie, ghostly quality. Devon felt a shiver run down his spine, the flesh of his exposed arms raised in tiny goose bumps. He turned to face down the length of Main Street, noting that he stood directly in the middle, his feet slipping slightly on the white line dividing the right side of the street from the left. A traffic light in front of him blinked yellow, a reminder that Devon should remain cautious. He began walking slowly, though the downward slope of the hill drove him forward at a pace that became a little too quick for him. Dark shapes that were main street businesses, passed by as he walked. The buildings, however, remained shadowed and nondescript as the thickness of the fog saturated everything about him. Ignoring the buildings, for he felt no threat there, he trudged onward, hoping he was alone in this "dream". But he knew, somehow he knew, that there was another presence there. Someone, or something, that loathed him, that despised him beyond words or description.

Devon continued walking, wanting to wake up, but feeling compelled to push on, though fear rose from his bowels like a sickness that threatened to explode in a rush of vomit. He came, finally, to a familiar spot. The Captain's restaurant was located just a block ahead, and Zelda's Book Store was only a building or two past that. To his left was the gate that restricted non-boat owners from entering the private marina. However, as he turned to look he saw that the gate stood open, its gaping entrance beckoning him to cross the threshold. Devon felt a momentary rush of surprise. The marina was private property. Only those who owned businesses on the seaside could enter. Devon remembered a few months ago when he, Zeke, and Taylre had entered the marina to search the Captain's boat for clues to the Korrigan. At the time the entrance through the bookstore was the only option. Now the gate yawned open, and again, Devon felt compelled to enter, although his reluctance was substantial. He felt another shiver of fear run the length of his spine.

Passing through the gate, Devon began the steep walk down cement steps that eventually gave way to wooden docks where small boats, tied to rusted cleats, bobbed with the lapping tide, their hulls slapping at the smooth surface of the green water. Walking farther on, Devon made his way beyond the familiar docks and proceeded to a section of dock that was new to him, though the wood that floated on the green surface appeared rotted and withered with age. The sides of this pier were empty. As Devon peered down the length of the docks, the slated wooden surface faded into the distant fog, losing shape. *He made his way carefully along the broken lumber, feeling the slick wet exterior on the bottoms of his bare feet. A slight movement to his right caught his attention, and the dock shifted as a small wave hit its side. Devon steadied himself, widening his stance and spreading his arms in order to remain balanced.*

He looked up and suddenly a form appeared out of the fog, cutting through the mist like a dark specter. It loomed before him large and menacing.

The head of a serpent.

Its teeth resembled an evil grin; its long neck appeared to be overlaid in scales, its devilish eyes peering down at him, immoveable, without the slightest blink.

Devon reared back in terror causing him to skid on the slick surface of the dock and fall with a solid thump on his backside. Normally the pain of such a fall would cause him to wince and cry out, but his fear overshadowed any present discomfort. He began frantically working his way backward, crawling crab-like on his hands and feet. He slipped once on the slimy surface of the dock and again found himself perched on his butt, his arms twisted painfully behind his back. Devon looked up again expecting to see the serpent-like creature readying itself to pounce and devour him like a frightened mouse before a hungry cat. *However, the monster remained steadfast, looking not at Devon, but toward some distant vista beyond the fog. Devon realized that the monster was nothing more than a wooden serpent that adorned the prow of a large, ancient ship.*

He exhaled a sigh of relief, and laughed nervously at his own foolishness while pushing himself up from his precarious position, standing once again upon the unsteady surface of the dock. He tried to brush away the damp and dirt that clung to his pajama bottoms, then stopped abruptly - pajamas? He realized for the first time that he was actually standing in the same clothes he went to bed in that night -am I sleepwalking? Is this real or just a dream? He continued to gaze down at his clothing feeling a little silly and even a bit embarrassed. What if someone sees me like this? I'll be the laughing stock of the whole school. Then another feeling tugged at him, the feeling he had before of a presence. He knew it wasn't the serpent on the prow, but someone or something real, an entity of flesh and bone, that hid in the darkness.

Moreover, darkness was its power. Darkness and fear.

Devon looked up from his soiled clothing and gazed down the length of the fog-covered dock. From the mist, there appeared a shape, a man, who slowly took form just beyond the serpent's head. He stood motionless, his head bent, his chin resting on his chest. Then, slowly, he raised his head and stared.

Devon gasped. The man appeared to have no eyes, just deep empty sockets where blackness swam, sucking light and energy into them. His facial features were shadowed and unidentifiable, though his hair appeared long, smooth and black, running down the length of his back. His shoulders were broad. Thick muscles emphasized his chest, and the tight-fitting turtleneck sweater he wore appeared to accentuate it all. Then the man began to raise his muscled left arm until he was pointing his finger at Devon.

"Bring them to me," he said, although his mouth made no movement. Devon shuddered inwardly while fear danced about him, mocking him from every recess of his mind. He stepped backward and again slipped on the slimy surface. He felt himself falling and waited for the inevitable thump on the hard exterior of the dock, but the impact never came. Instead, Devon continued to fall, a never-ending free fall into nothingness.

Behind his closed eyelids, Devon's eyes shifted rapidly back and forth, up and down. They stopped abruptly and slowly, ever so slowly, he opened his eyes and gazed at the ceiling of his bedroom. He gently pulled aside the blankets that covered him and sat up, swinging his feet over the edge of his bed and resting them on the cool, hard surface of the floor. He looked at his feet. They were dirty and wet. His pajama bottoms felt wet too, the hem of his pajama legs frayed and mud soaked. He ran his hands through tangled hair, ignoring the dirt that clung to them.

"Not again," he said, shaking slightly as he tried to stand. "Not again."

CHAPTER TWO
A Blocked Path

Alder Cove had been inundated with rain. August passed with the mild gentleness of a dove, but September entered the scene like an angry pack of wolves. This particular morning was no exception.

An old style alarm clock, positioned unsteadily on the edge of a nightstand, began to sound, its brass colored bells vibrating with the rapid beats of the tiny hammer. Zeke woke with a start from his deep, dreamless slumber. He sat up quickly, shook the sleep from his mind, and immediately walked over to his window. Drawing the curtains aside, he saw that this day proved to be as nasty as the previous ones: blustery, wet, and cold. He sighed in frustrated resignation. He realized he had no choice but to enter the fray and get to work.

Zeke had decided early on that if he were to join the Alder Cove High School cross-country team he would have to give it his all. The interim coach, Mrs. Freya, had challenged the team to run everyday; to spend time in the school's weight room building their leg muscles, focusing on eating right, and getting plenty of rest. She said that if they committed themselves to a rigorous program they would be ready for the upcoming season where the competition was fierce. She also hoped that the new coach, whomever that might be, would be impressed with the team's progress and wouldn't have to work so hard to get them in shape later on.

Zeke turned from the window and the depressing view and trudged his way across the floor. He tried opening the closet door quietly so as not to awaken any other members of the household, but the hinges squeaked in protest as if the door's own restful slumber had been disturbed. Zeke made a mental note to locate the WD40 and squirt a little on the hinges. Inside the closet he found his Nike running shoes, his running shorts - freshly laundered and folded (compliments of his mother) - and a white t-shirt emblazoned across the front with a picture of the school's mascot: A blond haired, muscle bound Viking, wielding a large hammer and wearing a helmet with horns protruding from the sides. Underneath the picture were the words "The Thunder Makers".

Zeke dressed as quickly as he could and made his way out to the hallway. Rufus stood outside the door, his tail wagging eagerly, as if he had expected Zeke to open the door at that very moment.

"Not this morning, boy," Zeke said, petting Rufus roughly on the top of his head. "Maybe when I get home after school." He began to tiptoe across the sparsely carpeted floor, stepping tenderly on the first step of the stairway leading down, when he heard a faint squeak behind him. He stopped and turned abruptly. In his own doorway stood Devon, his hair standing on end, his eyes slightly puffy, and his pajamas wrinkled and covered in a thin dusting of soot and mud. "What the heck have you been up to?" Zeke said. "Building sand castles in bed?"

Devon shook his head, partly to shake off the cobwebs that pervaded his tired mind, and partly to express an emphatic negative response.

"No," he said, almost mumbling the answer. "I need to tell you something."

"Not now, goober face. I have seven miles to cover before breakfast and school. No time to chat."

"Wait," Devon begged. "This is really important. You might want to hear this."

"Important?" Zeke responded. "Yeah, so is learning how to do your laundry and take a shower." Then with a wave of his hand and a snort of laughter, he bounded down the stairs and out the front door.

Devon followed until he reached the top of the stairs where he remained fixed, his hands opening and closing into tight fists of anger. He looked down at Rufus, who now stood leaning up beside him, his wet nose urging Devon to consider taking him for a walk. Devon ignored the nudge.

"Goober face?" he said to the empty staircase, his eyes narrowed and his mouth turned into a thin-lined frown. "Fine, then. See if I care. Just don't come running to me when you find yourself in a whole butt load of trouble."

Devon turned and headed back into his room, closing the door quietly behind him. He stood for a moment staring at the blank wall and sighed. He wanted to climb back into bed and feel the warmth and safety of the blankets surrounding him again, but sleep abandoned him. Instead it was replaced with a constant nagging feeling of impending doom; a looming premonition of catastrophe hovering over his thoughts like a vulture gazing hungrily upon its dying prey.

�઼

Alder Cove sits on the northeastern tip of Nova Scotia. Its rocky shores and shear cliffs, set to the north of the town, make for very treacherous boating. Mooring a sea-going vessel along these shores would spell disaster. The inlet that gives Alder Cove its name, however, is a perfect, natural port. The water is deep and the surrounding mountains - Odin's Peak, Mt. Balder, and Mt. Sif - provide protection from the fierce storms that can ravage the area, especially during the long, cold winter months.

The town edges the inlet, hugging tightly to its cold waters where fishing is supreme. In fact, the town's economy depends on the fishing business. The harvesting of cod, halibut, and lobster brings riches and stability to the inhabitants along with the tourism industry; Alder Cove is a perfect location for summer getaways. Travelers from across Canada and the northeastern United States flock to these rocky shores for the salty breezes, the beautiful scenery, and the scrumptious fresh fish.

The business district of Alder Cove skirts the cove and marina as well, where anglers and pleasure craft owners moor their boats. Main Street, which runs directly through the business district and is adjacent to the water's edge, connects Alder Cove with the rest of the province by means of the Cabot Trail and then Hwy 105.

Nestled directly behind Main Street and up into the surrounding foothills sits the town proper, where the residents of Alder Cove build their houses and raise their families. Here, with the recent growth of the town, the homes stretch high up into the hills where some enjoy an impressive view of the town, the Cove, and the open ocean beyond. Behind the newest of these homes are hiking trails and old logging roads which extend farther up the hills and into the mountains themselves. It was toward these trails that Zeke made his way on his early run, battling the elements on this cold, wet Monday morning.

Normally, Zeke enjoyed the challenge of the hills that provided a chance to build his stamina and helped raise the bar in his workouts. However, today's run proved to be more than Zeke had bargained for. With a fierce wind barreling down from Odin's Peak, and a torrent of chilly rain to accompany it, Zeke found the incline to be almost too much. However, with his head bowed, his eyes closed to narrow slits to keep out the rain, and his hair matted to his forehead, Zeke pressed on, his legs screaming with each forward push.

Zeke's chosen route headed up Pike Street where his own house stood, quiet and sleepy, like its inhabitants. The road stretched for a quarter mile before taking a slight left turn and coming to a dead end. Zeke entered a cul de sac where the homes seemed to circle in a protective arch. However, in between two of the homes there stood a paved walkway where hikers, walkers, or, in this case, a runner, could easily slip through the neighborhood and reach the forests and hills that lay beyond in the undeveloped regions. Zeke passed through the cleft between the homes, still bent against the force of the wind and rain and found himself on a sodden trail where muck, fallen leaves, and pinecones littered the ground. He tried hard to keep to the edges of the path where the ground was more firm, but instead kept finding himself slipping into the middle of the trail where the rain accumulated, causing his feet to slosh and stick with each step. When he lifted his foot, the earth emitted a disgusting farting sound that, despite the discomfort he felt, made Zeke laugh, a tight smile etched across his strained face.

The path continued to ascend with tall evergreen trees towering on either side providing limited shelter and blocking the wind. Zeke felt the wind slacken and welcomed the cover and protection the trees provided. As he continued upward, the trees thickened, their cover darkening the trail and turning the hazy light of a stormy morning into a gloomy dusk. He rounded a tight switchback, slowing his pace so as not to slip in the mud. He glanced upward along the route, planning his steps, huffing and puffing with each stride, when he suddenly saw something move in the shadows ahead of him. At first Zeke assumed it was the movement of the shifting vegetation in the blustery wind, but something in his mind caused him to reject this idea. The small hairs on the back of his neck stood on end, and a shiver ran down his spine. Zeke slowed his pace to a jog, and then finally to a slow, even walk. He stared hard into the mist before him, waiting for the movement again. When nothing happened, he chuckled to himself inwardly.

"Too many memories of things that go bump in the dark," he said aloud.

Zeke picked up his pace again, feeling the burn in his chest and an equal, but gratifying, sting in his legs. With each painful sensation, he knew he was becoming stronger.

Again, there was movement. Zeke stopped abruptly in the middle of the trail.

Up ahead, in the gloom and mist, Zeke could have sworn that he saw what appeared to be a large dog, perhaps even a wolf, standing in the center of the path. It was watching him hungrily as its tongue lolled from the side of its mouth. The animal suddenly careened to the side, crashing through the wet foliage and disappearing from sight. Zeke waited for a moment, trying to take in what he thought he had just seen, but wondering if in fact the wind, rain, and shadows were simply playing games with his exhausted mind.

He moved cautiously, wanting to continue his run, but the fear of danger ahead pulled at his heightened senses. Zeke inched forward, measuring each step with vigilance. Finally, after trudging across the muddied ground, he reached the spot where he thought he had seen the animal. Zeke looked at the path but saw no tracks. He looked to the side, into the thick green growth where it appeared the creature had run through, but, again, saw no indication of the animal's presence. Standing still in the drizzle, Zeke chuckled again, chiding himself for his paranoia and blaming his recent encounter with the Korrigan, the monster he had successfully battled with the white stones, whose surfaces were etched with the ancient runes, for his overactive imagination.

Feeling his legs and arms stiffen from the sudden lack of movement, Zeke bent forward and stretched his limbs. Then, once again feeling ready to continue his run, he headed up the path, realizing that he'd only managed to cover one meager mile of the seven he had to traverse before he headed home for breakfast and then on to school.

Zeke began with a slow, easy jog, working his limbs hard to build back the momentum he had established upon first reaching the steep incline of the trail. He edged past the place where he thought he saw the large dog, and made his way to another switchback, this one taking a sharp turn to the left. With his head down and his mind focused on the strenuous physical exertion, Zeke was in no way prepared for the sudden shock he felt when he ran into a man standing in the middle of the path.

Zeke screamed, something he would later reproach himself

for; he thought his cry sounded like a little girl's, and he found it hard to shake the total embarrassment he felt.

When Zeke hit the man with his forehead, it felt as if he had struck a brick wall. The impact caused him to fall backward, tumbling over in an awkward reverse somersault. When he came to a sudden stop at the base of a large tree, Zeke found himself leaning unsteadily on his left knee, his right leg wedged uncomfortably behind him. Mud and remains of twigs, leaves and pine needles clung to his body. For a moment, Zeke had lost all sense of direction. His head was swimming in a swirl of stars and drifting shades of light. It was not until Zeke heard the laughter that his thoughts slowly came together.

The laughter continued, raspy, deep-throated, and raucous. Zeke looked up to see the silhouette of a man standing before him, his head pulled back as he continued to roar, the falling boy an obvious source of amusement. Slowly, the man's mirth subsided to a soft giggle as he wiped away fresh tears. He looked down at Zeke and approached him, offering his hand as he neared.

CHAPTER THREE
Almar Loden

Zeke looked up from his crumpled position on the ground and was at first startled to see the man advance toward him. However, as the man drew near, Zeke noted the sparkle of cheer that seemed to illuminate his bright blue eyes, coupled with the obvious look of concern written across his face. Zeke also saw that the man was extremely large in stature: incredibly broad and muscled in the arms and shoulders, and stood well over six feet tall. His hair was blond and long, and extended down the length of his back, but pulled in a tight ponytail. His features were stark, with high cheekbones, a faded scar ran the length of his left cheek, and a well-defined nose that seemed to shift one's attention to his piercing blue eyes. His chin was also sharp, with a discolored cleft accentuating the middle. Zeke thought that perhaps it, too, was a faded scar from a long past injury. The man wore dark clothing: a pair of new looking denim jeans, a black leather jacket, and a heavy black wool turtleneck sweater, one that gave him the appearance of a seasoned sailor. On his feet were a pair of heavy, mud stained hiking boots. Thick yellow laces ran crisscross through the dull copper eyes up to the middle of his calves. Above the boots, his pant legs puffed out unevenly, the hems tucked tightly into the tops of the boots.

"Loden," the man said as he extended his large, smooth hand, his voice betraying a slight accent that Zeke could not quite place. "Almar Loden, at your service."

Zeke took the offered hand and was gently but quickly lifted from his precarious position.

"I'm Zeke," he said, wincing as he spoke. "Zeke Proper."

' A sharp pain stabbed at his right knee, and the sensation that a thousand tiny pins were being jabbed into his leg sent Zeke reeling to his left. Almar Loden held onto him easily, steadying him before he could fall back to the muddied ground. Zeke felt the unusual strength in the man's arms.

"Looks like you might have a dislocation there," Loden said, as he gently placed Zeke down in a comfortable seated position on the side of the path, out of the mud and water. "Let's have a look here, shall we."

Almar Loden began to probe Zeke's right leg with an expert's touch, paying close attention to his knee. Zeke remained silent, the shock of the encounter and the pain of the twisted knee rendering him mute. He watched with a kind of detached fascination as the man gripped his leg, one hand resting underneath the knee, the other clutching his calf. Zeke kept his gaze centered on the man's face, but when Loden lifted the leg ever so slightly, Zeke flinched, his focus now on his own knee. He observed the obvious deformation of his kneecap. Instead of sitting on the top of the knee, which was normal, the kneecap had slid to the inside, making his leg look like an appalling rendition of a Picasso painting.

With deft, lightning-like speed, Loden lifted, turned, and pulled, all at the same time. A sharp, searing pain ripped through Zeke's leg, across his thigh and ended abruptly in the back of his brain. The pain was quick, even, and very intense. Just as quickly, it ended, leaving Zeke with a sense of relief.

Zeke exhaled a rush of air, realizing that he had been holding his breath.

"You should be fine now," Loden said. "You may want to have a doctor look at it just to be sure, but I don't think you'll have any problems."

Zeke examined the knee skeptically, still feeling a bit of soreness, but certain that he could now stand without any debilitating pain.

"Thank you," Zeke said, his voice shaky, but his confidence around the stranger growing. "You did that just like a doctor," he mumbled. Then added, "I'm really sorry about running into you. I didn't figure there'd be anyone else on the trail this early in the morning."

"Don't think twice about it. It was the best laugh I have had in a long time. And no, I'm not a doctor, just someone who's been around and knows a thing or two, you see," Loden explained, standing and brushing some of the accumulated mud from his jeans.

Again, he extended his hand, helping Zeke to his feet. Standing next to the man, Zeke felt dwarfed; Loden seemed to tower over him.

"Well, I should probably continue my run," Zeke said uncomfortably. "I still have a few miles to cover to get in my workout."

"Be careful on that knee," Loden said. "It's weak; it'll take some time to feel normal again."

"I will," Zeke said, lifting his hand in an awkward, self-conscious wave. He turned and continued up the path, a slight twinge of pain penetrating his right knee each time he took a step.

Loden watched as Zeke limped up the trail. His eyes followed Zeke's clumsy movements, but his head never moved. Then Loden's mouth turned up into a tight-lipped smile, his eyes turning from bright blue to black.

Zeke managed his way up the path to where the trail took another tight switchback. He turned quickly to look back at Mr. Loden, expecting to see him walking down the pathway hopping over puddles and mud filled holes. Instead, he saw what appeared to be the tail and hindquarters of a large dog entering a tangle of lush fern and ivy-filled forest. He stopped abruptly, ignoring the nagging tug of discomfort in his leg. Zeke narrowed his brow and pursed his lips. "He must have been walking his dog," Zeke said, wondering where the dog had hidden itself the whole time he was with Almar Loden.

After a few moments of staring into the wind-tossed foliage, Zeke continued his painful run.

CHAPTER FOUR
The New Coach

The long, hot, hectic summer was over and school was back in session. The high school's parking lot was packed. The older students, at least the ones who could afford them, drove up in their old, run down clunkers, parked them in their designated areas, and let their engines run to keep the insides warm, the windshields clear of mist, and the CD players playing, their tail pipes issuing a blue, torrent stream of choking exhaust.

Rain continued to fall, pressing heavily toward the already sodden ground, the gray skies shaping an atmosphere of darkness, depression and routine.

The morning bell, signaling the beginning of first period, was about to sound; students were starting their exodus toward the large front doors. Some escaped the confines of the big yellow buses that pulled up in front of the school next to the wet curb.

Others reluctantly left the safety of their warm cars to trudge through the soggy haze and begin another day of reading, writing, and arithmetic. Among the group of backpack toting students was Zeke Proper and Taylre Anders. They huddled together, their heads bowed against the blowing elements as they made their way into the school. Both moved with trepidation, but especially Zeke, who found the first few days in a new school nerve racking. Trying to find his way around an unfamiliar building was one thing, but making new friends was quite another. However, both Zeke and Taylre felt emboldened by their recent experience with the Korrigan; although they faced the challenges of a new school year, they felt the bond of friendship and the union of an unspeakable secret.

The hallways were crowded as students filed through, some talking loudly in stairwells, while others noisily slammed locker doors closed. The floors, trodden by many rain-soaked shoes, were slick and potentially hazardous. As Zeke left Taylre, who had to make her way to her first period history class, he found himself teetering with the weight of his backpack, wary of the slippery, tiled floor. Accompanying the discomfort of the pack was an ache that still nagged at him from his injured knee. He thought briefly of the man, Almar Loden, who had helped him that morning and advised him to see a doctor just in case. Zeke felt he should probably heed those words of advice.

Zeke rounded a bend in the hallway, his focus intent upon his locker. There he would pick up his English textbook and make his way to his first class. However, as he turned the sharp corner, a stab of pain from his right knee jolted Zeke out of his thoughts; his feet slipped out from under him, his knee giving way. Then, like a slow motion scene from America's Funniest Home Videos, Zeke found himself falling, for the second time today, on his already tender backside. Zeke felt a sudden rush of breath escape his lungs as he met the solid floor, his backpack taking the brunt of the fall. The oversized lunch thermos tucked neatly in the bottom of the pack pushed its way into the small of his back. His neck snapped backward causing him to strike the base of his head on the floor; with it he saw what appeared to be a thousand tiny pinpoints of light floating across his mind and then passing his line of fading vision.

The next thing Zeke sensed was a sound, one that seemed to come from many miles away, like an echo pushing itself toward him in a windless rush from a distant tunnel. It became louder and louder with each passing second until it finally exited the tunnel and entered his ears with a note of familiarity. Zeke had heard the sound before, his spinning thoughts trying to make sense of it. Then he remembered. The sound was laughter: raspy, deep-throated, and raucous. Through slightly blurred vision, Zeke looked up to see Almar Loden standing above him; his head thrown back, his mouth open in a roar of amusement. Surrounding him were dozens of students who, seeing an adult laugh at the expense of a student, joined in heartily.

Zeke's sense of direction and vision rushed back to him, and as he looked about himself he felt a flush of redness and heat encompass his entire head. Zeke had never felt as much embarrassment as he did at that very moment. He wished he could be anywhere but there, on the floor, looking up at the fifty or so eyes that were looking down at him. He wanted to disappear, to fade out of existence, to have the building fall on him and bury his body forever. Unfortunately, none of those things happened, and Zeke, once again, looked upward to see Almar Loden's extended hand reaching down to help him out of his precarious position.

"Young Mr. Proper," Almar Loden announced as tears of laughter sparkled in the corners of his eyes. "You have once again been the source of extreme hilarity for me today. I must say if this continues I shall have to retire from teaching early due to excessive side aches, you see." Then he laughed some more, at the same time hefting Zeke to his feet.

Zeke stood unsteadily at first, but then quickly regained his balance, still favoring a sore knee coupled with an aching back. He smiled awkwardly, trying to pass off the intense shame that he was feeling, as if he had meant all along to fall like he did, but realizing no one would buy that excuse. Then, like a flash in a dark room, Zeke suddenly registered what Loden had said. He turned his head to look up at the imposing figure beside him. When Loden saw Zeke's expression, he smiled an impish sort of smile that was neither friendly, nor happy, but one that knew too much. Then he said, "That's right, Zeke. I am a teacher here at Alder Cove High. I have been hired to teach English Literature, Mythology, and to be the school's new cross-county coach, you see. It appears that you and I are going to get to know each other very well."

ᚴ

Lunch, for Zeke, was not just a chance to refuel or a chance to subdue the nagging hunger pangs that most students feel when noon comes around. For Zeke, it was his few moments of pleasure in a busy day. However, today was different. The enjoyment that comes with a hot meal after an early morning run, a walk through the drizzling rain, and three high school classes could not satisfy Zeke. Sitting next to Taylre on a bench seat that pushed up uncomfortably close in front of a picnic-style table, Zeke could sense the stares and hear the muffled laughter directed toward him from the other students who sat nearby.

The embarrassment of the incident in the hallway still lingered. The students who had seen the fall had spread the news of Zeke's accident. Now, it was common knowledge among the entire student body. Therefore, instead of chewing eagerly on each bite of his macaroni and bagel sandwich, Zeke poked at his meal with his plastic fork, peeling bits of crust off the edges and flicking them onto the side of his lunch tray.

Taylre watched Zeke's slow, methodical movements. His sulky frown seemed to cast a dark ring of depression that touched even Taylre whose attitude toward life always seemed to be accompanied by a glowing, silver lining.

"I think you're making too much of this," she said, eyeing Zeke's sandwich and wanting to ask if he was going to eat it, or just play with it for the entire lunch period. "It could have happened to anyone. The floor was slippery. Rainwater was everywhere. How could you have known?"

Zeke looked up from the destruction of his meal and glared at Taylre.

"I realize that slipping on a wet floor could have happened to anyone, but that's not the issue," he grumbled.

"Then what is the issue?" Taylre asked, tilting her head slightly to one side, a look of concern evident on her face.

"The issue, Taylre, is that it was embarrassing. The whole school thinks I'm the biggest dork that ever lived. This is definitely not the way I wanted to start out this year."

"Again," Taylre repeated, "I think you're making too much out of this. You just wait; tomorrow it will all be forgotten. Nobody will even remember any of it happened."

"Right," Zeke said sarcastically, a scowl continuing to crease his face. "You have no idea how humiliating that whole episode was. Next thing you know people will be dubbing me the 'great, uncoordinated one.' I'll never live this one down."

"You're wrong, Zeke. Kids around here have too much else to think about," Taylre said reassuringly. "They got their laugh for the day, and then tomorrow, it'll be something else. You'll see. This incident will blow over as fast as it started. In fact, I bet before the end of the day someone else will have slipped on the wet floor. It happens all the time."

Zeke shrugged his shoulders slightly and let out an exasperated breath. "You're right, I guess. Maybe I am making too much of this..." then Zeke stopped. "But you know the thing that really bothers me about all this? It's Mr. Loden."

"Mr. Who?" Taylre asked.

"Loden," Zeke repeated. "He's the new English teacher. Plus, he's the one who's going to be taking over as coach of the cross-country team. I met him earlier when I was out for my morning run. Funny," Zeke said, "I landed on my back when I met him then, too. And," he continued, "it was an odd sort of encounter. I mean, how many people are out in the woods, in the rain, at six o'clock in the morning?"

"Well, it's obviously not that strange," Taylre responded. "You were out there. How often do you see a high school freshman out running, voluntarily, on a day like this. *Especially* at six o'clock in the morning?"

"You've got a point there," Zeke said. "But still, there was something about meeting him, both times, that seemed odd. I mean, he smiled at me. He was pleasant, thick accent and all. Shoot, he even fixed up my knee after I fell. And yet..."

"You're being paranoid," Taylre interrupted. She shifted in her seat and turned so that only Zeke could hear her speak. Then, she lowered her voice to a soothing whisper. "The stuff that happened this summer has gotten to you. It's gotten to all of us. We have to let it go. Everything's fine now. The town is finally back to normal. I can even sense that the depression that hung over this place is gone. You took care of that. We all did, so stop worrying. Give this guy a chance. From what you've said, he sounds like a pretty cool guy. Maybe he just seems odd because he's from some other country and he feels a bit awkward about meeting new people. You mentioned yourself that he had an unusual accent."

"You know, you're right," Zeke said, sitting up a bit

straighter. "I am being stupid. I'm letting little things get to me, things that never affected me before. This morning I even imagined seeing a big wolf out in the woods. Crazy, uh?"

"You see?" Taylre said reassuringly. "By tomorrow this will all be a bad memory. And then," she said with a smile and a quick nod toward Zeke's mutilated sandwich, "you can eat your lunch instead of torturing it."

Zeke laughed and pushed his plate away. He smiled, and with an extraordinary effort shoved away the thoughts of the other students who surrounded him. He knew Taylre was probably right, that tomorrow most, if not everyone, would have forgotten the incident. Yet, as he thought this, Zeke's mind suddenly twisted back to the memory of Almar Loden's face, his exaggerated features bearing down on Zeke like a vision from some demented nightmare, his mouth open in riotous mirth. Zeke felt an involuntary shiver run the length of his body.

CHAPTER FIVE
Teddy

Teddy Walford, Jr. sat in the back row of his 5th period Algebra 1 class. The math teacher stood at the front of the room moving lithely between her desk and the white board. She spoke enthusiastically about slopes, x's and y's, and intersecting lines, but seemed to be failing in her attempt to engage the thirty or so students who stared up at her, some of their minds blank, while others thought about anything other than arithmetic. Teddy just glared, his eyes narrowed into tiny slits of malice, his mouth curved in a snarl, like an angry junkyard dog planning an attack upon its trespassing victim.

Teddy loathed math. Teddy hated his teachers, his school, and the students who surrounded him asking stupid questions. He despised the ones who talked incessantly about boyfriends and girlfriends, about this TV show and that TV show. He detested the girls who constantly looked at themselves in the mirror, and the boys who flexed their muscles in an attempt to attract the opposite sex. He hated the ones who listened to their iPods, talked on their cell phones, or texted constantly when they were sitting in the same room with someone else. He hated the town, the lousy weather, and he hated the smell of fish. He even hated his own reflection in the mirror. In short, Teddy Walford, Jr. hated everything and everybody.

However, Teddy wasn't always like this. Recent events had caused a change to come over him, producing a bitterness that took hold of his soul, like a deep scar that marred an otherwise beautiful complexion.

Teddy was only fifteen years old, but compared to the other boys his age he was a giant. Sitting in desks designed for the "normal sized student" was a challenge. Teddy had to squeeze himself into place. His knees pushed up against the bars that held the desk together, and the frame howled in protest every time he shifted his weight. His arms were thick and muscular. His belly, though large, was firm, a solid mass of strength. His feet were size sixteen and the source of a common argument with his mother, who dreaded the continual search for new sneakers. She found that her best option was to order online, since no local shoe stores carried footwear that large. Teddy also had a broad, muscular chest, shoulders that exceeded any normal size that a clothing store would carry, and a head that simply denied every hat that tried to fit its dimensions. His size made him both an object of ridicule and a presence to be feared. When he walked down the hallway, the corridors literally parted. No one wanted to mess with Teddy.

For Teddy this was a kind of relief because at times he preferred solitude, but the isolation came with a price, the cost of both grief and frustration. Teddy was practically friendless, which was not always the case. His friends were abandoning him. Those who did associate with him were only temporary relationships. The fear he instilled in others was simply too much of a barrier. His temper had become quick, and at times very violent. Nobody wanted to bear the brunt of a misplaced word or an accidental, untoward look. It just wasn't worth it. And so, Teddy remained alone. He was a solitary form in a sea of grumbling, cell phone talking, iPod listening, attention seeking students who avoided the boy who stood heads above everyone else.

Until he met Almar Loden.

When Mr. Loden came into Teddy's life, things really began to change...for everyone, but not necessarily for the better.

This day had been a particularly bad one for Teddy. Attending math class hadn't helped his foul mood. To him, the numbers and lines drawn on the board were a foreign language.

He could make absolutely no sense of them. Then, he realized at the end of his last class of the day that he had a ton of new homework, along with the work that was already overdue. He thought, for just one brief moment, that he should go home and get to work on his assignments, but then reality sunk in and he realized that going home would be futile. There, in the house he had grown up in, he would find nothing but darkness. He could envision the scene: he would walk into the house, the heat would be off, there would be no food in the fridge, and there would certainly be nothing cooking on the stove or in the oven. His mother would be gone, at work as usual, and wouldn't be back until late, probably sometime around midnight when her shift at the Surf Motel would end. He would have to scrounge up some food for himself, watch TV alone in the dark, and go to bed without saying goodnight to anyone. Teddy just couldn't stomach the idea of going through that tonight. Things were gloomy enough without adding another lonely evening into the mix.

Two months ago, Teddy Walford, Sr., Teddy's father, had disappeared. He left no note, no message, and no phone call. Rumors had been flying around the town like gnats over a garbage heap. And why not? His father had been the town's chief of police. It was hard to imagine why someone with such a prominent position in the public eye would suddenly leave without even a hint of his whereabouts. To Teddy, this had been a source of intense frustration and sadness. His mother, who had always been a stay at home mom, was forced to go to work to pay the bills. She was constantly on the verge of tears, feeling abandoned by her husband of twenty years. This left Teddy with the burden of fending for himself most days and dealing with his own shattered emotions as well as those of his mother. The worst part, however, was all the finger pointing from the townspeople themselves: reports of embezzled money from the town's treasury and conspiracies with the town's former mayor and Peter Roberts, the previous town manager, who were also missing. The authorities had been called in. Questions, embarrassing questions, had been asked, and many accusations had been made, but still there were no answers.

With the final sounding of the bell, a line of school busses and cars began streaming out of the parking lot in what appeared to be a desperate attempt to flee the bonds of education, a chance for teenagers to find solace in front of their TVs, or in the presence of friends. All of these escaping students were taking advantage of a chance to shake off the pressures of school for a few hours before returning the next day. Teddy stood just inside the main entry to the school watching with detached indifference the exodus before him. As the last of the vehicles departed the lot, Teddy turned and began walking back through the silent, abandoned school hallway. Bits of trash lay strewn across the tiled floor. He kicked at a crumpled piece of paper, turning it into a game of trash soccer, watching the discarded parchment collide with an empty garbage can then bank off a wall of lockers. He jogged heavily toward the makeshift ball and gave it another mighty kick, sending it sailing in a perfect arc. The trash ball landed momentarily on the top of a rusted drinking fountain, spraying droplets of water across the wall before descending once again to the muddied floor, rolling awkwardly to the opposite side of the hallway, then finally coming to rest at the feet of Almar Loden.

Teddy looked up in surprise at the unexpected appearance of the tall, blond haired man. He stared at Teddy, his eyes piercing blue, and Teddy, normally able to withstand any kind of stare down, even with an adult, found he could not keep looking at the figure before him. He dropped his gaze to the floor. When the man spoke, Teddy jumped slightly, as if the sound of the voice was a rushing magical force striking him in the chest, breaking some long lost silence.

"You," Loden said sharply, "look like a young man who needs something to do." Teddy found himself entranced. He was unable to speak, capable only of nodding, affirming the man's statement.

With the wave of his hand, Loden beckoned Teddy to
follow, then turned and proceeded down the now darkening
hallway toward the other end of the school. Teddy followed
obediently, his head bowed slightly, his arms hanging uselessly
down the sides of his body, like a soul that had suddenly given
up all hope.

The school had emptied quickly of its students, but teachers
remained working quietly in their offices and classrooms. Loden
led Teddy past many of these open doors and came finally to a
small classroom, its lights dimmed, a scattering of tables and
chairs intermixed with desks making up its only furniture. Along
the far wall a large window faced a football field that was
surrounded by an oval running track. Beyond it were some small
spectator stands, the wooden benches waterlogged from the
incessant rainfall.

Teddy looked past Almar Loden, who stood with his back to
the window gazing at him, and peered out toward the bleak,
weather-beaten day. He noted, with some pleasure, a sullen
group of students standing near the stands on the gravel-covered
track. Most were shivering in the cold, their arms wrapped about
themselves, their bare legs pocked with goose bumps, and their
hair matted down from the dampness. Teddy gave a slight
chuckle at their displeasure, then noted the t-shirts they wore, all

uniform, bright yellow in color, and depicting the head of a long blond-haired Viking with the words The Thunder Makers inscribed underneath it. Below that, in small blue letters, were the words, ACH Cross Country Team. The small group of boys and girls, twelve or so, seemed to be waiting for something to happen. Occasionally, one or two of the team members would look up expectantly toward the window where Teddy and Mr. Loden stood.

"You seem amused at my team," Loden said, turning to look out the window and bringing Teddy's attention back to the present. "They're waiting for me to come down and give them instructions, to guide them, to help them hone their skills and be the best they can be," he continued. His voice had a kind of mesmerizing quality that pulled at Teddy's senses, giving him a feeling of calm. "But, before I do that, I must ask for your assistance. For you see... Teddy," then Loden paused, smiling eerily toward him, and sensing Teddy's shock in the silence, "Yes, I know your name, Teddy. I know many things about you. For that reason, I think that you and I can help each other."

Loden turned back to face Teddy, his head tilted slightly to one side, as if he were examining him more closely and measuring his worth. "I have a very weak team down there, you see," he declared, turning to look across the dampened field again, staring with a kind of loathing at the small assemblage who

THE SERPENT'S SHIP   43

stood trembling in the wet chill. "I need you to be my team manager. I need you to help me put some of the team members in their place, to make sure they are not slacking off. Some of them have bad attitudes, you see. They think they are better than everyone else. They need to be set straight, and *that's* where *you* can help me, you see?" Loden walked slowly toward Teddy, who stood fixed, his voice seemingly lost. Loden reached his arms out and grasped Teddy by the shoulders, his grip strong and unyielding. "Will you help me, Teddy? Because if you do, you see, I can make things go very well for you. I, Teddy, can fulfill your wildest dreams. So, will you, Teddy? Will you help me?"

Loden's height forced Teddy to look up to his face, and when Loden grasped him by the shoulders, a stab of pain coursed through his body, like a small current of electricity. The feeling was unpleasant. Teddy tried to shrink away from the touch, but Loden's clutch was firm. "Yes," Teddy finally said, his ability to speak coming from some unknown source, as if he had not even spoken the words, but instead had only been the conduit of another entity's voice.

"Good. Very good," Loden declared. "Now, put your coat on, Teddy. We have some lives that need a little disrupting."

CHAPTER SIX
Swinging Branches

Teddy set the whole thing up, at least that's what he was led to believe. He thought he was simply pushing the team to run harder, to help them keep ahead of the pack. Little did he know Teddy was merely a pawn in a much bigger, nastier, evil design.

Almar Loden supplied Teddy with the necessary tools: a long piece of nylon rope, a small hatchet, and a shovel. The rest of the diversion, as Teddy named it, was all his idea. It was a stroke of genius that occurred in a moment of startling realization. Loden's instructions were simple: keep the team on their toes and make sure they are aware of their surroundings. He wanted to make sure that the team learned how to stay ahead of the pack when opponents got in their way. The rest was all Teddy, or so he assumed.

Teddy made his way along the path that Loden mapped out for him, noting that one part of the group, led by the team's fastest and youngest male runner, Zeke Proper, would be running through a tight patch of dark forest. The trail where the small troop would be running was narrow and surrounded by woods. Teddy had situated himself high up on the limb of a nearby tree so that he could witness the effect of his diversion. He had no way of knowing just how perfect the outcome would be.

Rain continued to fall, but at this point in the day, it had turned to a light mist. The ground was soggy, and standing water pockmarked the slender path where Zeke and the rest of the team ran. Zeke was ahead of the group but only by a small margin. Normally, he would be a good quarter of a mile in front of the next runner, but his knee was still a bit tender and swollen from his accident earlier in the day, and his back spasmed every time he lifted his left leg. Nevertheless, Zeke pushed through the pain and discomfort, keeping his mind focused on the road in front of him and pushing aside any soreness. With three more miles to go on the route that the new coach had outlined, Zeke felt a surge of determination flow through him, one that would allow him to get on Mr. Loden's good side. Rounding a short curve in the trail, Zeke saw the darkened entrance to the small wooded area up ahead. He turned slightly to one side and could see from the corner of his eye his teammate, Chaz Nelson, closing in quickly. With a burst of strength, Zeke rushed on, pushing a bit farther ahead of Chaz and the rest of the group and entered the grove of trees.

The already dimming light of the late afternoon became even more sullen when Zeke came into the thick forest. For a brief moment, he lost his sight; the darkness seemed to envelop him. He slowed his pace, feeling for the path beneath him, when suddenly he tripped over what he thought was a root or a small branch. Then, as if he were a piñata hanging from the limb of a tree, Zeke was struck in the face. The branch that hit him was as wide as a baseball bat. The force behind the branch was like that of a major leaguer swinging his way out of the ballpark. It happened so fast, Zeke barely had time to close his eyes. Coming in an upward motion, the branch walloped him just below the jaw line sending him flying, his head snapping back and his arms splaying outward in a helpless pose. He landed with a resonant thud on the mud-covered pathway, striking the back of his head on an exposed root. Carried by his own momentum, Zeke found himself rolling into a tangle of berry bushes and a mesh of white nylon rope.

Just before Zeke passed out, he heard what he thought was a scream of laughter coming from somewhere high up in the branches. Through a blurry haze of vision, Zeke saw the outline of a boy descending from the trees and running off farther into the forest. He couldn't be sure, but Zeke thought he had seen the boy before. That was when Zeke's world went dark.

ꙮ

The mini-van, driven by Zeke's father, Percy Proper, drove carefully into the driveway. Percy tried his best to keep the arduous journey from the hospital emergency room to the house as smooth as possible; any type of jarring or bumping caused Zeke to cry in pain. Percy made sure that each stop was calculated well beforehand and that every turn was taken with precision. Nevertheless, he couldn't help the occasional bump that jarred his tender passenger.

When the van finally pulled up in front of the Proper house, a sense of relief flooded the inside; the grueling excursion was finally over. Percy stepped out of the driver's side and moved to the rear sliding door, opening it slowly and cautiously. Inside, lying on the seat, was Zeke, his head, leaning against a pillow, was bandaged like an ancient mummy; his leg, slightly elevated, was cast in a swathe of tape and medical gauze.

Vivian Proper, Zeke's mother, practically launched herself from the front porch as the van pulled into the driveway. She ran and stood by her husband, her hands shaking with stress and worry; mascara-stained streaks of tears ran the length of her cheeks.

"Careful," Percy said. "He's pretty sore and quite drugged up. The doctor gave him something to ease the pain, but it doesn't seem to be helping all that much." He leaned into the van and gently took Zeke by the head and shoulders and slid him out of the vehicle part way. Vivian took Zeke's legs and the two of them carefully carried Zeke in the house to the waiting couch that had been made up with pillows and blankets.

To Zeke, that first night on the couch was agonizingly long. Tossing or turning was not an option. The pain that poured through his body with any movement was unbearable. His knee, the one he'd dislocated while running during the previous morning, was damaged more than he thought. And his jaw, well, it was broken. A hairline fracture, running the full length of the right side of his face, shot jolts of pain down his neck into his upper torso and upward to the top of his head. As a result, Zeke's jaw was wired shut. For the next few weeks, Zeke's nutrition would be through a straw, his food pureed to a smooth liquid in the blender.

Zeke's home became the couch. He would occasionally get up from his cushioned retreat, fighting the tangle of blankets and sheets that wrapped themselves around his limbs like fishing nets pulling in their catch of the day, and limp his way across the living room floor and down the hall to the bathroom. He always did this with the help of his mother who took on the task of nurse and caretaker. The process was always agonizing, but the pain pills that the doctor had provided had a way of tempering the worst of the discomfort.

And then, there were the dreams.

Like his body, Zeke's thoughts were ravaged with pain. These, however, were in the form of torturous images. They appeared almost as soon as Zeke closed his eyes. So now, for Zeke, the thought of drifting off to sleep in a drug-induced stupor became a physical battle as he struggled to keep awake, his mind revolting against the inevitable descent from consciousness to unconsciousness.

The dreams had been coming for the last three weeks, all during Zeke's recovery. They always began and ended the same way, but tonight was different and Zeke could tell as soon as he closed his eyes that something was unusual. For that reason, he struggled even more to remain awake. Nevertheless, as always happened, sleep won out, and Zeke was once again plunged into a spiral of images, their impact somehow all too real.

CHAPTER SEVEN
Entity

Zeke was actually feeling comfortable in the darkness. At first, he was terrified; he had never felt blackness so thick, so complete, but now, though still feeling a twinge of trepidation, he felt as if he might begin to finally move, to investigate his surroundings.

Though Zeke recognized that he was only a character in this dream, that realization in and of itself caused him to question his predicament: was this really a dream? For a moment, Zeke reflected on Devon's description of dreams he had experienced with the Korrigan and with his Grandpa John. He wondered if this was a similar encounter.

Zeke began walking. The darkness he trudged through seemed to hold a weight of its own and he could feel its burden resting on his shoulders, but he ignored it for the time being and concentrated only on walking, shuffling his feet forward a bit at a time, feeling for any unseen obstacles or drop offs . He walked with his arms outstretched, waving them around in an attempt to prevent himself from running into anything. Finally, after walking for what seemed like hours, Zeke began to see shapes forming ahead of him as the darkness slowly dissipated, as if a small amount of light was being allowed to seep in from underneath some imaginary doorway. He continued walking but picked up his pace now that he could see there was nothing to hinder his progress. The light increased with each step until he could see that he was standing on a beach, yet the white sand he stood upon felt firm, as if he were standing on a solid tiled floor. He stopped to get a better look at this new environment.

To his left Zeke saw the ocean, its waves lapping up gently on the pearly beach, and yet their soothing ebbing and flow made no sound. It was as if someone had pushed the mute button on this dream. To his right stood a rocky cliff, its rough, rust colored exterior displaying its torturous exposure to centuries of wind and rain. Then, directly ahead of him, Zeke could make out the figure of a man approaching.

At first, he appeared like a mirage, a shifting, wavy, shimmering form, like heat rising off a hot surface. As he got closer, Zeke could make out the definitive image of an older, white haired man, his face pale and his short beard peppered with streaks of red. The man wore a plain white shirt that looked as if it had survived several years of wash and wear. It was clean, but tattered and faded. The pants he wore were also faded, the thinning knees and frayed hems testament of hours of toil. However, though the man appeared ragged and aged, he did not seem to be frail. He walked with purpose; his head held high and his stride was confident, a gait that remained consistent as he strolled toward Zeke and eventually stood before him. Zeke gazed curiously at the man's face, noting the color of his eyes, their bright green centers gleaming brightly like a fresh spring morning.

Zeke felt at ease in the presence of the man. He seemed familiar, and Zeke found himself frantically searching his memory for any kind of recollection. However, his search was quickly forgotten when the man suddenly smiled, a pleasant and completely guileless smile.

"Good morning, Zeke," the man said, his feet planted firmly and squarely, his arms hanging at his sides. His voice echoed as if it were being projected from the distant past. "What is it that you want?"

To his complete surprise, Zeke answered the man very quickly, not even realizing he had a question to ask.

"How do I destroy it?"

The words escaped like a sharp exhale. Zeke had no chance

to retrieve them, and he was shocked by the sound they made as he uttered them. He had no idea what "it" was. He had no idea what needed destroying.

"Very well," the man said, apparently unfazed by Zeke's response. "But you must follow me. There is much to show you, and I have very little time. I'm afraid I'm going to have to dispense with the pleasantries. In addition, you must be careful to stay on the path at all times. For there is an entity in your midst that desires to have you, Zeke; it will stop at nothing to exact its vengeance."

"An entity?" Zeke asked, his voice sounding strained and awkward. "What entity? What do you mean?"

"Darkness," the man answered simply. "The entity is darkness, chaos, and fear. It is the thing in the closet, under the bed, and within the darkest recesses of your mind. The entity is depression, hate, and violence. It is loneliness and betrayal. The entity goes by many names, and he will answer to all. A mischievous imp who cares for nothing but itself and its devious lies. Moreover, it wants you, Zeke. It wants to destroy you and make you pay for killing its daughter. So be vigilant. There will be those close to you who will betray you, but make no mistake; they are being deceived. Trust no one, at least not yet." Then the man turned and began walking before Zeke had a chance to say anything more, his pace quick and even.

Zeke followed closely, but was always mindful of the narrow path below him that seemed to appear out of nowhere. He was amazed again at the "realness" of this dream. Zeke actually felt tired, his breathing coming in ragged bursts. He thought back to his recent accident and blamed his sudden exhaustion on the fact that he had been lying on the couch too long, that his extended recuperation had sapped all of the conditioning he had worked so hard to build up.

After what seemed like hours of walking, constantly moving from one unusual landscape to the next, the man came to an abrupt stop. He looked back at Zeke for one brief moment then turned again, extending his arm and pointing his finger.

"Look!" he said.

Zeke looked past the old man in the direction he indicated, and there, lying on his back, his face partially obscured by the flowing dress of a crying woman, was a young man, writhing in pain and anguish.

The man, his cries sharp and resonant, was naked except for a thin and tattered loincloth. He rested on a bed of sharp rocks; two perched uncomfortably beneath his shoulders, one beneath his buttocks, and one balanced under his ankles. Bound in place by a heavy chain, its thick links wrapping themselves over his chest and around his arms and his legs, the man was severely restricted in his movements. Above him, hanging from the gnarled ancient limb of a tree directly over the man's face, was the largest snake Zeke had ever seen. Its mouth gaped open, its massive fangs exposed, dripping huge drops of venom onto his exposed skin while the crying woman frantically tried to catch each and every drop in a small earthenware container.

"What do you see?" the old man asked.

"I see a tortured man," Zeke replied. "One who's paying a heavy price for a costly mistake." Again, he was astonished at his own response. He felt as if the dream were somehow injecting the answers into his own thoughts, ones he would have never thought of on his own.

"You are correct, Zeke. The man is being punished, for he is a fallen god. He has destroyed that which was beautiful. His own treachery has caused his downfall and he has become darkness. However, there is more. Look!" Again, the old man pointed a stern finger in the direction of the punished god.

Zeke saw that the clay jug catching the toxic drops began to spill over, and the woman holding it turned, her face streaked with centuries of tears and lined with years of worry. She emptied the venom into an impression in the ground. When she turned to drain the container, the poison continued to fall, striking the still unseen face of its victim, sliding down his left cheek, oozing over his exposed neck and shoulder, and finally streaming onto the rocks. As each drop struck its intended target, the liquid sizzled like acid, burning away flesh and turning pink skin into a charred mass of burnt meat. Screams rose from the sufferer like those of a terrified child waking from a nightmare.

Zeke turned his face from the scene. Hot tears ran down his own cheeks as he listened to the tortured cries. He could no longer stomach the sounds of anguish, and he began to feel nausea rise within him. Then the old man called to him, forcing him once again to turn his attention to the gruesome scene.

"Behold," the old man beckoned, "the Darkness begins to break its bonds!"

As Zeke turned, a mist began to gather, and the scene before him became shrouded in fog. No longer could he see the entity struggling with his bindings, but could only hear a change in the cries. At first, it was the familiar cries of pain, but then the pitch changed, becoming frustrated and angry. Then finally there issued a cry that signaled a surge of strength.

The sound of twisting metal echoed through the air. The clang of steel striking the exposed rocks followed. The mist that had risen to conceal the scene began to settle and Zeke could see the back of the entity, his strong frame and muscled shoulders now standing high above his bed of torture. Beside him hung the snake, its eyes wide with fear as the entity extended his arm in one quick fluid motion, grabbing the serpent's head, *pulling it in, and smashing it repeatedly with a fist. His blows rained like a blacksmith pulverizing white-hot iron. The snake fell to the ground, its form now unrecognizable.*

The entity bent to look at the dead heap of flesh that was once a venomous serpent and he laughed: a raspy, deep throated, raucous sound, one that sent a shiver up Zeke's spine.

Then the entity ran, racing off into the distance with purpose.

The woman who stood by the entity's side, attempting to catch each drop of venom, stood dumbfounded, her mouth hanging open in disbelief; her recognition of the wasted years of devotion striking her like a solid slap in the face.

Suddenly the dream location changed, and Zeke found himself standing once again on the beach. Before him stood the old man, his head tilted slightly to one side looking at Zeke intently.

"The entity seeks the ship Naglfar," the old man said, "built from the painfully extracted fingernails and toenails of the dead. With his devilish crew, he will seek the end of the world. But first, he will settle his vengeance against those who he feels have wronged him. Make no mistake, Zeke, his wrath is severe."

"But he still seeks me," Zeke said. "He still wants to destroy me. How do I stop it?"

"How to stop it. Yes. That is the correct question," The old man said. "Killing it is not an option, that task is for another to perform. Nevertheless, you, Zeke, must protect others from its influence and send it away, its purposes unfulfilled. In this, it will become weak, and its final intentions will be thwarted.

"It is enough that you know it exists," the man continued. "Your own strength will be added upon when you discover how to send it away, back into chaos where it must wait, taking time to gather its army."

The old man turned and began walking away from Zeke. However, after only a few yards, he looked back and said, "You can do this, Zeke. Just remember that it feeds upon fear. Without fear, it cannot thrive. And know this: anger will be your motivation. Beware that it doesn't overtake you. Instead, let it guide you. Your task will be difficult and very dangerous, but you've already proved yourself once. Don't let us down." Then he faded into the landscape, leaving behind a shimmering vision, like a stone tossed into the calm surface of a pond.

CHAPTER EIGHT
Ready to Listen

The living room was dark, except for a steady glow from a streetlight outside the large picture window, its pale beam casting shadowy images that, to Zeke, looked like ghostly apparitions standing over his makeshift bed. Zeke stared at the forms hovering above him, trying to make sense of the shapes; trying to figure out what or who they were, until he finally recognized that they were, in fact, only shadows. Then, with that realization, he recalled where he was and the incredible dream he had.

He sat up slowly from the sofa expecting the usual jolt of pain that followed any type of movement, but this time there was nothing: no pain, no wrenching ache from his knee, and no penetrating twinge from the mesh of wires that held his healing jaw together. In fact, Zeke felt normal.

The dream? he thought. *Could this have something to do with the dream?*

He stood up the rest of the way, his bare feet tingling from disuse, and discovered that he could move about freely, that pain was no longer a factor. Zeke felt a rush of relief and thankfulness. He whispered a quiet word of appreciation to the old man of his dream.

He moved about the darkened room slowly, testing each move, making sure everything was as it should be. When he was satisfied that he'd been healed, he sat down heavily in the family's large overstuffed chair, the one his dad seemed to favor most, and began to mull over his recent nighttime visions, taking care to remember as many details as he could. He was surprised to find that he had a vivid memory of the night's events. It was not, he thought, like his usual dreams, where the emotions and images faded quickly.

As he pondered, Zeke sat up abruptly, scooting quickly to the edge of the chair.

"Devon!" he exclaimed through his immobilized, clenched teeth. "He was trying to tell me something and I completely ignored him." Shaking his head slowly, he cursed himself. "How could I have been so stupid? Have I learned nothing?"

Zeke stood, leaving the comfort of the soft leather chair, and moved across the darkened hallway. He crept up the stairs, tiptoeing on each step so as not to awaken any member of the family. When he came to Devon's door, he turned the knob slowly, easing his way into the room. Once inside, he gently closed the door behind him and made his way over to the sleeping form of his brother.

Devon lay on his side. His breathing was regular and deep. Zeke sat next to him, slightly jostling the mattress, but otherwise leaving Devon undisturbed. Seeing his brother sleeping so deeply made Zeke rethink his decision to wake him, but he realized that time may not be on his side. Then, once again, the voice of the old man echoed in his thoughts.

There is an entity in your midst, Zeke, one that desires to have you; it will stop at nothing to exact its vengeance.

Zeke shuddered at the memory and felt a renewed determination to seek some explanation for the night's strange events. He nudged Devon lightly on the shoulder, but Devon neither moved nor changed his breathing pattern. Zeke poked him again, this time harder. Devon stirred. He opened his eyes slowly, blinking a few times as if he were trying to figure out where he was, then focused an accusing glare at Zeke.

"So," Devon said, his voice calm, but seasoned with an edge of sarcasm, "are you finally ready to listen?"

He was. Though Zeke was slightly astonished by Devon's lack of surprise or anger at being woken up so early. But he remembered that Devon had an unusually keen perception. Devon seemed to know and feel things that most normal twelve-year-olds would not. And so Zeke listened as he should have the first time Devon approached him in the hallway on that weary, blustery morning.

Zeke spoke first, or rather wrote, since speaking through the wires holding his jaw together required far too much effort. He began retelling his dream, and the two brothers compared experiences. After an hour of questions and answers, they sat staring at opposite walls, each trying to figure out the mystery, and if, in fact, there even was a mystery that needed solving.

Finally, after some moments of silence, Devon spoke again. "It was Grandpa, you know."

"What?" Zeke managed to mumble through his tightened jaw. "Who?"

"The man in your dream. It was Grandpa John. He was in my dream too, the one on the ship. He told me about the stones. He told me how to kill the Korrigan. So this dream you had could be just like mine," Devon answered emphatically. "We need to find out who or what this entity thing is. Maybe Taylre will know what to do."

Zeke nodded a muted agreement when the door to Devon's room opened. Their mother stood in the darkened entry, her hands on her hips, a scowl furrowing her brow.

"Do you two have any idea what time it is?" she asked, her voice coming out in a hushed but sharp whisper. "And Zeke, what in heaven's name are you doing up here? The doctor said to keep off your knee for four weeks."

"I'm better," Zeke responded, his lips moving awkwardly, but his teeth remaining clenched.

"Oh, please," his mother said. "You can't just suddenly be better."

"But I am," Zeke insisted. "Look." He stood up and began walking around the room. Moreover, there was no limp and no grimace of pain reflected on his face.

Vivian Proper watched Zeke march around the room with a doubtful expression. "Well," she said, "we'll let the doctor be the final judge since we have an appointment later today." Then she looked back at both boys. "Why *are* you two up so early?"

"No reason," Devon answered quickly.

"Really?" Vivian answered questioningly. "No reason. You two just decided to have a friendly little visit at three o'clock in the morning?" She leaned into the doorframe, arms crossed, a motherly expression of concern on her face, filling the room like a soft down blanket.

"We were just trying to catch up," Zeke lied. "Devon and I haven't had much of a chance to talk since the accident, so..." Zeke's eyes shifted, he found it hard to look at his mother while not being completely truthful.

"Right," his mother replied, a touch of sarcasm in her voice. "Just remember this: our family has been through a lot lately. We don't need another... event in our lives. A little sense of normalcy would be nice for a change. So if there's something you're not telling me, you'd both better come clean."

The brothers looked at one another guiltily, each waiting for the other to speak. Vivian Proper waited, but her patience was near its end. "Fine," she said, staring sternly at the boys. "But if something weird starts happening around here don't expect me to come running to help."

Vivian went to leave, but stopped and turned to look again at her two sons. "That's not true, you know. I will always be there for you. Just please promise me that if there's anything going on you'll let me and your father know before it's too late." Then she left, but not before she took another quick, unbelieving glance at Zeke's knee. She shook her head and left the boys, their mood suddenly silent and pensive.

CHAPTER NINE
The Visitor

Zeke managed to find his way back to his temporary bed on the couch, ignoring the urge to return to his own comfortable bed in his room. He hadn't been sleeping in his bedroom for three weeks now, and he sincerely looked forward to returning to his own space where life was familiar, both in sight and smell, and vowed that after today things would be back to normal. Or so he thought.

Zeke's mother had woken him early, and he rose from his short slumber with a nasty headache. Just as Zeke was swinging his legs off the couch Devon walked in, his hair standing on end, his face mottled with the residue of sleep, but his eyes wide with a sense of adventure. He gave Zeke a knowing wink before he headed into the kitchen for breakfast, mouthing the words, "Talk to Taylre."

Zeke stood unsteadily, once again expecting the familiar twinge of pain from his knee and jaw, but thankfully, there was nothing. He again thought about the dream, assuming that its reality was somehow the cause of his miraculous recovery.

Entering the kitchen, Zeke smelled his mother's extraordinary cooking, something that he had missed dearly over the past few weeks. With his jaw broken, and the wires clamping his mouth shut, Zeke had been forced to drink all of his meals through a straw, unable to enjoy a truly home cooked meal. At first, he was satisfied with milkshakes, yogurt, and the occasional cup of soup, but the novelty soon wore off. He began to crave something that he could sink his teeth into, something with substance. He hoped that his visit with the doctor later in the day would result in the immediate removal of the wires. In the meantime, Zeke was reduced to his usual glass of orange juice and a well-blended glass of oatmeal sucked through a large straw that was waiting for him on the kitchen table.

Zeke stared enviously at Devon who chewed ravenously on a piece of toast smothered in butter and strawberry jam. His father also sat at the kitchen table, munching heartily on a plump bran muffin. Zeke actually found himself beginning to drool. His longings, however, were quickly interrupted when his mother spoke.

"Devon, hurry up and eat, I'll be driving you to school today. I'm starting work at the book store this morning and I don't want to be late on my first day." She shuffled around the kitchen cleaning up small messes, wiping down countertops with a wet rag, and placing dirty dishes into the dishwasher. "And Zeke, make sure that you hurry and get yourself dressed, too. Your tutor will be here at 8:30 this morning instead of 9:00. She's coming earlier because I made an eleven o'clock doctor's appointment for you."

Zeke's dad looked up from his breakfast and his laptop computer.

"I'll be picking you up today, lover boy," he said, a small grin appearing on his face as he recognized the way his son's expression changed at the mention of the tutor, "so be ready when I get here. If you're healed as quickly as you claim, then we should be in and out of there like a flash and I can get back to work."

"Yeah, I'll be ready," Zeke answered, though he barely heard his mother's or his father's remarks. When his mom mentioned that the tutor would be over, Zeke's expression really did change. His eager thoughts for solid food had suddenly shifted. He now thought only of Miss Edda. The beautiful Miss Edda.

Due to the severity of Zeke's injuries and his inability to go to school, Zeke's parents decided that the best course of action would be to hire a tutor who would come over to the house each weekday to help Zeke keep up with his school work. The high school's principal was quick to suggest an excellent candidate for the job, a young college student by the name of Alicia Edda. Alicia had been a long time resident of Alder Cove until she left for college in another part of the country. Unfortunately, she had to return to the town due to the sudden and as yet unexplainable disappearance of her grandfather, the former mayor, David Vernon. The entire family had been distraught, and Alicia's studies were suffering due to her worry over the situation. She decided that it would be better to be with the rest of the family in their time of need and try to get back to her college studies later.

At first, Zeke felt a momentary rush of misery upon hearing the news that he would have to trudge through the next few weeks in the daily company of a tutor. Zeke felt that his hardships were bad enough without compounding them further by introducing a new, and possibly embarrassing element into his life. The thought of having to spend time with a teacher, in his own home, one who probably resembled the wicked witch from the Wizard of Oz, sent a shudder of despair coursing through his entire body. This, along with the pain he was already feeling, was almost more than he could bear. That was until he saw her.

Zeke was lying on the sofa the first day she arrived. His mom helped prop him up by placing pillows behind his back and scooting him rearward so that his back rested on the arm of his temporary bed. He was still in his pajamas, but feeling uncomfortable with the thought of meeting a stranger in nothing but his nightclothes encouraged him to drape himself in a ragged bathrobe. He waited for the inevitable knock on the door, anticipating that the next few hours would probably seem like an eternity. Finally, when the knock came, Mrs. Proper raced for the door and swung it open.

Alicia stood on the porch, her brunette hair blowing slightly in the wind. A reflection from the light colored paint on the side of the house shone on her face, illuminating it with an angelic glow. After greeting Vivian Proper, Alicia turned her radiant features toward Zeke. And he gasped.

Immediately he was aware of nothing but her face: her soft complexion, her thick luxurious hair, her green eyes and her perfect set of white teeth. The room, the house, his mother, the floor, the carpet, and the sofa, did not exist for Zeke. Everything had disappeared except for the perfect, radiant image of Alicia Edda.

In Zeke's eyes, Alicia could do no wrong. To him, her words and even her subtlest of movements were pure poetry. Her voice was soft, but confident. She was well versed in all of the literature Zeke had to read as well as the math and science he needed to learn. She was patient and kind. Above all, as far as Zeke was concerned, she smelled wonderful, like a field of lavender on a warm summer day. Whenever it came time for her to leave, Zeke felt a twinge of despair and began counting the hours and minutes until she would once again fill the tiny living room with her aroma, her glow, and her beauty.

Since today's meeting would be Zeke's last opportunity to visit one on one with Alicia, he was determined to look his best and perhaps, if the occasion presented itself, express his feelings of adoration to her. It never occurred to Zeke that a seven-year age gap could make that much of a difference. Besides, he thought, they'd become fast friends. And they laughed together all the time. In addition, she would often reach over and touch his hand when she was trying to encourage him to find the right answers to complex questions. Obviously, Zeke thought, she cherished him just as much as he cherished her.

As 8:30 slowly approached, Zeke situated himself on the sofa, its previous coverings of sheets and blankets now only a fading memory. He was freshly showered, his hair was washed and combed, and he was dressed in his best t-shirt and blue jeans. Surrounding him there wafted, ever so gently, the soft smell of his dad's finest cologne.

When the knock finally came, Zeke rose, smoothing his hair, straightening his shirtfront, and cupping his hand over his mouth to check his breath. He took one more deep lungful of air and let it out slowly, deeming himself ready. When he opened the door he was stunned to find Almar Loden standing on the porch, his crooked smile sending a shiver of surprise up the length of Zeke's spine.

"I'm assuming, from the look on your face, Zeke, that you were expecting someone else," Loden said. "I hope my visit doesn't come as a disappointment to you."

"I... I," Zeke stammered.

"I know," Loden interjected. "You were expecting Alicia. However, due to an unexpected illness she was unable to make it today, you see. And since I have just recently become good friends with the family, I felt I would be derelict in my duties if I did not offer my valuable services during their time of need. Therefore, since there was no pressing need for me at the school this morning I thought I could help by coming here and assisting you. It's really the least I could do." Loden smiled again and without waiting for an invitation, pushed past Zeke and entered the house.

Zeke was dumbfounded as he watched Almar Loden walk into his house and begin looking around as if he were a buyer considering the purchase of a home.

"Very nice, Zeke. I love what your family has done to the place. Your mother must be quite a decorator."

Zeke remained in place by the still open front door. "Yes," he replied awkwardly, "she likes to do that kind of thing." Then, before he lost voice again he asked, "How do you know Alicia?"

Loden turned sharply to gaze at Zeke, his eyes squinting slightly. "Well, I heard about the grandfather, you see, the former mayor, and I felt inclined to investigate things. Tragic, really, don't you think, Zeke? The mayor, all of a sudden coming up missing like that? It makes one wonder if there wasn't something malicious going on." Loden said, continuing his stroll around the room. His hands were clasped behind his back as he gazed at pictures on the wall and photos of the family balanced in small frames on end tables and shelves.

"What do you think of all that, Zeke? Surely you must have some opinion," Loden asked, turning once again to stare at Zeke.

"I really couldn't say," Zeke lied. "I didn't know the mayor, so how could I know anything about his disappearance?"

"Well, I just thought, with your father being so involved in the city's government, that there might be talk, perhaps around the dinner table," Loden said.

"No, no talk. No news," Zeke said, his eyes shifting downward involuntarily.

"Well," Loden responded with a slight wave of his hand, "it doesn't really matter. But I must say," he said, changing the subject abruptly. "You are certainly looking well. I honestly did not expect to see you bustling about so soon after the accident.

"And speaking of the accident, I never did get a chance to tell you how sorry I was. I mean, what are the chances that you'd be struck by some hoodlum's attempt at a prank." Then as a seemingly benign afterthought said, "By the way, did they ever find out who set that silly trap?"

Zeke shook his head and answered with an uncomfortable grunt. Questions about the accident always made him feel that way. And right now, he could feel his face heating up and turning a pale shade of red.

Loden noted the change with a tight grin and his usual squinting of the eyes, but said nothing about it. "Well, perhaps someone who has a conscience will step forward to either confess, or to turn the villain in, eh? In the meantime, it's good to see you up and around. You almost look whole enough to come back to school and get back to your running. The team could really use you."

"I... I do feel better," Zeke replied. "I have an appointment with the doctor later today, so hopefully I can get this brace off and these wires, too."

"I'm confident that all will go well," Loden said. "I'm sure that the doctor will give you a clean bill of health. However, in the meantime, we have some work to do. Why don't we begin with mythology, my favorite subject."

ᛦ

Later that day, after his appointment with the doctor, Zeke strode unencumbered by braces or wires to Alicia Edda's house, located in one of the more posh sections of Alder Cove. He was concerned about her sudden illness, but was mostly anxious to show her that he was now whole and healthy. When Zeke arrived at Alicia's house, he was dismayed to find that she was gone. Her mother, a thin, slightly older version of Alicia, informed Zeke that she'd suddenly decided to return to her schooling.

CHAPTER TEN
Wormwood

During the first two weeks of Zeke's recovery, Taylre had been, by far, his most consistent visitor. But then, something changed.

Taylre was walking to her third period chemistry class. Her mind was filled with myriad thoughts, ranging from homework assignments that would be due in the next couple of days to Zeke's accident, and, finally, to what she would cook her grandmother for dinner that night. She reflected on how busy her life was and wondered how she was ever going to get everything done. As she continued walking, muttering to herself as usual, she felt drawn to a particular part of the school, one she rarely visited, as if bidden to do so by some unseen influence. Taylre's eyes were drawn to a small poster on the wall, its colorful announcement shouting for her attention. She leaned in closely, taking in every word, feeling a slight tingling sensation begin to rise from the back of her neck and end abruptly on the very top of her head. It was a confusing feeling, one she wasn't sure she liked, but one she somehow couldn't ignore.

The poster was an advertisement for a new club. It read: **The Ferocious Fenrirs - Dedicated to providing random acts of kindness to those in need.** The club's advisor was Mr. Loden. Meetings were held twice a week, after school, in room 3366. At the bottom of the poster was a picture of a wolf, its back arched, its mouth open in a howl, and its eyes glowing a brilliant red. Then, in very small print on the lower right hand corner were the words: This club approved by ACHS Administration. Taylre was immediately intrigued. All previous thoughts of her busy life were now forgotten. And although Taylre was not one that would normally join clubs, she felt an immediate attraction to this one. All at once, she was determined to become a member of The Ferocious Fenrirs.

A meeting was being held that very day, and Taylre, in her sudden anxiousness, began watching the slow ticking of the clock, literally counting the seconds until school was over and she could attend her first meeting. When the last bell of the day rang, Taylre gathered up her books and backpack and quickly scampered her way to Mr. Loden's classroom. Upon her arrival,

Taylre was surprised to find the room packed with other students. Most of them she didn't know by name, but instead by reputation. These were the troublemakers of the school, the ones who actively looked for a reason to cause problems, the ones who made life for the rest of the student body at Alder Cove High School a living nightmare. She suddenly felt lost among this sea of errant bodies, and wondered if perhaps she had made a mistake in coming. Taylre was ready to turn around and leave when she unexpectedly felt a hand on her shoulder. She turned quickly, not because she was startled, but because the touch sent an unpleasant shock streaming through her body.

"Taylre," Mr. Loden said, his smile and the reflection in his eyes drawing Taylre in, causing her to forget the alarm she initially felt when he first touched her. "I'm so glad that you decided to come."

Taylre was taken aback by the greeting, experiencing a moment of uncertainty. "How... how did you know my name?" Taylre questioned.

"From Zeke, of course. He speaks of you often, you see," Loden responded. "When you walked into the room I recognized you immediately, though I'm sorry to hear that things have soured between you two."

It took a moment for Taylre to comprehend Loden's last

statement, but when she did, her head tilted to one side and her face clearly displayed confusion. "Soured?" she asked uncertainly. "What do you mean?"

Loden's face was the one that now showed a confused look, though his ability to act in such a way was well rehearsed and often practiced. "Well I..." he stammered. "I have been a frequent visitor of the poor boy, you see, and he mentioned..." then he paused, a soft shuddering sigh escaping his lips. "I can see that I've said too much. I really shouldn't meddle in such things. This is obviously between you and Zeke. But, I beg you," he pleaded, and this too was a well rehearsed performance, "don't let on that I mentioned anything to you. I wouldn't want my friendship with Zeke to be soured as well, you see."

Loden hesitated for a few calculated moments, and then patted Taylre sympathetically on the shoulder. He moved away, continuing to mingle among the crowd of students who had now become some of his faithful followers. Taylre just stood there, fixed in place by skepticism and perplexity. Her first impulse was to go to Zeke and ask him what, if anything, was wrong. But then she remembered Loden's pleading words. She wouldn't want to cause him any trouble, she thought, besides, wasn't he only trying to help? Wasn't he just attempting to be a mentor to all who needed one? She couldn't say anything, not now. She would just have to wait and hope that time would reveal the problem.

In the far corner of the room, amongst the hustle and bustle of students, Almar Loden stood with the ever-present Teddy Walford, Jr. standing beside him, a sentinel in tennis shoes, both watching Taylre. Loden's mouth was twisted up into a devious grin. From where he stood, he recognized the workings of the worm that squirmed and poisoned Taylre's mind. He could see it squirming its way into her brain and laying its eggs of treachery and vile deceit. Then he laughed a short, mirth-filled grunt of pleasure as another plot of destruction began to ripen.

And so, for the last week Taylre had avoided visiting Zeke. Instead, she allowed the worm of doubt to twist and turn its way into her brain where it pattered about, finally wriggling south until it reached her heart. And there it sat, waiting.

CHAPTER ELEVEN
La Cueva del Diablo

Ten miles north of Alder Cove, the landscape ascended abruptly forming high cliffs that overlooked the sea. Below the cliffs were straight, vertical walls of rock that reached as high as 300 feet above the water's surface. Here they crashed violently against the wind-swept terrain. Mooring a boat along these shores was impossible; the strong currents and the razor-sharp rocks that edged the cliffs could cause immediate and lasting damage to any watercraft that ventured too close.

The cliffs themselves were pockmarked with centuries of erosion. Here, among the sparse foliage, sea birds made their homes, flying in and out, flitting amid the small caves that made up the wall covering, and raising their families in scavenged nests. Farther north along the cliffs, about a mile or so beyond the tallest precipice, the indentations in the crag's face became larger, some big enough for a small mammal, and some even big enough to shelter a large man. And so it went, the farther north one traveled, the larger the caves became. Thus, if someone were to venture past the point, they would soon come across an inlet that hides an expansive cavern, its entrance guarded by sharp rocks that keep out even the most curious sea creatures. Nevertheless, although the hidden bay with its cavern was protected, it was not impenetrable. A mariner, who is familiar with the location and is correctly tutored, could direct a boat into the bay if he had to. It would take some time and effort, but it was possible.

And so it was that on the same day that Zeke had the wires removed from his jaw and the brace removed from his leg, Captain Bartholomew Gunner, better known to the general populace around Alder Cove as The Captain, was fishing for ling and yellow tail cod. His boat, an antique relic that contained a powerful motor and managed to provide plenty of fish for his expanding restaurant, cruised the rough waters of the Atlantic just a few hundred yards from the entrance to the hidden bay. Within the bay was the portentous grotto known to the locals and, in particular, the seasoned fishermen of the area, as La Cueva del Diablo. The Cave of the Devil.

The Captain had been fishing since very early in the day, long before the sun had risen. His labors had been successful for the most part, and he had all but decided to pull in his lines and head into port. However, just as he was turning the boat back to shore, the Captain glanced once more at his recently acquired fish finder and saw a large school of fish heading northward. The Captain, always considering the many mouths he had to feed each day in his restaurant, felt that the catch would just be too much to pass up, so he started giving chase, the fish always staying just ahead of his trolling boat and just out of reach of his fishing lines. As he continued to follow the elusive catch, he ended up in his current location, the bow of the boat facing the foreboding entrance to the bay.

While the Captain struggled near the stern with some tangled fishing lines, he felt a sudden unease as if someone were watching him, eyes boring imaginary holes into the back of his neck. He stood abruptly, releasing the lines he was bent over, and looked around, his own gaze finally resting on the narrow entrance to the bay.

Something moved in the inlet, a shadow that seemed to blend with the blackness of the cave.

The Captain moved quickly toward the bow, his heavy feet shuffling aside the fetid, brackish water that had accumulated on the deck. He stood, hips resting against the railing and raised his hand to his forehead to shade his eyes from the glaring sun as he stared toward the bay, frantically seeking the cause of the shadow. In his mind, the Captain worried that an inexperienced boater had somehow wandered into the treacherous cove, their life now suddenly in peril. He squinted, narrowing his weakening eyes to find the source of the movement, but he saw nothing, He convinced himself that what he really saw was nothing more than a trick of the light, an errant movement of some passing cloud, the inescapable deception that aging vision can start to play on a man who has spent too many days at sea staring into the dazzling sun shimmering off the water.

There! A murky shape crossed his vision, a gloomy trace of movement edging behind the rocks and entering the cave. The Captain felt compelled to take a closer look.

Bartholomew Gunner had entered the hidden bay before; in fact, he had done it several times. He was no stranger to the fact that sailing beyond the jagged rocks that stood as guards to the cove required experience and ability beyond that of a weekend sailor. Getting past those rocks required skill, and the Captain had it. Nevertheless, each time he entered, the challenge took its toll on him. The effort necessary required the eyes, the strength, and the coordination of a young man. The Captain realized that he had little left of any of these things. Deep within him, he dreaded the thought of making a run into the inlet. He knew that a life may need saving, but his courage was beginning to falter.

Suddenly his thoughts were hurled back to a memory, a time when his own lack of courage may have cost the life of a dear friend. Finding that courage came thirty years too late, it was a regret that he would never live down. His own confrontation with the Korrigan and the evil men who fed its hunger came about only because some very young friends of his finally convinced him that something needed to be done. The Captain knew that he couldn't let that happen again. And so he dug deep, finding the strength of will and determination necessary, marching his way forcefully into the wheelhouse, pushing the throttle of the aged boat forward, and setting a direct course toward the bay.

Perhaps, he thought. *Perhaps this time I won't be too late to do the right thing.*

The sea was agitated, typical for this particular time of the day and year. However, the sudden rise in the waves also seemed to be an ominous sign. The Captain steered the boat toward a well known out cropping of rocks, almost as if he were on a deadly collision course. But then, just as it appeared that the bow of the craft would be crushed on the needle sharp projections, he turned the wheel sharply, bringing it about to the starboard side. The sudden shift almost sent the Captain flying from his seat, but he managed to hang on, his knuckles white as his grip tightened on the helm. The chugging engine sent out a torrent of black smoke as it fought against the current, the boat now running parallel to the shore. The Captain held the direction for a few calculated seconds as he waited for just the right moment. Then, once again, he turned sharply, this time to the port side, bringing the boat around and pointing it toward a small opening in the rocks, its passage just wide enough for the boat to slide through. The Captain reached down to the throttle and gave it a final forward thrust sending it headlong into the hidden bay, its bow now directed at the gaping mouth of La Cueva del Diablo.

Within the confines of the hidden bay, the water was calm, its smooth surface protected from the battering Atlantic winds by the surrounding rocks and cliffs. The Captain took a moment to catch his breath, easing back on the throttle and allowing himself a short respite before directing the boat into the cavern's opening where the ocean's water settled in deep, undisturbed pools.

When he felt ready, the Captain made his way once again to the bow of the ship. Here he began scanning the area for the source of the moving shadow. However, after looking around the bay and seeing nothing, he determined that whatever caused the movement must now be in the cave. One glance into the cave's gaping mouth, however, made him realize that a casual glimpse would not suffice. He would have to enter the cave. Its interior was just too dark, an absolute contrast between the bright light of day and the pitch-black interior of the grotto.

Before returning to the ship's wheel and readying himself for the slow drift into the cave, the Captain hesitated. Something felt wrong. He couldn't place his finger on it, but something was definitely wrong. The short hair on the back of his neck prickled and he felt an irritating shudder climb the length of his back. In fact, the very air surrounding him seemed to be shouting at him to leave, to get out before it was too late.

And he almost did. How many times would he look back on this day and wish that he'd paid attention to those feelings?

Just then, he saw something stir from the corner of his eye, something in the cave like a white flash, purity among evil. He stepped closer to the bow, raising his hand once again as a shield against the glare from the water.

A small girl stood just inside the cavern's entrance, the hem of her white, flowing, antique dress soiled with bits of mud and debris, its frills dripping with seawater. She was standing at the precipice of a smooth, rounded rock where small waves ebbed and flowed over its even edges. Her head tilted gently to one side, and a small, sad smile creased her mouth. Her eyes glimmered an emerald green, while her long auburn hair fell across the side of her face like a faded watercolor painting.

The Captain stared in disbelief. How, he thought, did this girl get in the cave? Where were her parents? Where was the boat that brought her there?

Behind the girl, there was only darkness. She seemed to stand out like a beacon of light, the brilliant glare from the surrounding cliffs and the smooth water of the bay reflecting off her white dress. The Captain waved at the girl since she appeared to be looking directly at him. However, she made no movement, no gesture. She only stared and smiled, her pale arms hanging limply at her sides.

The Captain moved deftly to the ship's controls and expertly floated the boat into the cavern, ever mindful of the shallow water and the rocks that could easily puncture a hole in the bottom of his vessel. As he coasted closer to the spot where the girl stood, he eased up on the throttle and brought the boat to a standstill in the calm water. The Captain then moved quickly to the side of the boat and dropped a small but heavy lead anchor over the side. He pulled hard on the rope when the anchor finally reached the bottom, its hooks catching on some sharp crag beneath the surface and keeping the vessel from drifting any farther. He looked up at the girl who now stood only a few yards away, her pose still unchanged, like a storefront mannequin.

"Are ya alright, lass?" he asked. "Is someone with ya?"

Nothing. No movement, just the stare, though the Captain knew she was alive; her eyes followed his movements.

He exhaled a grunt of frustration. "I'm comin' over to get ya," he said, making a mental measurement of the distance between the side of the boat and the rock. In his younger days, the Captain could have easily made a leap like the one he was considering. But now, with arthritis stiffening the joints in his back and knees, he knew that he could never make it. Instead, he would find himself falling into the cold water, rather than dropping safely onto the smooth rock. The Captain scanned the deck of the boat and found a wooden plank, its weathered surface and rotting edges a testament of its age. He grabbed the board and secured it on the edge of the boat, the other end he rested on the rock, thus building a temporary bridge between the boat and the shore. Balancing himself like a man who had spent many years at sea, the Captain walked across the bridge, stepping safely onto the rock.

Though the girl remained frozen in her standing position, her eyes shifted, surveying the Captain's every move. The Captain stood before the girl and squatted down, his eyes now level with hers.

"Ya look cold, wee lassie. Let me put this blanket about yer shoulders." The Captain reached around behind himself to gather the gray woolen blanket he'd carried from the boat when he felt the solid grip of a hand on his shoulder.

"There's no need to go to all that fuss, Bartholomew," the quiet voice of the girl said.

The Captain turned his head in surprise, shocked to hear his own name uttered. "How did you ...?" the Captain began to say, but he was interrupted by the painful pressure of a vice-like hold upon his shoulder, its grip causing him to cry out in agony. The Captain fell to his knees, his eyes closed against the pain, and reached for the hand that grabbed him, his own strength useless in the attempt to release its hold.

"You're such a silly man." The voice of the small girl said, suddenly changing mid sentence from the innocent melody of youth to a deep bass, its tone dangerous and threatening. "You should have never ventured into my cave, you see. This is no place for a coward such as yourself."

The Captain opened his eyes, ignoring the anguish that coursed through his shoulder and neck, and looked up to see a man now standing above him, his long blond hair hanging in smooth strands down the length of his back, some of it brushed across his face, slightly obscuring his sharp features. Bartholomew Gunner stared up in disbelief. One moment there was a small, innocent looking girl standing before him and now there stood a large man, the power of his voice turning the

Captain's blood cold and his face an ashen white. An unstoppable terror materialized in the Captain's mind. His body began to shudder.

"Oh yes," the man said, his grip remaining firm, his head turned upward as he began to sniff the air. "I tend to have this effect on people. I do love it when fear rises; its aroma is so pleasant." He stared back down at the Captain. "Your fear is so thick that I can actually see it. Its sickly yellow hue reminds me of just how cowardly you really are. Nevertheless, *Captain*," he said sarcastically. "I have no further use for you. You weren't invited here, you see. You must now be punished, Bart. You don't mind me calling you Bart, do you?" He said with a sly smile.

The Captain continued to stare at the man before him, his mind and his voice paralyzed by fright. "I'll take your silence as a yes," the man assumed, his wicked smile drawn across gleaming white teeth.

"Entering the cave of the devil requires a very special invitation, you see." the man continued. "And since I'm the owner of this particular cave, that invitation can only come from me, *Bart*. I am quite certain that I didn't give you one, so that must mean you are trespassing. My policy has always been: all trespassers will be punished to the fullest extent of the law." The man began laughing for the first time, raspy, deep-throated and raucous, as if he had just told the funniest joke on Earth. "The best part is that since this is *my* temporary dwelling, I can make the law, you see."

The man released his grip on the Captain's shoulder, transferring his hold to the Captain's throat. He squeezed slightly, and with one muscled arm raised the Captain off the ground, his feet squirming below him like a drowning man treading water. The Captain gagged, gasping for breath as his face turned a bright red and his hands groped in vain to release the grip that the man had on him.

"Quit messing around in my affairs, Bart." The man said slowly, giving the Captain one last squeeze with his powerful hand and then, as if the Captain were nothing more than an annoying bag of trash, he tossed him into the darkness of the cave, with barely a grunt of effort.

The Captain flew through the air, his mind a whirl of shock, panic, and helplessness. All about him was darkness and the thrash of wind as he awaited the inevitable collision against the rocks. Just before his mind fell into the inescapable blackness of unconsciousness, a brief flash of reflected light from the cave's entrance revealed the severe outline of a serpent, its long head and neck making up what appeared to be the prow of an ancient sailing vessel.

CHAPTER TWELVE
A Course of Action

Zeke woke earlier than usual, discovering that he was actually excited about going to school. He washed up quickly, rinsed the sleep from his eyes, and dressed in the clothes his mom had bought at a late August Back-to-School sale. He put on his tennis shoes eagerly, tying the neon laces into a double knot and then found himself bounding down the stairs two at a time, entering the kitchen with enthusiasm, his appetite excitedly anticipating a hearty breakfast, something he had dearly missed over the past few weeks of recuperation. However, when he entered the kitchen he was disappointed to find the table empty and the air filled with the odor of burnt toast.

Percy Proper stood near the stove, his back turned to Zeke, his attention focused on a sizzling frying pan that issued an occasional puff of brown smoke. Zeke's father cursed lightly under his breath as he tried in vain to scrape some of the overcooked eggs off the bottom of the pan. He turned slightly to his right and noticed Zeke standing behind him.

"Whoops, sorry about that," he said, a slight red tinge shading his cheeks. "I didn't know you were up already. Would you like some breakfast?"

Zeke leaned in to glance at his father's attempt at cooking, noting the slightly askew plate of charred toast, the rubbery yellow stained eggs, and the watered down pitcher of orange juice perched on the counter. He frowned and looked up at his father.

"Where's mom?" he asked.

"Your mom had to go into work early," Zeke's dad said, returning his attention to the charred food. "Karen, her boss, had to go on some kind of book buying conference. Your mom is running the bookstore on her own until Karen gets back. So, in the mean time I'm in charge of the breakfast. But I'm assuming by the sour look on your face that the gourmet meal I've prepared doesn't meet with your approval," he said, looking at Zeke and then glancing back at the food he'd arranged, a disagreeable look now drawing itself across his own face. "I guess I don't blame you."

Percy Proper pushed aside the ruined breakfast, a playful smile curling his lips. "How does a nice bowl of Captain Crunch sound?"

Zeke nodded, "Perfect. It's exactly what I was hoping for."

As father and son sat down to their cold cereal, Percy Proper began talking about his idea of buying a sailboat, his excitement bubbling over as he related his own childhood memories of sailing up and down the coastline. He started to tell Zeke about the specific boat he had been looking at when Devon stumbled noisily into the kitchen, his hair disheveled and his face lined with pillow crease marks. His flannel pajamas were awry and wrinkled, and the large Toronto Maple Leaf logo printed across the front was faded, almost unrecognizable. When he yawned small droplets of spittle glitted onto the floor. Zeke and his father edged back slightly to avoid the mist of saliva. Devon sat down at the table, but it took a moment before his eyes focused. When they did, he looked around the room with a look of concern and confusion.

"Where's mom?" he demanded. Then, before anyone could answer, "Why are you eating cold cereal? And where's mine?"

Percy Proper chuckled and then rose from the table. "I'll get it for you, Devon. I'm not quite certain, considering the way you look, that you'd be able to get it on your own."

This time Zeke laughed, shaking his head and rolling his eyes, "Yer such a goober," he said.

Devon was too tired to respond to Zeke's taunt, but he was awake enough to recall their latest conversation. "What did Taylre say when you talked to her?" he asked, rubbing his eyes with the heels of his hand.

"Taylre?" Zeke responded, wiping away a spot of milk from his chin. "I didn't get a chance to talk to her. I tried to see her yesterday afternoon but her grandma said she wasn't home. Said she was at some sort of club meeting at school."

"Taylre in a club? Hmm..." Devon pursed his lips. "Joining a club doesn't sound like Taylre; you know how anti-club she is. She thinks they're stupid. She wouldn't even join the cross country team." Then thinking it over more he said, "Maybe we can catch her on the way to school. Let's finish our breakfast and then head over to her house before she leaves."

Zeke shrugged a tentative agreement. He was just as anxious as Devon to interpret his recent dream, but he had definite doubts about Taylre having any answers.

"Whatever," he said. "But I've an idea that she's not going to care too much. She hasn't exactly been 'miss friendly' lately. She hasn't called or visited in over a week. My guess is that she's discovered some new friends. That's why she's all of a sudden gotten involved in some new club."

"Well it's worth a try," Devon replied. "We've all been through too much together to start ignoring each other now. I'm sure she's just been busy. You know Taylre, she would never forget us."

The brothers left the house prepared for a cool day, but found the weather surprisingly warm for a mid-October morning. They ran across the street and knocked at Taylre's door. In a few moments Marjorie Anders, Taylre's grandmother, stood at the door, her smile warm and inviting. "Hello, boys. You are certainly here early." She looked back over her shoulder, evidently expecting to see Taylre sitting at the kitchen table. "That's funny," she said, turning her attention back to Zeke and Devon. "Taylre was here just a moment ago. Let me go get her."

While Marjorie left to find Taylre, the boys stepped into the small entryway, closing the door behind them. In a moment Taylre's grandmother returned, the once cordial smile gone and replaced with a subtle look of concern. "Taylre wanted me to let you know that she's ... busy." Her pause revealed a hint of anxiousness. "She wanted me tell you that she'll see you later ... maybe." A tight expression now etched itself across her face.

Zeke and Devon looked at each other, their expressions confused.

"Okay," Zeke finally said after a few moments of uncomfortable silence. "Well ... tell her ... tell her we'll see her later, then." Marjorie nodded, gently pushing the boys out of the door and closing it behind them without another word.

"That was weird," Devon said as the brothers descended the steps and continued their walk toward school.

"Yeah it was," Zeke replied, his hands shoved into his pockets, his backpack swinging slightly from side to side. "I got the strange feeling that she just didn't want to see us, as if she were angry for some reason."

The boys continued to walk, their path coming to a division in the road where Devon would turn left to the middle school and Zeke would turn right to the high school. As they approached the corner the boys stopped, their heads down, their minds both adrift in serious contemplation. Devon kicked absentmindedly at a stone, watching it tumble in the dirt.

"It's funny," he finally said, breaking the silence of the moment. "It's almost like I'm feeling betrayed. I'm not sure why, I just do."

Zeke abruptly stopped his own musing and looked at his brother, his hard stare causing Devon to step back. "What did you just say?" Zeke questioned sharply.

"I ... I didn't say anything," Devon stuttered, a hint of fear sounding in his voice.

"No, you did," Zeke said. "You said 'betrayed'. You said that it's almost like you're feeling betrayed."

"Well, yeah, but I didn't mean anything by it," Devon said, his thoughts racing, wondering how it was that he offended Zeke so easily. "I was just thinking out loud. You know, trying to work out the problem. That's all."

"No, it's okay," Zeke said, resting a comforting hand on Devon's shoulder. "It's just that when you said the word betrayed it reminded me of something that the man said in my dream. Something about people betraying me. People that are close to me."

Zeke turned to face Devon placing both of his hands on his shoulders, his look intent as he spoke slowly and carefully. "Listen, I need you to do something for me. After school go to the bookstore where mom works. When you get there use those research skills of yours to find out everything you can about 'fallen gods', 'punishing gods' or 'gods and snakes', anything along those lines. Write it all down and we'll meet tonight."

"Okay ..." Devon said hesitantly. "But why can't you do that?"

"Because I've got a meeting to find and attend after school," Zeke said, turning quickly and walking purposefully toward the high school, leaving Devon standing on the corner, confused.

CHAPTER THIRTEEN
Meeting Crasher

Zeke sat in his fifth period chemistry class. He watched the clock anxiously, anticipating the club meeting where he hoped he would finally be able to speak with Taylre.

Zeke had spotted Taylre earlier that morning dressed in her usual short overalls, but wearing a black t-shirt instead of her usual red and white striped one. He wanted to speak with her then, but the occasion never presented itself. She had been standing next to her locker with the door open hanging up her coat. Zeke was just rounding the corner where he had fallen on the wet tiles nearly four weeks ago. He tried to call to her over the tumult of the noisy crowd of students who lined the hallway, but she either couldn't hear him, or (and he had a hard time believing this) ignored him completely. As she turned to leave, Zeke tried to follow, but the horde of students was too thick and he eventually lost her in the crowd.

Throughout the rest of the day, Zeke tried to find Taylre. He walked past her locker several times without success and finally settled on the lunchroom, but again, she was nowhere to be found. Zeke began to think that she really was avoiding him, especially after the cold, unusual reception he and Devon received when they tried to visit her at her home earlier in the day.

At the sound of the final bell, Zeke pushed past the dawdling students who lingered to talk to the teacher and each other, and proceeded up the hallway toward the section of school that housed the English and Social Studies departments.

As he approached Mr. Loden's room, Zeke saw that the door was shut and that its exterior was covered with poster paper. On it, in bright, distinctive colors, was a well drawn depiction of a wolf's head, its teeth bared, its eyes glowing a brilliant yellow-red, and its ruddy fur standing on end as if it were bracing itself for an attack. One look at the creature sent a shudder of fear racing through Zeke's mind. Logic told him that there was no reason to be anxious; it was only a picture. And yet ... there was something eerily familiar and real about the drawing that caused a tremor of dread to run through him. To make matters worse, the eyes of the beast actually seemed to follow him as he moved. He reluctantly pulled his eyes away from the drawing and reached for the door handle when it suddenly opened on its own. With it came a hiss of stale air that smelled like incense and old wax. Zeke stepped back quickly, to avoid being hit by the swinging door, when a hand reached out from the darkened interior of the room and grabbed hold of his shirtfront, pulling him inside in one quick motion. Zeke barely had time to blink before he found himself standing inside the room, the door slamming shut behind him, the dim light causing him to squint.

Before him, their bodies forming unrecognizable silhouettes, stood a group of students. There were perhaps twenty-five to thirty in all, their shadows drifting about the room, silent, eyes fixed steadily on Zeke.

The shades over the windows were closed leaving the room in semi-darkness, allowing just enough light to seep through and give the room an ethereal character. The desks were lined up against the walls, a large empty space in the middle. Within this space lay cushioned mats. Beside each mat was a stick of burning incense perched in an intricately carved holder, engraved with a Viking warrior at battle, his sword piercing his enemy in some ghastly, gruesome manner.

The air was smoky; nevertheless, Zeke was able to make out a glint of light that reflected off Taylre's glasses. She was standing among the group that was staring at Zeke. She, like the rest of the group, wore a black t-shirt. Across the front was the familiar illustration of the wolf, the same one that appeared on the poster outside the door, the words *The Ferocious Fenrirs* written clearly across the front. Zeke made a move toward her, hoping to find comfort in her presence, but she stepped back, only a short stride, but enough to let Zeke know that he was not welcome.

"Why did you come here, Zeke?" she said through gritted teeth. "You weren't invited. You have to be invited to be here. It is the way. It is the law."

Zeke stared at her uncomprehendingly as the others around her nodded their heads in muted agreement.

"Taylre's right, Zeke. You must be invited," a voice proclaimed behind him. "But he said you'd come, and he was right. He's always right." Again, the group of students nodded their silent agreement in unison as if following some hidden direction.

Zeke turned, startled by the sound behind him, to see who had spoken, but the light was too dim to make out exactly where the declaration came from.

"Who is that?" He asked, his voice quivering with fear.

"I'm Teddy," the voice said. "Teddy Walford." Then, from the smoky shadows near the door, there emerged a large boy. He moved wraithlike toward Zeke, his giant form looming like a dark tower. "I was told to start the meeting without him. But he said to be prepared. That you would be coming. I didn't believe him. I couldn't imagine that you'd actually come. But here you are. Just like he said." Teddy then seemed to falter slightly, his face twisting with pain. "I hope he doesn't get angry at me," he said through a tightened jaw. "He hates it when we lose faith." The others around him nodded, their movements robotic, as if they'd been rehearsed.

"*Who* told you?" Zeke asked, his skin crawling with fright. "*Who* said I'd be coming?"

"Loden, of course," Teddy replied. "He's the club's advisor. He's the one in charge. He tells us what to do and we do it. It is the way. It is the law." More muted agreement came from the circle of staring students.

Zeke looked around the circle trying to identify faces, hoping to see Loden among them, but they were all strangers to him with the exception of Taylre.

"Where is Mr. Loden?" Zeke asked, a momentary curiosity taking over his fear.

"He said you would ask that," Teddy responded. "I was told to tell you: 'he is going to and fro on the earth, and walking up and down on it'. That's what he said to say."

Zeke shook his head and furrowed his brow in confusion.

"What is that supposed to mean?" He turned again to look

for Taylre, his hands outstretched as if he were pleading for an answer, but when he looked at her she slunk back into the crowd, shielding herself from Zeke's stare as if she were ashamed to be in his presence.

"None of that is important right now, Proper," Teddy said, bringing Zeke's attention back on him. "What *is* important is that you realize that you will continue to suffer for what you did. You have made a big mistake, and you must pay for that." Teddy suddenly stopped speaking, his head tilting awkwardly to one side, as if he were listening to a distant sound outside the door. His eyes seemed to lose focus, and an opaque glaze fogged their surface.

A few tense moments of silence passed, and then Teddy came out of his trance-like state, peering once again at Zeke.

"Where's your brother, Zeke?"

"Wha ...what?" Zeke responded, taken aback by the unexpected question. He looked among the crowd, trying to find Taylre, seeking for any help he could get in the hostile environment. None came, however, and Zeke returned his attention back to Teddy. "What does that have to do with anything? I just came here to join a club. I didn't see any signs that said this was an invitation only event." Teddy ignored Zeke's minor outburst and continued his questioning.

"What is he up to, Zeke? What are you up to?" Teddy's

voice was rising, his tone, once a flat robotic kind of inflection, began to take on an angry tone. "Are you snooping? Huh? Are you meddling where you shouldn't? He hates snoops you know. You need to mind your own business. It is the way. It is the law."

By now, Teddy was screaming, his voice reaching a distressing howl. Zeke could think of nothing but getting out of there as the pack of students began to close in on him. Then, they began to chant in unison, their bodies moving in a slow sway.

"It is the way. It is the law. It is the way. It is the law." Above the measured incantation was the voice of Teddy, his screams pressing against Zeke's mind like a vice.

"What is Devon doing? Why is he snooping? He must be stopped! He's an interfering little brat!"

Teddy reached for Zeke, grabbing hold of his shirtfront and shaking him violently. The rest of the Ferocious Fenrirs reached for Zeke too, their hands pulling at his back, tugging on his hair and slapping the back of his head. Zeke cried out in pain, his arms thrashing the air in an attempt to protect himself. Overcome by the pushing crowd, Zeke fell to the floor and felt the tips of several shoes kicking into his sides, the back of his head, and his face. He instinctively brought his arms up to cover his head, fearing another fracture to the jaw, but the kicks continued to come, relentlessly hitting him as he fought to breathe.

Suddenly, the booming voice of Teddy froze the onslaught. "Stop!"

The crowd of students immediately moved back to their places, building once again a tight circle that surrounded Zeke, his cowering form bunched up in a fetal position on the floor.

Teddy moved toward Zeke and bent down, his face only inches from Zeke's. Zeke pulled back, partly from fear, partly from Teddy's overpowering breath that smelled of raw onions and garlic.

"Where is Devon, Zeke?" Teddy hissed. "Where did you send the little brat off to? What kind of snooping do you have him doing? Huh?"

As Zeke continued to shy away from Teddy, he suddenly felt another presence beside him. He turned his head slightly to the side, startled by a voice that whispered delicately in his ear.

"He's with your mom, isn't he, Zeke? You sent him to the bookstore. Why?"

Zeke stared incredulously up at Taylre, her face impassive and expressionless. He tried to speak, but his mouth moved wordlessly. Then he felt it.

An overwhelming wave of betrayal.

How could Taylre do this? How could she be so cold; so filled with hatred, especially after everything they'd gone through? What had he done to cause her to turn on him?

Zeke watched as Taylre sat up and looked at Teddy.

"He's at the bookstore," she said. "I can see it in his eyes. That's where you'll find Devon."

Teddy nodded once, then turned and waved his hand at another boy who stood just inside the circle. Together they picked Zeke up, carrying him outside the room. The two boys marched Zeke down the vacant hallway and out a rarely used door that led to the football field. Beyond the field was the grove of trees where Zeke had suffered the blow to his jaw, and where the two boys were taking him now.

For the second time in his 14 years, Zeke actually felt fear for his life. He was sure that the two boys who lugged him across the field fully intended to take him to the forest and kill him. Nevertheless, Zeke, realizing that he'd defeated death once, knew he could do it again. He had to. He couldn't let these two thugs ruin his life. He wouldn't let them.

Hanging limply in the grasp of the two boys, his feet dragging behind him as he was pulled across the field, Zeke recognized a complacency that had settled in on his captors, their feelings of control overshadowing their need for vigilance. So, pushing past the pain that rushed through his body, Zeke took control, twisting free of the two boys by pressing his feet firmly into the ground and pulling away with a quick jolt. Zeke landed flat on his back but regained his feet quickly, turning in the opposite direction and running with the speed he'd acquired as a cross-country runner. Though he was out of shape from his weeks of recuperation, Zeke easily outran Teddy and his accomplice. The boys tried to give chase, but their legs quickly gave out, their tongues hanging out of their mouths like exhausted dogs.

CHAPTER FOURTEEN
Research

Vivian Proper sat amid the musty smell of old book leather and varnished wooden shelves. In her hand was a roll of binding tape. Before her sat a number of damaged books that had been donated to Zelda's Bookstore. Vivian's task was to repair the books, to bring them back to a sellable condition and then place them on the bargain shelf where an avid reader could pick up a copy of a like-new novel for cheap. To most onlookers this task might appear as tedious and boring, but to Vivian the labor was nothing short of divine.

While she placed strips of tape onto the damaged spines and ripped pages of each book, Vivian hummed to herself, content in her work as a handful of customers mingled amid the aisles, perusing the new and used books that lined each shelf. Her long auburn hair hung down the length of her back, but her short bangs allowed her pleasant, pale face to remain open, revealing blue eyes, tender pink cheeks, and soft red lips. With a smile, Vivian handled the task at hand with care, always aware that among the greatest loves in her life, first and foremost was her family, but second would forever be the love of books and reading.

When Vivian Proper first saw the advertisement in the newspaper declaring an opening for an assistant at Zelda's Bookstore, she had jumped at the chance. Taking the job would allow her the opportunity to spend some time away from the routine of housework and bring in some extra income as well. Percy and the boys were supportive of Vivian's decision, each of them keenly aware of her deep love for literature. She appreciated her small family even more for their support and their willingness to take on extra chores around the house. So, when her youngest son, Devon, appeared in the doorway of the little shop, her smile broadened even wider. Vivian always loved it when one of the boys visited; it allowed her to keep a close connection even while working.

"Hi, Devon," she said, standing up from her slouched position at the worktable and arching her back, stretching out the kinks that had developed. "How was school today? Did you ace that math test?"

Devon ambled into the shop, removing the heavy backpack that held his textbooks and binders. "School was great," he announced. "And the test was a breeze. I think I got one hundred percent on it, plus, I think I was also able to get some extra credit points by answering the bonus question."

"I don't know where you get it," his mom said, sitting again at the worktable. "Both your father and I struggled with math, and for that matter, anything to do with school, but for you it's so easy. Glad at least one of us has the smarts.

"What brings you in?" she asked, her voice taking on a serious tone. "You know you have chores at home, right? Just because I love it when you visit doesn't mean that you don't have to finish the work at home."

"I know," Devon said, exasperated. "I just came in to look some things up. I'm doing a..." he paused. "A project at school," he lied. "I need to check out some information on mythological gods. Do you have anything here I could look at?"

Devon's mom nodded her head slowly, eyeing her son suspiciously. "Mythological gods, uh? Anyone in particular?" she asked.

"Nope," Devon shrugged, attempting to look and sound nonchalant. "It might be nice to look up something about..." he paused again, trying to remember what Zeke had asked him to look for, "oh, anything to do with gods that get punished, gods that are fallen, or gods that have anything to do with snakes."

"Well," his mom said, now smiling slightly, though her suspicious look had not left. "That sounds pretty specific for someone who isn't looking for anything in particular."

"I might have been giving it a little thought," Devon admitted.

Vivian Proper rose from her seat, still looking at Devon with narrowed eyes. "Follow me," she said. "There's a section over here that has several books on mythology. The key is knowing what culture you're looking for." She guided him toward the rear of the shop where wooden shelves extended to the ceiling, their ledges packed with books of every size and shape.

"There are stories here from the Greeks, the Romans, and the Mayans," she said. "There are even mythological stories here about the Native American Indians, the Hindu gods, and the Norse gods. So," she continued, waving her arm at the mass of books, "take your pick."

"Wow," Devon said, his mind considering the enormous amount of research ahead of him. "I didn't realize there were so many. I knew the Greeks had their myths, but I never imagined everybody else had myths too."

"I'll leave you to it," Vivian said, turning and heading back to her work. "Just remember, this doesn't get you out of chores at home."

Devon watched his mom leave, and then looked back at the many titles that faced him, contemplating where he should start. At first, he just stood there, mulling over Zeke's instructions and the contents of his dream. Then, after a few moments of thinking he began running his fingers across the spines of each book, as if the titles themselves could speak, instructing him where to begin his investigation. After a few minutes of this tactile search, Devon stopped, his hand coming to rest on a book titled, *Norse Legends - Stories of the gods and the North People.* He pulled the book from the shelf, a shiver running the length of his arms causing his hair to stand on end.

Devon took the book and slipped it under his arm protectively, moving to a small, tattered couch that the owner of the bookstore had provided for patrons. Its faded fabric bore proof of the many customers who, over the years, had sat, relaxed, and read a good book. Devon sunk into the couch, the worn springs squeaking their own kind of protest. He reached into his backpack, took out a notebook, and turned to a clean page, then began flipping through the textbook. He studied the contents, hoping that something would catch his attention and scribbled down notes as he read.

While he sat scrutinizing the book, the small bell that hung over the door to the tiny shop jingled, its chime announcing the entrance of another customer. Devon looked up briefly to see two large boys walk in, his momentary glance turning into an all out stare. The first boy to enter was tall, very broad in the shoulders and chest, had extremely short, closely cropped hair (something Devon imagined he might see on a soldier) and a scowl on his face that sent a shudder of fear into Devon's mind. The boy that trailed was also large, but nothing in comparison to the first. He was lankier, slender in the shoulders and chest, and had a shock of black hair that appeared almost purple, contrasting drastically with his pale skin. Devon also noted that the boy had a silver nose ring pierced through his septum, like a large, angry bull. Both boys wore t-shirts depicting an enormous gray wolf, its teeth bared, its back arched, its mouth open in a howl, and its eyes glowing a brilliant red. Below the illustration were the words: **The Ferocious Fenrirs.** The letters looked like fresh drops of blood.

The boys mingled among the shelves, their attempt at trying to remain inconspicuous becoming plainly obvious to Devon. They appeared uncomfortable in the bookstore, as if the prospect of reading were a disease that one needed to avoid rather than embrace. Devon noted that they only pretended to look at the books, their interest actually lying somewhere else. Occasionally one of the boys would look over at Devon, and though he tried to focus on his research he couldn't help but look up from time to time, his own curiosity overwhelming him.

When they did look over at him, Devon sensed a kind of disapproval, anger, and even an intense dislike. Though he couldn't understand why, since he had never met either of them, he felt somewhere deep within him that it had something to do with his current task.

While the two watchers continued to circle the store, darting in one aisle and out through another, Devon wrote, not knowing if the information he was finding would be important or just a bunch of nonsense. Nevertheless, he kept at it, letting his intuition guide him.

The light of day was quickly fading and Devon was finding it hard to see the book he held; the daylight coming through the window behind him just wasn't enough. He felt it was time to pack things up and head home, deciding that he had enough information to keep Zeke happy, at least for a while. When he got up from the couch, he saw that his mom was still at work on the book repair and that the two boys were still in the store standing near the entrance. Vivian Proper had attempted once or twice to ask if the boys needed any help, but her offers were quickly shot down with curt, unfriendly responses. Eventually she went back to her work, always keeping a wary eye on the two strangers.

Devon placed the book back on the shelf and tucked the notebook in his backpack, but folded the paper he had written the notes on and shoved it in his back pocket. He walked past the two boys to say goodbye to his mom, aware that they were watching his every move. With a passing tap on the counter and a quick wave at his mom, Devon turned to leave, "I'll see you when you get home," he said.

"Okay, honey," his mom responded, calling after him as he slipped past the two boys who stood like sentinels in front of the door. "And don't forget your chores."

Devon glanced back at his mom, rolling his eyes. "I know. I know. You don't have to remind me."

When Devon walked out into the purple evening light, the two boys followed, slamming the door to the bookstore behind them. The sudden sound caught Devon's attention and he turned to look over his shoulder. He was surprised to see that the larger of the two boys was right behind him, the image of the wolf on his t-shirt staring Devon in the face. Devon turned quickly and picked up his pace, his steps echoing off the nearby buildings. Before long, he was standing at the intersection of Main Street and Odin's Parkway, a section of town that suddenly reminded him of his own ominous dream. Both boys continued to follow, the tallest of them still within arm's reach of Devon.

Devon crossed the street, now stepping up his stride to an easy jog.

The boys kept pace.

Devon began the slow incline that inched him toward his own neighborhood, passing the alley that he, Zeke, and Taylre once ventured up to witness the spectacle of the young boy who crouched animal-like in a stranger's backyard, a phenomenon that still remained a mystery. Both he and Zeke were now sure that the event was somehow connected to the appearance of the Korrigan. Devon decided to take a short cut through the alley, thereby reaching his home and safety quicker.

As he turned onto the gravel roadway, Devon felt a hand seize his shoulder, the grasp firm and unyielding. He was spun around violently and struck hard in the face. He fell to the ground striking the back of his head. Starry shapes appeared in his vision, but he fought hard to remain conscious, his eyes flying open wide, his arms flailing out in front of himself to ward off another attack. However, his attempts at defense were ineffectual. Both boys grabbed Devon, easily deflecting his weak blows and lifting him effortlessly to his feet as hot blood poured from his nose, its saltiness and copper-like taste clinging to his lips and dripping off his chin.

The larger of the two boys held onto Devon's shirtfront, bringing his face within inches of Devon's.

"What do you think you're doing, brat? You think you're smart? You think you're clever?"

Devon tried to pull back from the boy's grip, but it was just too strong, and the boy's breath sent Devon's mind swirling with the odor of raw onions and garlic.

"I ... I don't ..." Devon tried to answer.

"Shut up, brat!" The boy yelled. Then, turning to the other boy said, "Grab his backpack, stupid."

Devon felt his arms being pulled back and the pack forcefully removed, its contents chaotically dumped on the rocky surface. Once again, he was shoved to the ground, this time scraping the side of his face on the small gravel and feeling the tiny sharp pebbles penetrate his flesh. Fresh blood began to flow as his cheek split open, minute lacerations filling with dirt and filth. In the confusion Devon managed to raise his throbbing head, his vision slightly blurred by tears, and saw the textbooks and notebooks that were neatly organized in his backpack, being tossed, kicked, and ripped apart. Small pieces of paper lifted in the slight breeze and scattered themselves along the alleyway, the sidewalk, and into the surrounding yards. Finally, the large boy took hold of Devon's pack and with his bare hands tore it in half, tossing its remnants among the already littered ground.

Having destroyed the backpack and its contents, the boy lumbered back to Devon, his large hiking boots kicking up bits of stone and gravel as he moved. Behind him, the other boy giggled and snorted, taking obvious pleasure in the taunts and violence. Devon, still lying on his stomach in the dirt, was once more lifted by the back of his collar, his body suspended in the air by the boy's muscular arm. Again, the face of the boy came into focus, the odor of garlic and sweat mingling with his senses.

"You're a snoop, Devon Proper," the boy growled. "The Fenrirs don't tolerate snoops. So, here's a little message for you. And you'd better pay very close attention.

"You and your brainless brother are going to pay for what you did. It's going to be slow and painful. And when you can't take the agony any longer, we're going to add to it, making it ten times worse until you finally drop dead. If you keep meddling in places where you shouldn't, we're going to kill your parents, too. Think about that, Devon Proper. Do you really want your parents to suffer and die, too?" The boy shook Devon, expecting the answer to fall out of him. But, Devon merely shook his head; his brain was too jumbled; his thoughts were clouded behind a thick curtain of confusion. Devon was only able to comprehend a portion of what the boy said, though he remembered it all clearly enough later.

Finally, Devon felt himself falling. He landed with a solid thud on the gravel of the alleyway, his face and chest taking the brunt of the impact, pushing more dirt into his already swelling wounds. He lay there for several minutes, vaguely aware of laughter that dissipated into the evening air until it became a silent nothingness.

CHAPTER FIFTEEN
Revelation

A cold autumn night descended on Alder Cove, and with it came a blustery, late October wind that shook the remaining leaves off the trees that lined the barren streets. Hunkered down against the wind, appearing like a weakened soldier returning from battle, was a small stumbling figure. A slight limp accentuated his walk. As the figure approached the quiet house on Pike Street, the glow from the overhead streetlight pushed aside the shadows and revealed the bloodied, tired features of Devon Proper. Tears and blood stained his face. His expression still showed a grimace of pain, and each labored step seemed to bring on another stab of discomfort.

Finally reaching the house, Devon slowly ascended the front steps, taking each one deliberately and cautiously. He tried the front door but found it locked. He instinctively reached for his backpack where he kept his key, but then remembered with a shuddering sigh that his pack was now just a torn piece of fabric strewn among the rest of the litter that filled a nearby alleyway. He tried the doorbell even though he knew the house would be empty; his parents were still working and Zeke was attending a club meeting with Taylre, but a sense of desperation overwhelmed him. All he really wanted right now was to clean up in a nice hot bath and crawl into bed.

Devon moved to the top step on the porch and sat down heavily; the pain from the bruises on his back sent jolts of pain streaming through his body. He was preparing to wait and deliberate his next course of action when he heard the familiar shuffling walk of Zeke as he made his way up the sidewalk, cut across the lawn, climbed the porch steps, and then sat down heavily next to Devon.

Zeke was breathing rapidly; panting like a dog. He leaned forward, resting his arms on his knees, and hung his head low, gulping in air. After a few moments, Zeke began to regain his composure, his breathing slowing to a manageable rate. With his head still down and the darkness of the early evening shrouding Devon's wounds, Zeke glanced over at him.

"I'm glad I caught you in time," he said, still trying to slow his breath. "This could've been a really bad night if I didn't."

Devon sat quietly for a moment, and then turned his face fully toward Zeke.

"I don't think you did, big brother."

Zeke lifted his head, taking a close look at Devon. "What the hell?" he gasped. "Wha ... when did this happen? Who did this to you?" Zeke moved quickly, crouching in front of Devon, grabbing his shoulders firmly, and examining more closely the cuts and bruises that covered his face. "Devon, who did this to you?"

Devon shrugged off Zeke's grip, wincing with pain as he did. "Two big guys," he said. "They came into the bookstore and waited for me to leave. They attacked me on the way home, ripped up my books, tore up my backpack, and beat the crap out of me. A real pleasant afternoon," he said sarcastically.

"I'm so sorry, Devon," Zeke said. "This is my fault. I should have done more to stop them."

"Stop them?" Devon responded incredulously. "You mean you knew this was going to happen?"

"I didn't know what was going to happen," Zeke replied. "I knew they were looking for you, but I thought I could get to you before they did. When I saw you sitting here on the porch I assumed that everything was fine. I've had my own struggles over the last couple of hours, too. Obviously not as bad as yours, but bad just the same."

Zeke stood, extending his hand toward Devon. "Come on," he said. "Let's get you inside and cleaned up. After that we can talk and try to get this whole mess figured out."

ᛦ

Steam settled like London fog in the bathroom as the hot water from Devon's shower fell upon his aching body. He stood under the showerhead, letting the water pour over him in a comforting rhythm, allowing the soothing stream to wash away the dirt, grime, and dried blood that coated his skin.

Sitting on Devon's bed, listening to the rush of water that emanated from the bathroom down the hall, Zeke studied the wrinkled piece of notebook paper that he'd found in the back pocket of Devon's jeans. Smoothing the sheet of paper on his pant leg, Zeke considered Devon's chicken scratch scribbles and found himself examining each printed word closely. Some of the items were easy to read and even familiar. Phrases like Odin, the leader of souls, and Thor, god of thunder. But for the most part the words remained confusing, the names unfamiliar.

Devon entered the room with a colorful beach towel wrapped around his waist, his hair still dripping wet. His face was clean, revealing deep scratches on his cheeks, chin and forehead. When Zeke looked up and saw the injuries, he shook his head and sighed.

"I have no idea what we're going to tell mom and dad," he said.

"How about the truth," Devon responded.

"Not a good idea," Zeke said abruptly. "You know mom. She freaks out with stuff like this. And dad. He would want to get too involved. He'd try to solve everything and he'd be pulling City Hall into this. Next thing you know we'd be having big meetings in the principal's office, mom would be crying, and we'd have the Ferocious Fenrirs coming down on us like flies on molasses."

"The Ferocious what?" Devon said, balancing himself as he lifted his foot to put on his socks.

"Fenrirs," Zeke replied. "It's the name of the club that Taylre joined. The one I made the mistake of walking in on today."

Devon dressed quickly, tossing aside his wet towel in the corner of the room. "That's the name that the two jerks had written on their t-shirts. There was a picture of a wolf on them too."

"I know," Zeke said. "It was Teddy Walford and Chaz Nelson. They were the two that tried to do me in, too."

"Walford?" Devon questioned. "Why does that name sound

so familiar?"

"Think hard, Devon my boy. Remember the adventure by the river and the four dudes that tied you up? One of them was a cop. The chief of police, to be exact," Zeke said matter-of-factly.

"Chief Teddy Walford," Devon said, almost as if he were talking to himself, a moment of painful recollection appearing on his battered face. He looked at Zeke, confused, a myriad of questions forming in his mind. "This is all connected, Zeke. You know that, right."

"Yeah. But connected how?" Zeke replied. "Big Teddy's dad hasn't been seen or heard of since the night at the river. Is he somehow communicating with his son? Letting him know that we destroyed things? Is this some kind of a revenge thing?"

Devon sat next to Zeke, taking the wrinkled notebook paper and examining the words written earlier. "No. There's more to it than that. I've become a strong believer in dreams. Both of us have had major dreams lately. Not just your run of the mill visions either, but real eye-openers. This goes beyond simple revenge of a father and a son. Still, I believe revenge is a major thing."

"Where's it coming from, though?" Zeke said, standing and pacing the floor. "There's just too many questions, top among them is why has Taylre turned on us? I mean, whoa, dude.

What I saw at that meeting was, well... Let's just say she is not the same Taylre that we've come to know and love."

"Listen," Devon said, his expression stern with a look of authority that was too old for such a young face. "We've got three things to help us. Two dreams and this," he held up the paper, waving it in the air.

"I can't see how that's going to help," Zeke said, stopping his pacing to glance over his shoulder at Devon. "Your hand writing is so illegible that I don't even think you can read it."

"I can read it," Devon said curtly. "Sit down and I'll translate."

"I can't wait," Zeke said sarcastically. "But, we still have the issue of Mom and Dad. They're bound to be home any minute, and they're going to want to know about your injuries. What are we going to say?"

"I'm still for the truth," Devon said. "I hate the idea of lying to them. The last time we kept stuff from them it caused all sorts of problems."

"You're forgetting that we don't know anything yet," Zeke retorted. "That was the case last time, too. If we start spouting off all of our woes and worries with nothing to back it up, then we just end up causing all sorts of problems for everyone." Zeke sat down on the bed next to Devon, squaring his shoulders and looking him in the eye.

"This has got to be one of those wait and see times. If we reveal too much to Mom and Dad, and let's remember, we don't have that much to reveal, then it may ruin our chances of solving whatever's going on." Zeke softened his gaze, a tactic he always used when he was trying to win a serious debate. "Trust me, Devon. Not saying anything to Mom and Dad right now is a good thing. They'll thank us later."

Devon looked at Zeke with narrowed eyes, his mind working quickly trying to find the gap in Zeke's logic, but he could find nothing. At least nothing that he thought could win him the argument.

"Alright," he said reluctantly. "We tell them I came home from the bookstore, that I took my bike for a quick ride and wiped out while trying to do some BMX moves. But we eventually tell them the truth. I can't hang on to guilt like that for too long."

"Fair enough," Zeke said. "Just as soon as we get things figured out we tell them. Besides," he continued, "they may be able to help us if we come up with something really juicy."

Devon shook his head, "Let's hope we don't have to cover that ground again. One Korrigan is enough to last a lifetime." The boys settled themselves on the bed. Devon fluffed his pillow with practiced exactness and set it up against the wall behind the bed; Zeke simply smoothed out the rougher edges of the comforter and plopped his feet on top, mindless of the dirt that he scattered on the fabric. Devon looked at the mess and almost said something, but decided to let it pass.

"Okay, check it out," Devon began, returning to the crumpled paper. "I discovered some interesting things today. One is that there are a lot of names from mythology that we're already familiar with."

"Yeah, like Zeus and Poseidon," Zeke said, trying hard to stifle a yawn. "I know, I've read a bunch of stuff on that."

"Right," Devon retorted. "But those are from Greek myths. What I'm talking about is Norse mythology.

"Do you remember when the Captain told us about the Northern People that came over here hundreds and hundreds of years ago?" Devon continued as Zeke nodded, his expression drifting into boredom. "Well those were Norse people, or at least close relatives of them. They had a completely different set of gods that they worshipped; their names are all around here."

"Yeah, like what?" Zeke asked, his interest just slightly piqued.

"Like Odin's Peak, Mt. Sif, and Mt. Balder," Devon said. "All of them are names of Norse deities." He waved the notebook paper in front of Zeke's face, then pointed to some scribbles he had made. "See here, Odin is the main god. He's referred to as the Leader of Souls, plus about a million other names. Sif is a goddess. She's the wife of another god you may recognize: Thor."

"Thor?" Zeke said, now paying a little closer attention to the conversation. "As in 'The Thunder Makers' Thor?'"

"The very same," Devon stated.

"And Odin?" Zeke repeated. "That is definitely a name I've heard, and not just because of the mountain. Remember the writing on Grandpa's box? The carvings that made the mayor freak out and throw the thing into the fire?" Devon nodded, recalling the night and its terrors with vivid clarity. "The carvings said Odin's light."

"Yeah, goober. I was there, remember," Devon responded, dabbing at the corner of his mouth where it had begun to bleed again.

"What about this Balder dude?" Zeke asked. "Assuming it is a dude."

"He is," Devon assured him. "He was the son of Odin. His other name was 'the Beautiful', but he was killed by another god, a really bad mischievous guy named Loki."

"Whoa. Just wait a minute," Zeke said, sitting up a little straighter now. "You're saying that a god can die? That's not what I've read."

"I'm saying that the Northern People believed that their gods could die," Devon said. "They didn't think that the gods were immortal, like the Greeks or the Romans did. They believed that their gods fought battles against evil forces and tried to keep mankind safe, but in the end they would die."

"Okay. That sounds tragically ominous," Zeke said sarcastically. "But go back for a second. Who was the guy that was killed? What was his name?"

"Balder. He was considered the pure and peaceful one, so when he died all the gods were extremely upset."

"But there was another name you said he had. One that sounded kind of familiar."

Devon consulted his scribbled notes for a moment then looked up. 'The Beautiful', he said. "Balder was referred to as 'The Beautiful'."

"Hmm," Zeke mused. "There's something about that name that reminds me of something the man said in my dream. What about the guy that killed him? What's his name again?"

"Loki," Devon answered, after perusing his notes. "He has a lot of names, too, but I only wrote down a few of them. For instance, he's called 'The Sly One', and 'The Shape Changer'," Devon looked up from his notes. "Apparently he can change into anything he wants: a horse, a wolf, or even another person. Also, he's called 'The Trickster' and 'The Sky Traveler'. But then he's called ordinary names too, which seem to be an offshoot of Loki: Loder, Loden..."

"Stop!" Zeke sat straight up, reaching for the notepaper and tearing it out of Devon's hands, his eyes scanning furiously over the sloppy writing, his frantic brain making no sense of the scribbles. "What did you just say? What was that name you said?"

Devon grabbed the paper back, smoothing it out again on his leg. "Relax, monkey boy. What are you, mental?" Devon looked over his notes quickly. "The trickster."

"No, not that one," Zeke said. "Go further down."

"The Sky Traveler." Zeke shook his head, twirling his finger to push Devon to continue. "Loder, Loden..."

"There!" Zeke said, raising his hand like an overzealous traffic cop. "Loden. Did you just say Loden?"

"I did, monkey boy. Why does that make you so excited?"

"Loden," Zeke exclaimed. "He's the new teacher at the school."

"Yeah. So?" Devon said, shrugging his shoulders.

"He's Loki. He's come here to avenge the death of his daughter."

Devon stared. His face held an expression of disbelief and bewilderment. "What the hell are you talking about? These are myths. They're not real. These people don't exist."

"Right," Zeke said. "And the Korrigan wasn't real either."

Devon opened his mouth to say something, but then stopped. He tilted his head slightly to one side. "You've got a point there."

"You're damn right I do. And I do believe we are in serious trouble."

CHAPTER SIXTEEN
Naglfar

Water was dripping. Its splash on the rocks made a tinny echoing sound that carried a melancholy tone. The Captain raised his head, the thrumming reverberation waking him from his dark dreams. As he looked up, a shock of pain struck him like a jolt of electricity, gliding down his neck and ending in his belly. He lurched forward, sending a cascade of vomit spewing across the rocks. He sat up slowly, dizziness threatening to empty more of the contents of his stomach. Steadying himself, he reached up, felt the side of his head, and touched something slick. He looked at his hand reluctantly, knowing in his heart that it would be smeared with red, but hoping that the gods would somehow spare him, that the slickness would simply be accumulated sludge from the surrounding seawater. He sighed when he saw the crimson slime. He knew the wound was serious. He needed help quickly.

The Captain looked about him. Mostly there was darkness, but a glint of light reflected off the ceiling of the cave, and then he remembered where he was. His last few moments of memory came back to him, and the encounter with the small girl who was not a small girl at all came rushing back to him. A shudder of terror coursed through him causing his already chilled body to shake even more. He remembered the frightful man who took the place of the girl; his malevolent look, his incredible strength as he hurled the Captain through the air, across the cave, and against the solid rock. He remembered something else, too. A fleeting vision that etched an indelible image in his mind. One that, even now, he found hard to believe.

A ship in the cave, its presence hidden from prying eyes or curiosity seekers, resting like a sinister apparition.

However, this was no ordinary boat. In fact, the Captain could recall seeing only one like it, and that was merely a rough sketch, a charcoal impression of what some inspired artist had conceived in his own mind.

"No," the Captain said aloud, a whisper that sent a resonant hum through his aching head. "It can't be. There's no way in God's universe that it could be that ship."

He moved slowly on the slippery rocks, climbing clumsily upward out of the small cleft that he found himself wedged in.

A wave of nausea splashed over him and he was forced to stop, breathing deeply to settle the rush. He suddenly realized that the cause of the nausea was the head injury. A severe concussion. The Captain understood, from his many years at sea among men who could often get hurt for one reason or another, that remaining conscious until help came was his only hope. If he were to drift into a pleasing slumber, as he so desired to do at that moment, he might not wake up. And so, steadying himself and pushing away the cobwebs that filled his mind, he continued the short climb to the top of the jagged rock where the glint of light he had seen earlier first appeared.

Upon reaching the narrow crest, the Captain paused; voices sounded from the other side of the rock, their echoes reverberating off the nearby cavern walls.

Sharp, angry shouts along with cries of pain made the Captain's short neck hairs bristle and his grip on the uneven rock tighten with a sense of trepidation. He inched himself slowly over the crest of the rock and peered out into the large, open cavern. A quick intake of breath almost caused the Captain to lose his grip as he beheld the sight before him. There, huddled amongst the walls of the cool, darkened cave stood a small group of children, perhaps twenty in all. Surrounding them were twelve of the largest men the Captain had ever seen. Giants. Their huge bodies were covered in thick leather armor, their long hair was braided, and their beards hung the length of aged sages. Among the giants who surrounded the brood of youth, the Captain recognized four figures, their presence bringing back a memory that the Captain would have just as soon forgotten. Sweeping back the curtain of time to just a few months previous, the Captain saw the familiar face of the errant ex-chief of police, Teddy Walford. Beside him stood the three other nameless thugs who once wore the black robes of the Korrigan ceremony and who assisted the past mayor, David Vernon, in his dark task of calling forth the monster and drawing it toward its intended prey, Devon Proper. The Captain felt he should be surprised to the see these men, considering they had been the talk of the town over the past few months. Their disappearance was a mystery that was quickly becoming legend. Nevertheless, his surprise was tempered with curiosity; the Captain accepted their presence as appropriate, sensing that this series of events somehow connected with the other curses that had afflicted the town.

The youth, heads bowed and their shoulders hunched, cowered before the towering figures in obvious fear, as did the four men who labored among them. Indeed, they seemed to be captives here just as much as the terrified youth. Each child wore an identical, dark t-shirt. Each child also wore an expression of dread and forced obedience.

Before them, standing on an elevated rock, its surface flat and smooth, stood a tall blond man. The Captain recognized the man as the one who had literally picked him up and thrown him across the cavern. He was yelling at the assemblage, his words coarse with a violent undertone. Beside him stood a gangly youngster whose black, shoulder length hair was seized in the man's unyielding grip. The boy screamed when the man tugged on his hair and, as a result, received a skin-chilling slap. The Captain turned his head and cocked his ear to hear the man better. His accent was difficult to understand, especially with the echo that sounded off the cave's walls.

"... as a consequence, this one will be punished, you see. As you all will be if I catch any of you trying to escape. Must I continue to remind you how important this work is? Must I continue to force upon your minds what a magnificent honor it is to be able to render your service to me? It is the way, it is the law! You are all fools if you cannot see that! Fools!" Again, he turned to the struggling boy and tugged violently on his hair, causing another sharp scream. He dragged the boy from the rocky platform, the assembled group separated, allowing an opening for the man to walk through as he towed the child behind him. The boy's ankles dragged on the ground, his feet kicking helplessly as he tried to regain his footing, but the man moved too quickly. The boy continued to whimper with pain, his exhausted screams fading like dying embers on a cooling fire.

The Captain watched the youth's hopeless struggles and felt a pang of regret at his own helplessness. He was obviously too weak and far too outnumbered to offer any help to the boy, but managed to pull himself up enough to watch where the man took the lad.

That's when the Captain saw it. Now he knew that it was not some wild dream or a vague shimmer of some foolish subconscious fantasy. The thing he had seen while flying through the musty air of the cave *was* the ship of nightmare: Naglfar.

As a child, Bartholomew Gunner's mother taught him to revere all the gods. It was her belief that one could never be too careful. If a god did exist, and he or she was neglected, then the afterlife might become a horrific place. It was her motto, one she tried hard to impress upon Bartholomew, that a god remembered was a happy god. As a result, the Captain was educated very well in the ways of the Norse gods, the Greek and Roman gods, the Mayan, the North American Indian, Hindu, and Christian gods. Nothing, it seemed, was left to chance. The Captain was familiar, at least to some extent, with all of the stories associated with the gods of differing cultures, thanks to his mother. Now, as he stared dumbfounded at the infamous ship of Norse mythology, he couldn't help but shudder as his mother's words seemed to echo off the cave's walls along with the shouts and cries from below.

"*Remember this, Bart. All of the stories and legends have some basis in truth. One day you may be surprised to find that myth is actually reality.*" And indeed, there it was, Naglfar, the ship that would carry the wicked remnants of the underworld, led by their evil leader, Loki, to the gates of the gods in Asgard. There the final battle would begin, the war to end all wars: Ragnarok.

To the Captain's mind came a poem that ensnared his thoughts as a youth and which now seemed to give answer to his childlike intrigue:

> From the east comes the giant with shield held high;
> O'er the waves he twists, and the tawny eagle
> Gnaws corpses screaming; Naglfar is loose.
> O'er the sea from the north, there sails a ship
> With the people of Hel, at the helm stands Loki;
> After the wolf do wild men follow,
> And with them, the brothers of Loden go.

Now the Captain began to understand. The ship and its helmsman were here in La Cueva del Diablo.

"How appropriate," muttered the Captain, "that Loki, the devil himself, should be resting in *his* cave, preparing his ship and his minions for the battle to come."

Another sharp, piercing scream filled the cave and the Captain watched as Loki tossed the lanky youth onto the deck of the enormous ship, its port side oddly reflecting the scattered light from the mouth of the cavern. A giant who stood on the deck grabbed the boy and swiftly took him below, his cries becoming distant, muffled entreaties. The Captain returned his gaze to the gathered youth and suddenly realized something that sent a shiver of fear coursing through his veins. Taylre stood among the bowed and huddled group, her clothing identical to all of the others, but her curly red hair and oversized glasses making her appearance unmistakable.

CHAPTER SEVENTEEN
Skipper Jack

Saturday morning presented itself in the form of a gray leaden marine layer that settled heavily over the town of Alder Cove, its gloominess enveloping the town like a thick shroud. Zeke woke from a deep, intense slumber, his journey to consciousness feeling as if he was wading knee deep in syrup. His head throbbed, his neck felt stiff, and his abdomen reminded Zeke of what a punching bag must feel like after a run in with Mohammed Ali. He rose slowly, slipping his feet from the covers and placing them gently on the solid floor.

For just a moment, Zeke forgot the beating he had received the day before as he tried to figure out why he was feeling so sore. But then the painful memory came back in a flash of reality. He began to wish he had stayed asleep.

Looking out the window, Zeke felt the weight of the morning gloom. At that moment, he knew something was terribly wrong. He didn't know what that was exactly, but without a doubt he knew that the day held despair. Zeke looked back at his bed and seriously considered crawling back under the covers when he heard a knock. The door creaked open slowly.

Devon stood in the doorway. The look on his face was one Zeke had seen before. "Yeah, I know," Zeke said. "I feel it too."

The boys crept down the stairs, Rufus quick at their heels, their stomachs calling out for nourishment despite the depression that was thick in the air. Half way down the stairs, the door to their parents' room squeaked open. They stopped and looked up. Their father was standing above them peering over the railing.

"Hey, guys," he whispered. "Glad you're both up. I've got a surprise for you. Go get some breakfast and then meet me at the car. Make sure you dress warm." He smiled, rubbing his hands together in anticipation.

The boys continued to the kitchen, brows wrinkled in confusion.

"What do you think he's up to?" Devon wondered.

"I'm not sure," Zeke responded. "He definitely doesn't seem concerned about the story we told him and Mom last night. They actually seemed convinced that you got into a bike accident. Fortunately, none of my bruises showed, otherwise I'd be trying to explain that, too."

When the boys reached the kitchen, Zeke pulled open a cupboard, grabbed a box of cold cereal, and filled two gigantic bowls. Devon busied himself by filling Rufus' dish with dry dog food. Rufus looked up at Devon imploringly. He would rather have had the cereal.

"Still," Zeke continued, pausing before stuffing a heaping spoonful of Captain Crunch into his mouth, "Mom did seem a little suspicious. You can always tell when she thinks were lying, her eyebrow lifts while the other one stays put. It's kind of creepy."

Devon nodded, his mouth working furiously to chew the wad of cereal that filled his cheeks. "Dab seembs preddy habby dough."

Zeke looked up from his breakfast, his face a mask of wonder and bewilderment, "What'd you just say?"

Devon stopped chewing and swallowed. "I said, dad seems pretty happy. He must have something really exciting to show us."

"I guess," Zeke shrugged. "But I'd rather be spending my time figuring this Loden thing out. I have an aching feeling that time may be running out."

ᛦ

Percy Proper was waiting in the car, its engine rumbling with a low growl, reminding Percy that a tune-up was long overdue. Beside him lay a damp towel he had just used to wipe down the windshield and the outside mirrors that had become victims of the heavy morning dew. Rufus sat beside him, content to be going somewhere, anywhere.

Zeke and Devon climbed in slamming the door solidly behind them, Zeke taking the front seat since he had called shotgun just moments after stepping outside the front door, and Devon clambering in the back seat with a sullen expression of defeat. He always hated losing to Zeke, especially when it came to giving up the front seat.

Zeke tightened his seatbelt and then turned toward his dad, he saw that he wore, what Zeke had aptly named "the goofy Devon grin". When Devon wore it, Zeke despised it, but on his dad, Zeke saw it as warm and inviting.

"Are you boys ready for an adventure?" Percy asked, his face lighting up with expectancy.

Zeke glanced back at Devon. When their eyes met, the same thought raced through their minds: *This day will inevitably be full of adventure, one way or another.*

"Absolutely," Zeke said. "Obviously you've got something fantastic planned. I haven't seen you this excited in a long time."

"It is pretty cool," Percy responded. "I'm dying to spill the beans and tell you guys what it is right now, but that would spoil the fun. In the meantime, I know you both just ate breakfast, but I also know that you've both never turned down an invitation to eat, so I thought before I show you the secret I have in store maybe we could head over to the Captain's place and start the day with a hearty meal. What do ya say?"

The mention of more food, especially at the Captain's restaurant, made the boys' mouths water and they both nodded their heads enthusiastically.

"Perfect," Percy said, turning up the fan on the defroster. "Then the first stop, Typhoon Jack's."

Percy pulled out of the small driveway and drove slowly down Pike Street, over the hill that separated the residential part of town from the commercial and drove the van up to the curb in front of the restaurant. All three passengers looked out at the darkened windows of the Captain's café.

"That's funny," Percy exclaimed. "The place seems closed."

Percy stepped out of the van while the two boys and Rufus waited inside, watching as their father drew closer to the restaurant. He cupped his hands to the sides of his face and leaned up to the window to peer inside. Turning to the boys, he gave a slight shrug of his shoulders and had an odd, confused expression on his face. He walked back to the van and took his place in the driver's seat.

"It *is* closed," he reported. "I wonder why? It's not like Bartholomew to have his place closed, especially on a Saturday morning. I hope he's not sick or something."

Zeke turned from his father and looked back at the empty restaurant. A rush of that same gloominess that he had felt earlier that morning washed over him. Something wasn't right. He could feel it in his stomach, in his very bones, and the voice from the man in his dream echoed in his thoughts.

It wants to destroy you, Zeke, so be vigilant.

Percy started the van and pulled away from the curb, driving slowly toward the marina gate while both Zeke and Devon watched the Captain's restaurant fade in the distance.

"Well, here we are," Percy announced.

Zeke and Devon shifted quickly in their seats looking out the front windshield. Before them was the locked gate to the marina.

"What are we doing here, Dad?" Devon asked, leaning forward from the backseat, stretching his arms over his dad's shoulders. "We can't go in there unless we own a boat and have it parked in the marina."

"Oh really," Percy said, drawing out the words sarcastically. "Well then, maybe we'll have to just walk in there... with this key... and get on our new boat!" Percy produced a key from his pocket with a flourish, his 'goofy-Devon-grin' becoming wider than ever.

"No way!" The boys shouted, both of them reaching for the key at the same time, their voices full of joy and excitement, while Rufus barked his enthusiasm.

"Yes way," Percy said. "But I'll take the key. We don't want it dropping over the side of the dock on the first day out."

The boys and Rufus scrambled out of the car, Devon slamming the large sliding door shut behind him. They trailed their dad to the locked gate like eager dogs anticipating a long walk in the woods. Percy fiddled with the key in the lock making it seem like he was having trouble getting it to turn, knowing all the while that his stall tactic would cause the boys to become even more anxious. He smiled at his own childish game.

"Come on, Dad," Devon complained. "The anticipation is killing me."

"Almost got it," Percy said playfully. Then with a subtle click, the lock was released, the gate swung open, and the four of them began running over the wooden docks like children racing to the playground swings. As they ran, they passed all manner of ancient fishing vessels, sturdy tug boats and large pleasure crafts until they finally stopped abruptly in front of one particular sailboat. Zeke stood in silent awe, his breath coming in short gasps as he studied the smooth white surface of the hull, took in the polished wooden deck, and gazed almost lovingly at the stalwart masts. Then, as he slowly made his way around to the stern, he noted the name painted in bold letters that read: Skipper Jack.

"Skipper Jack," Zeke said thoughtfully. "What a cool name."

"I thought so, too," Percy agreed. "I got the name from an old book that my dad used to read to me when I was a kid. I always said that when, and if, I ever got a boat of my own I would name it the Skipper Jack."

All three now stood admiring the boat, their excitement growing as they anticipated the first voyage. "Time for your first sailing lesson, boys." Percy said as he put his arms around their shoulders and drew them in close. "First off, names and specifications."

"Can't we just go out on it?" Zeke asked. "I wanna see this baby ride the waves."

"Not until you've got the basics down." Percy answered. "The fundamentals of sailing are imperative, especially around here. The waters in this area can be pretty scary. If you don't know what you're doing and you come across a touchy situation, you could find yourself in trouble really fast. Many seasoned sailors have lost their lives out here simply because they lost focus and didn't remember the basics. As long as you have that, you should be fine.

"So," he said, stepping in front of the boys with his back to the boat, its sleek outline acting as an effective backdrop. "Lesson one: this," Percy said, waving his hand toward the boat like a model on *The Price is Right*, "is a 35 foot Island Packet. You could live on this boat if you wanted to. It's equipped with a shower, two bedrooms, and a roomy head that allows you lots of room when you have to use the bathroom, a 27 horsepower diesel engine, and a 90-gallon water tank. Plus, it also has a refrigerator and a stove, though the refrigerator seems to suck a lot of energy from the battery, so we use that only when necessary."

Percy stepped over the rope that circled the outside of the boat and stood on the smooth, polished wooden deck. "What I'm standing on here is the called the deck. The left side is referred to as the port side. The right side is the starboard. The front of the boat is the bow, and the back is the stern." Zeke and Devon listened, or at least put on their best 'listening faces', but they were quickly becoming bored as their father droned on. "...called the main mast, and this is the jib..."

While his father spoke, Zeke's mind drifted, his thoughts tracing through the odd closure of the Captain's restaurant, to the strange way that Taylre was acting, then to the Ferocious Fenrir meeting that he unintentionally interrupted the day before. He knew there was a connection and that it was all linked to Loden. He was sure of that. The dream was the key to figuring it all out.

"...Zeke, did you hear the question?" Percy asked, interrupting Zeke's thoughts.

Zeke was startled out of his thoughts. "Wha...what was that?"

"I said," his father repeated, pointing at the sail near the front of the boat, "what is the name of this sail? It's a bit of a test. A right answer gets you on board."

Zeke looked up and for the first time noticed Devon standing on the deck next to his father. "How'd he get up there?"

"He answered the question," Percy stated. "Where were you? In La La land?"

"No," Zeke said, a bit defensively. "I was just thinking. School stuff, ya know."

Devon scoffed, "Ya right. More like you were thinking about your girlfriend. You know, the one you *don't* have."

Zeke narrowed his eyes giving Devon an accusing look. "So, what's the answer?" his father repeated, still pointing to the foremost sail.

"Um...the grib," Zeke answered, his voice shaky and unsure.

"Close enough," Percy responded. "It's actually called the jib, but I'll let it go this time." Then, extending his hand toward his son, he said, "Welcome aboard, Zeke. Welcome aboard the Skipper Jack."

CHAPTER EIGHTEEN
The Devil's Domain

The sea was calm and the wind was light as the small inboard engine on the Skipper Jack puttered out of the marina and pushed the small crew into open water. Percy had the sails folded, knowing that the time for wind would eventually come as they got farther out to sea. In the meantime, he stood proudly at the helm, steering the boat and staring at his boys who looked on at the open water, their bright eyes marveling at the rising light that reflected off the ocean's surface. Percy also reflected on how much he loved his family, his boys, their love for life, their energy. Thinking of it infused him with life. *I would do anything for these boys,* he thought. *To think I almost gave it all up for some crazy, misunderstood curse.*

The last few months had brought many changes to the Proper family. With the "disappearance" of Mayor David

Vernon and his chief Alderman, Mr. Roberts, Percy was elected the town's interim Mayor. The change had been stressful considering the fact that he knew little about the actual running of a town, and he couldn't say anything about the whereabouts of the two men, or the errant Chief of Police, at least not yet. Maybe never; who in their right mind would believe that a monster in the river ate one of them, drowned the other, and scared the third away. Therefore, he was forced to keep the status quo in the mayor's office while all around him government officials were trying to discover where the missing men might have gone and if there were any improprieties connected to their disappearance.

Percy suffered no feelings of guilt regarding the two men. As far as he was concerned Roberts, Vernon, and Walford got exactly what they deserved. They dabbled in evil and it turned on them, as it always seems to do, eventually. Of course, he felt bad for the families they left behind, the ones who would always question what had happened, going to bed each night wondering if they were alive or dead. But there was nothing Percy could do. The best he felt he could do was to love his own family, to cherish every moment with them and look forward to a bright future. He had to find a way to settle his own mind into believing that justice was served in this event; that good prevailed over evil; that life could now go on.

"This is so awesome," Zeke said, interrupting Percy's thoughts. "I had no idea you knew how to sail. Where did you learn?"

"My dad," Percy answered. "Along with the boat that he and Bartholomew owned, dad had an old worn out sailboat that we used to take out in the summer. I got so that I could take it out on my own with a few of my friends. Mostly Dad taught me the basics; I figured the rest out for myself. A lot of trial and error, if you know what I mean."

"You didn't sink it did you?" Zeke said, a sly smile crossing his lips.

"You might think that's funny, but there were a few times when we came pretty close," Percy responded. "These waters can get scary really fast. If you're not careful, they can sneak up on you. And believe me when I tell you, this water is cold. I've been dumped a few times. If it weren't for the fact that I'm a good swimmer and that my friends were, too, I would've been a goner on more than one occasion."

"Really?" Devon said, now standing close enough to hear the conversation. "I'm surprised you still came out. I mean, being dumped overboard is not anything I'd want to happen twice."

Percy looked at Devon, a familiar look in his eyes.

"Uh oh," Devon said, rolling his eyes to look at Zeke. "There's that look. Dad just came across a 'teaching moment'."

Both Zeke and Devon laughed and Percy couldn't help but smile, too. "Am I that transparent?" he asked.

"Completely," Zeke answered.

"Well you have to admit there's something to be said about never giving up. I know this sounds like a stereotypical dad thing to say, but think about it," Percy said, now turning serious. "Quitting is the coward's way out. If it's important, at least to you, you fight. You keep going until you've acquired the skill, met the challenge, or, and you boys both know what I'm talking about, defeated the monster. You don't give up. You don't let anything get in your way. No matter what."

Both boys were silent for a moment, their thoughts turning to their father's mention of the monster and how its appearance had changed their lives.

"Dad," Zeke began, breaking the momentary pause, "you know we've been through a lot in the last little while."

Percy nodded his head pensively. "We certainly have," he said, unconsciously gripping the solid steering tiller a little tighter. "In fact, I'd venture to say there's not many families out there that have experienced anything quite as adventurous as we have. Wouldn't you agree?"

Both boys nodded, and Zeke even smiled a little. Then he looked at his father, his thoughts shifting back to the day they sat around a small fire, where charred trees stood as testaments to a vicious battle against the Korrigan, and where their father embraced them both in love and warmth. He took a deep breath.

"There's been some things happening lately," Zeke continued, his eyes shifting toward Devon who looked at Zeke with a bewildered stare, silent questions shooting at him like fiery darts from his eyes. "Things maybe you should know about."

"Yeah, like what?" Percy responded, his focus turning to the sudden tossing of the boat as the wind picked up.

Devon reached a strong hand toward Zeke and grabbed his arm.

"What are you doing?" He whispered sharply. "I thought that..."

Zeke pulled his arm quickly out of Devon's grip, his own tone of voice echoing Devon's.

"I have a feeling the time is right. We need to say something. Dad will listen."

Zeke turned back to his father whose gaze focused on the stowed sails, their unfurled material tucked neatly and securely on the sturdy boom. "There's this new teacher at school, and..."

"Hold that thought," Percy interrupted. "I'm going to need you to grab the tiller while I untie the sails. The wind is starting to pick up and I want you boys to feel what it's like to really sail, not just motor out onto the sea."

The once calm sea began to rise, and the wind blew with a steady breeze filling the sails that Percy unfurled. The billowy whiteness of the canvas was almost magical as they puffed open like proud peacocks, filling with the shifting air and pushing the Skipper Jack north along the coast line, the ship's hull tilting with the weight of the overflowing sails.

Percy returned to the helm, taking the tiller from Zeke's sweaty hands and expertly directing the bow so the wind and sails could work together creating a marriage of speed and momentum. Under his hands, he could feel the life of the boat. He called his sons to join him, to experience the energy that the Skipper Jack seemed to radiate.

Devon and Zeke stood beside him, both extending a hand and placing it on the vibrating tiller, their senses taking in the very being of the boat as well as the beauty of the passing coastline, its rising cliffs and pockmarked features giving way to an eerie foreboding.

The wind shifted unexpectedly, pulling at the sails and forcing the rudder to turn by some unseen current. Percy's heart raced as he gently pushed aside the boys and took control of the helm. Rufus, whose muffled whining drew the attention of the two boys, skidded along the deck, claws clicking unevenly along the wooden surface. Devon left his father's side to grab hold of him. As he grasped Rufus' collar with one hand and steadied himself with the other on the boom, the wind shifted again, but this time in an entirely new direction. The boom turned, swinging out to the port side, pulling Devon and Rufus with it. Devon, still holding firmly onto Rufus' collar with his left hand, swung over the side of the boat, his other hand still holding tentatively onto the boom, while the icy cold of the Atlantic Ocean roared beneath them.

"Hold tight!" Percy called, his muscles straining as he tried to pull the tiller to the starboard side. "Zeke, grab hold of the line and pull the boom in. Hurry!"

Zeke moved quickly but unsteadily toward the pulley where a length of rope connected the solid beam of the boom to the deck of the boat. He grabbed it and began to pull, but the wind's force was too much. He was left holding the rope helplessly as he watched the side of the boat tilt and Rufus' hindquarters dip into the freezing water.

"I can't!" he shouted. "I can't budge it! The damn thing won't move! The wind's too strong!"

Percy looked once more at Devon and imagined the worst as he pictured his son falling into the waves.

"Just hold the rope, Zeke! Don't let it slip! I'm coming over!" He left the tiller, securing it to a modified lock system that allowed him to leave the job of steering for a brief moment, and inched himself toward Zeke and the rope. The boat's violent tossing made walking on the deck almost impossible.

Together Percy and Zeke pulled on the rope, and inch by inch the boom moved. The dangling Rufus and Devon finally swung over the safety of the boat's deck. While Zeke held tightly to the rope, securing it firmly onto a cleat, Percy jumped up and placed one arm around Rufus while reaching up to grab onto Devon's belt. Devon let go of the boom, falling into his father's arms as they melted low onto the deck, both shaking from the rescue effort and both sighing with relief. Making sure that both Devon and Rufus were protected from further danger, Percy returned to the tiller as all former thoughts of spending a pleasurable day on the sea disappeared.

Devon leaned his back against the door to the galley, his body still shaking with cold and fear.

"Go inside," Percy said. "I've stowed some warm blankets in the forward bedroom. Wrap yourself up while I turn this around to head back home."

Zeke watched his brother open the galley door and step inside. He was filled with a sense of relief, but it was mingled with an edge of disappointment. He wanted to stay out on the sea. He knew they'd just had a narrow escape but he felt at home here. Now that the danger was over, he felt there was no reason to abandon their excursion.

"Do we have to go back, dad?" he asked. "We should be okay now. We'll just be more careful."

Percy shook his head. "Not today, son. My nerves are a bit frazzled right now. I was obviously not cautious enough. We'll come out again, but we need to get in before the wind gets any worse."

Percy pulled hard on the tiller, bringing the Skipper Jack around, the bow now pointing at the rugged coastline and the entrance to La Cueva del Diablo which was now visible, its ragged opening pulsing with violent waves. Recollections of warnings from his father to stay clear of the site echoed in Percy's mind.

The boom swung around and once again the sails filled with wind, pushing the Skipper Jack southward toward Alder Cove. Zeke, resigned to the eventual return to shore, looked up from his seated position near the tied off boom rope and relished the feel of the wind rushing through his hair. He had just remembered that he was about to tell his father about Loden and what he and Devon had recently discovered when he suddenly heard a faint cry. He tilted his head slightly to one side, trying to decide if what he heard was real or not.

Again, he heard the cry, but this time it was louder, and the voice seemed familiar. "Did you hear that?" he asked his father.

Percy turned to Zeke. "Hear what?" he said.

"That voice. There was someone calling for help."

Percy, his eyes squinting, began to look around at the rolling sea. "I didn't hear anyth..." he began to say, when he suddenly stood, his focus drawn toward the rocky shoreline.

Zeke also turned to look, his eyes scanning the water near the rugged shore when he saw a woman, her flailing arms and body bobbing up and down with the roll of the turbulent water, her faded cries for help coming in short gasps.

"There's a woman in the water!" Zeke shouted.

"I see her," Percy responded. "How in the hell did she get out here?"

Percy turned hard on the tiller, the bow now aimed directly at the woman. "Pull the sails down, Zeke. I'm going to switch on the engine. Then, hold tight. We've got another rescue to perform."

Zeke eased himself toward the ropes that secured the main sail. "This one?" he asked, pointing at the taut rope.

"Yeah, just release that and the sail should fall. Don't worry about tying it up. Just let it fall then get back here where you'll be safe."

Zeke pulled back on the rope, and the pulley that held it released, letting the rope slip while the sail dropped, the wind that filled its canvas slipping away like a forgotten dream. The engine rumbled to life, taking over the push of the boat and sending it briskly toward the drowning woman.

As they neared the target, Zeke stared in disbelief at the flailing figure.

It was Alicia Edda.

"How...?" He muttered to himself, trying hard to accept the reality of the situation.

"Grab the life saver, Zeke. Make sure it's tied off, and then throw it toward her when we get close enough!" Percy shouted, his hands still clinging tightly to the tiller, his muscles fighting the current and the high rolling waves in his attempt to keep a clear line toward the girl.

Zeke reached the white flotation ring and tied a line to it, testing its strength to make sure it held. As they neared Alicia, her face pale, her lips blue, and her strength ebbing quickly, Zeke tossed the lifesaver toward her.

"Grab on!" he yelled. However, Alicia seemed to be oblivious to the nearing boat and the rescue device that floated just a few inches from her.

"She doesn't see it!" Zeke called to his father, a pervasive sense of impending doom shrouding his mind.

Percy looked at his son, then back at the struggling woman. *Something's wrong,* he thought. *She's in shock. If I don't do something quickly, she'll drown.* Percy pulled back on the throttle, bringing the Skipper Jack to a near standstill. With quick, deft hands, he once again locked the tiller in place and without a second thought, dove into the water, the bite of its chill sending a reverberating shock through his system.

Zeke looked on in horror as he witnessed his father enter the cold, tumultuous water. The door to the galley swung open and Devon stepped out, Rufus quick at his heels.

"What's going on?" Devon asked, looking around the deck of the boat. "Where's Dad?"

Zeke pointed a rigid finger at the water where Percy Proper swam frantically toward the drowning woman. Devon gasped, "Who...? How...?" he said, searching for words to convey his scattered thoughts.

Rufus began barking, and Percy Proper turned slightly to peer behind him, the view of his sons and his dog watching him struggle through the cold water etched an eternal last impression on his mind. He was now within a few yards of the woman when she suddenly stopped her battle with the violent water and stared at Percy, her gaze fixing upon him like a ravenous beast.

"You're in my domain now, Percy," she said, her face slowly changing from an innocent beauty to a man with sharp, strong features and long golden hair.

Percy abruptly stopped his own struggle with the waves and stared at the entity before him. A chill, deeper than the surrounding water itself enveloped him. He recognized the man, but where was it from? A dream? Or perhaps a nightmare.

Then the man began to laugh, and Percy felt something brush his leg. At first, it felt like a gentle nudge, as if something, or someone, were testing its reality, its flavor, its substantiality. Then there was a pull, as if sharply clawed hands were scraping down the sides of his legs. Percy panicked, kicking his legs, trying to push away the unseen menace that taunted him.

Percy felt something sharp penetrate his skin. It tore at his flesh, and he fought to keep breathing, flailing his arms and splashing at the icy water. Then finally the thing below seized him, pulling hard. Percy went under, but by continuing to kick, managed to escape the razor-sharp bonds that held him. His head pierced the water's surface and he sucked greedily at the fresh air. Once again he stared into the eyes of the entity before him.

"Just one of my friends, Percy. You're the gift I promised him when I asked for his help. I hope you don't mind."

Percy was pulled under a second time; this time only his thrashing arms managed to brush the surface. His lungs screamed for air. He opened his mouth hoping another rush of air would cool the burning, but all that filled his lungs was the chilly water of the Atlantic. He felt the thing drag him deeper. Darkness engulfed him, and the chill seemed to fade from his tired limbs.

Percy's last thoughts were of his wife. In his mind she smiled sadly, her lips whispering a final farewell. *It's okay. They're waiting for you. Go in peace, my love.*

Finally, after another brief struggle, Percy Proper was silenced forever.

CHAPTER NINETEEN
Shock and Denial

Devon and Zeke just stood there, their fingers frozen to the bulwarks as if an arctic storm had suddenly driven in from the north. Their hands gripped the flimsy railing, their knuckles white, their open mouths issuing nothing but snowy silence.

Alicia Edda, the girl, had faded like a passing rain, revealing the entity. Zeke's sudden comprehension of the dream and the dark figure that lay upon the jagged stones suffering the violent drops of venom suddenly became crystal clear.

Loden was Loki.

He was the thing that filled the darkest recesses of one's mind. He was the thing in the closet. He was the punished god who now, after his bold escape, wandered to and fro on the earth, walking up and down on it seeking revenge for the death of his daughter, the Korrigan. But none of that mattered to

Zeke, not now. He'd have to deal with Loden later. For now, it was the horrible image of his father sinking to his death in the cold Atlantic that held Zeke frozen in place. As this thought took hold, Zeke found his voice, but it sounded like someone else's, someone in excruciating pain who dwelt far away. It took Devon's tight embrace to bring Zeke back to reality, a shared moment of deep, unbelievable anguish.

"No!" Zeke wailed. "No, no, no!"

Devon hugged his brother hard, not to stop the scream that fled Zeke's lips, but to join him, to partner in this moment of suffering, because there was nothing else that could be done. Percy Proper was gone, buried, and probably still sinking to the bottom of the deep current. Loden was gone, too, vanished like a snake slithering away in the tall grass.

Devon dropped to his knees, still clinging to Zeke's leg. He looked about him and found a second white lifesaver stowed on the railing, its round surface printed with the familiar name: Skipper Jack. In a futile effort, Devon reached for the flotation device, one hand bracing onto Zeke, the other clutching the feeble white life saving apparatus, and threw it into the waves, hoping for a miracle, hoping that his father would somehow reach up from the depths and retrieve the gift. But nothing happened. Zeke and Devon both just stared, their cries of grief softened as they watched the pale circle bob up and down with the tide, wondering what to do next.

"Such a pity, you see." The voice came from behind them, its tone irritably soothing.

Zeke and Devon swung around, their bodies turning at whiplash speed. Zeke almost fell over as Devon still held tightly to his leg, reaching mechanically for the rope-rail to control his spin. Devon gasped at the sound of the voice, feeling an electrical resonance sparkle through the air, as if the atmosphere were charged with an irritating static electricity. Rufus cowered in a corner, a throaty growl escaping his quivering lips as he tried desperately to hide himself under a layer of unfurled sails.

Before them, balanced on the boom, his back resting on the main mast, sat Loden, one knee raised with an arm resting on it. His long blond hair fluttered in the wind, and his face looked eerily sad as he stared out over the empty surface of the water, as if he were truly upset over the loss of Percy Proper.

"What the hell..." Zeke began, stepping forward as an inner anger began to rise. But he was interrupted by the forceful thrust of Loden's hand as it hung in the air, like a policeman halting traffic.

"Don't speak, Zeke," Loden said calmly. "I'm quite sure you'll only make matters worse, you see. You are a stupid, reckless little imp sometimes, and that worries me. It's going to get you into trouble. You should be more like your father is...or rather, was," he said, smiling briefly. "Percy was a brave man. You should return home and mourn him. Mourn him as I have mourned for my daughter.

"You remember her, don't you? She's the one you killed. The one you thought you were so brave in destroying," Loden said, the words spewing from his lips like a profane accusation.

"We'll meet again, Zeke, I can guarantee you that. For now, however, you should just leave. Because if you stay, I will kill you too, you see. You and your precious little sacrifice," he said, looking directly at Devon.

"We mustn't hasten things. I really don't think it's your time yet. But it will be. Soon. For both of you. When that is done, my work here will be finished, and then I can move on to more important things, you see. So, in the meantime, go home. Go home and tell your mommy that Daddy is dead," Loden continued mockingly. "I'm sure she'll have a good cry over it." He slipped down slowly from the boom, standing squarely on the wooden deck, his pale face and firm jaw set firmly, taunting Zeke and Devon.

Zeke said nothing, but he could feel his jaw tighten and his hands, which lay stiffly at his sides, clench into fists of rage. But just as quickly as the rage built, it was suddenly silenced by a mounting fear, one that completely enveloped him causing him to step back. He reached down, grabbed Devon by his jacket collar, and pulled him along with him, as if he were protecting him from an inevitable attack.

Loden is Loki, Zeke thought. He was swallowed again by paralyzing fear.

Loden stared at Zeke, his eyes widening, his mouth lifting into an evil grin. "That's right," Loden said. "Let it fill you, Zeke. Let the terror have its way. Feel it. Taste it. Let it melt into your very soul." Loden closed his eyes and lifted his head, breathing deeply from the surrounding air. "Ahhh," he said, his eyes opening and turning to look once again at the two boys. "It's wonderful, isn't it?" The smile faded from his lips, his eyes narrowed, and there was silence. Even the wind seemed to stop.

Then he left, as if he'd never really been there, like someone flicking a light switch on a wall. One moment Loden was there, the next he wasn't, and the brothers were left staring at nothing.

Finally, after several long moments, Devon came to his senses and touched Zeke on the arm, startling him out of a terror-stricken paralysis. Zeke turned to his brother, his hands shaking, his mouth trying to form words.

"What did you say?" Devon said, an intense look of concern painting itself across his face as he leaned his ear in closer to Zeke. "I can't hear you. You've got to speak up."

Zeke tried again, but managed only a sharp, incomprehensible whisper.

Devon took hold of Zeke and guided him by the arm to a nearby seat like a nurse leading an aged invalid. He sat Zeke down and placed a blanket around his shoulders protectively. "Talk to me, Zeke. You've got to talk to me."

Then, in a voice that sounded to Devon like a declaration from a distant mist, Zeke said, "This is a dream. None of this is really happening. It's all just a bad dream." He looked at Devon, his eyes welling up with tears. "Tell me this is just a dream, Devon. Dad isn't dead. He's in his bed sleeping and when I wake up everything will be all right again. Tell me that's what's going to happen. Please. Tell me that's what's going to happen."

Devon's own eyes began to tear up, too. He bowed his head, unable to look at Zeke any longer.

"C'mon," he said, lifting Zeke's arms, forcing him to stand. "We've got to get this thing home."

CHAPTER TWENTY
Pain and Guilt

The voyage back to the marina at Alder Cove went surprisingly well, especially considering that the boys had just watched their father drown right in front of their eyes, and the devil himself had just appeared to them. Devon handled the tiller as if he'd been sailing all of his life. He considered using the radio to call for help, and although he knew nothing about how to work it, he knew that if he fiddled with it long enough he would eventually contact someone. The Coast Guard, perhaps. But then he thought, *Why? What would be the point? No one is going to save Dad now. We certainly don't need saving.* But then he looked again at Zeke as he sat huddled in a corner, a thick blanket still wrapped around him, Rufus lying next to him, his head resting comfortably on Zeke's lap, and he wondered if perhaps they did need saving after all.

Neither Zeke nor Devon spoke a word during the short trip, but Devon continued to glance toward Zeke, concern for his mental welfare mounting. Occasionally Zeke would let out a muffled moan and Devon would look up to see fresh tears flood Zeke's eyes, his blurry gaze set once again upon the empty, open ocean. However, Zeke remained mute, as if speaking would release a spell, a curse perhaps, that would envelope the boat and its inexperienced crew and wrap them in a pall of darkness that the light of day could never penetrate.

As the Skipper Jack pulled into the marina, Devon finally did encounter some challenges. Turning the boat in the small area was difficult, and adjusting the throttle so that the hull didn't crash into the pier presented even more of a problem. He pushed, and then pulled on the throttle several times, as he tried to work the boat into the small slip, but in the end, he managed to settle it in place with only minimal damage.

His dad would have been proud.

After securing the boat to the cleats mounted on the ancient pier, their rusted, paint chipped edges proof of their age, Devon helped Zeke step out of the now steadied Skipper Jack. As Zeke stepped over the bulwark, his movements were stiff and slow and his expression was vacant. Together they walked slowly to the gate, trudging their way through the threshold and directing their steps toward home, leaving the family van abandoned in the parking lot.

It took the two brothers nearly forty-five minutes to make the trek home. Devon often found himself dragging Zeke along, tugging at the blanket that was still wrapped around him. Rufus followed obediently, but his movements were also slow, his head hanging low and the brightness of his eyes dulled, as if he were somehow aware of the great loss the Proper family had suffered and that his role as man's best friend was being put to the ultimate test.

When they reached the front porch, Devon looked upon its newly painted surface and recalled the work that his dad had just put in restoring it to its current like-new condition. Zeke tried to sit on the wooden steps, but Devon pulled at him, urging him to stand and enter the house, a task that neither of them really wanted to perform; telling their mother about what had just occurred would surely be the most difficult chore either one of them had ever had to do.

ᛉ

A strong northerly wind had been blowing hard all morning, and the temperature had dropped several degrees during the night. The windows in the house rattled with each gust of wind,

and the doors kept banging against the door jams as if someone
were trying to escape the confines of the empty rooms. A cold
draft whistled through the upstairs hallways, jostling pictures
hung on the walls and accentuating the loneliness and despair
that pervaded the house. In the living room, an open but as yet
unread book lay on Vivian Proper's lap. Rufus was snuggled up
beside her, his head resting on her leg, an occasional sigh
escaping his curled up form.

Vivian had a blanket wrapped around her in an attempt to
ward off the chill in the house. She refused to turn on the heat,
believing that it was still too early in the year to have the furnace
switched on. She knew that Percy would agree, he would have
kept the heat off, too. Saving money was always one of his
specialties. At the thought of this, Vivian began to cry again. Her
failed attempts at wiping away the many tears that had already
fallen were abandoned and she allowed the wetness to soak her
reddened cheeks and fall to her lap, some of the tears falling on
the pages of the open book.

Across from Vivian Proper, sitting in a worn and faded
leather chair, one that Percy Proper used to favor as he studied
manuals, wrote down notes for upcoming meetings at City Hall,
or read from works about famous men who had changed the
world, sat Devon. He, too, was bundled in an oversized blanket
that he had pulled up over his head, covering his ears but leaving

his face exposed. He seemed to be staring at nothing as his blank gaze and tired red eyes scanned the grooves and knots in the wooden floor. He listened to his mother's sobs feeling helpless to comfort her. He had tried many times over the past several hours and throughout the long sleepless night, but nothing seemed to help; her pain was deep, her anguish a throbbing, endless beating drum.

On the floor, curled up in the fetal position next to the cold and empty fireplace, lay Zeke. He seemed oblivious to the chill as he rested on the bare rug, still in his clothes from the day before, the twisted, wrinkled material proof of his own wake-filled and restless night. His eyes were closed, but his mind was alert and completely awake. He tried to tune out the mourning cries coming from his mother, finding the grief too painful to bear, especially when coupled with his own misery. But the chore was impossible, especially considering all that had happened during the last twenty-four hours.

Almost an entire day earlier, when Zeke and Devon finally climbed the front steps and entered the house, Vivian instantly recognized that something was wrong. Call it a woman's intuition or a mother's gift, but somehow she knew that something terrible had happened. Then, when Devon spoke the words informing her that Percy Proper had died, the sound that she made, the howl of pain that rose from her lips, reverberated throughout the house. And Zeke, lying with his eyes closed next to the cold fireplace, could still feel the shiver that coursed through his body touching him not only physically, but also mentally and spiritually as well.

After her initial expression of grief, Vivian Proper called the authorities, sending out everyone she could think of to search the area where Percy had been lost. A representative from the Coast Guard returned hours later with the sad news that no body had been found. They would continue the search, of course, but things did not look good. Most likely, the Coast Guard Captain said, the body would wash up on shore somewhere, until then they would keep a close lookout. Eventually, he said, they would find their husband and father.

Zeke remembered those words, that vacant promise. He knew they weren't true. He knew they would never find the body; it was gone forever.

"I need to hear the truth," said Vivian Proper, her voice now calm and even, breaking the prevailing silence that filled the room. "What really happened out there? And don't spare any details. I want to hear it all because I believe there's something you two aren't telling me, something you're keeping to yourselves that needs to come out now."

And she was right. There were many things she had not been told. As far as she knew, Percy had simply fallen out of the boat. When he did, the rising waves entangled him and he had drowned. Neither Zeke nor Devon had said anything about Loden or Loki, Taylre's unusual behavior, the beating that both Zeke and Devon had received at the hands of the Ferocious Fenrirs, or the dreams.

Most importantly the dreams.

Zeke sat up on the cold floor. Devon pulled the blanket away from his face, dropping it down around his waist. The brothers looked at each other, realizing the time had come to tell the truth, to bare their souls and free themselves, at least from *this* burden.

Zeke was the first to speak, though he did so quietly and reluctantly. "It's all my fault. All of it. If I hadn't..." he said, his voice trailing off as he forced his mind to think, to gather his thoughts. "If I had only spoken up sooner, none of this would have happened. Dad would still be here and we would be a happy family again." Then as if to accentuate the point, he spoke louder, "It's all my fault!"

Devon pushed aside the blanket wrapped around his waist, letting it fall to the floor. "That's not true and you know it, Zeke," he said, his voice rising with a mixture of anger and empathy. He turned to his mother. "Dad's death, along with everything else that I'm going to tell you about, happened because of the Korrigan. Zeke killed it. We were all involved in that event in some way, and we've all been made to pay. This whole thing is about revenge."

Devon stood and walked over to his mother, pushing Rufus aside and sitting down next to her. He looked at Zeke and beckoned him to do the same. Zeke rose obediently, though halfheartedly, and took his place on the other side of his mother, squishing himself in between her and the arm of the couch.

Sitting beside his mother, inhaling her fragrance that he associated so much with warmth and love, Devon continued his narrative. "I know we haven't talked about this much. In fact, hardly at all. I'm not sure if that has been a good thing or not, but either way we've chosen to ignore it. The reality is that supernatural events have happened here and this family has been a big part of them.

"Mom," Devon said, taking his mother's hand in his own, "I know you weren't there that night, the night that the Korrigan rose, but you know about it. I know dad told you everything. I wish I could tell you that that was the end of it. That with the death of the monster and the death of Vernon and Roberts, all the nonsense had ended. But it didn't. In fact, it's only gotten worse."

Devon continued speaking, relating everything he could think of concerning the strange and often painful events that had taken place during the last month and a half. When he came to the part about Zeke's dream, he let him take over. Zeke did so, but his normal enthusiasm and energy had left him. And though he told his mom about the dream with amazing clarity, he still insisted that his father's death was his fault. That if not for his own foolish bravado in trying to fix everything, Percy Proper might still be alive.

Vivian Proper listened carefully to everything she was told. Several times she wanted to interrupt the account to scold her children, to tell them they were being silly, that their imaginations were taking over, but mostly, she wanted to do what she did best, to comfort. She began to realize what a harrowing experience both of her sons had been through and she felt deep sympathy for them. Nevertheless, she managed to hold her tongue, letting the expressions on her face and the nodding and shaking of her head do the talking for her. Finally, after both boys had spoken and the room once again fell silent except for the battering gusts of wind that continued to pummel the outside of the house, Vivian spoke.

"I think that if this were the first time that I'd heard something like this, and hadn't seen for myself the results of this story you both have told, I would've laughed and called you both crazy. But I know what you've said is true. I feel it in every fiber of my being. I suppose the question now is: what do we do?

This Loden character isn't going to stop, you've made that very clear. So, *what* do we do?"

Zeke and Devon both considered the question, but it wasn't new to them. They'd reflected on it before, but there were no convenient answers, no manuals or textbooks to look at that would have directions on what to do in case your life was suddenly entrenched in the vengeful plot of an angry fallen god. A god who is able to change into whatever shape he wants or appear in any location he desires. The boys were stumped. They had nothing to offer, and this made the situation even more unbearable and frightening. Vivian Proper feared for the life of her two sons. She feared that she might lose all of her boys if they weren't careful.

In the midst of their silent thoughts, there came a sudden, frantic knock at the front door. All three jumped at the sound, and Rufus barked a quick but frightened yap, sitting up quickly from his curled up position on the couch, but not brave enough to step down and run to the door. For a moment they each, in turn, assumed that their worst fears were realized, that Loden, Loki, was now standing at the door waiting for it to open so he could pounce on them and have the matter over and done with in one fell swoop.

Mother and sons looked at each other and a silent argument seemed to ensue between them as to who would go to the door and open it.

Zeke was the first to stand. He walked toward the door cautiously, his legs shaking, wobbling actually, and he had a hard time keeping his balance. Behind him was Devon, following at an arm's length, his body tensed and ready to run at the slightest movement. Zeke reached for the knob, turning it slowly and pulled the door open. He felt a sudden draft whip through the opening, pushing his hair back and forcing his eyes to squint shut. As he regained his sight - though it was slightly blurred from the windy tears that welled up in his eyes - Zeke recognized Marjorie Anders, Taylre's grandmother, standing on the porch.

"Zeke," she said, an edge of panic rising in her voice. "I'm so sorry to bother you and your family, especially at a time like this, but have you seen Taylre? She seems to be missing."

CHAPTER TWENTY-ONE
The One That Got Away

Thirst. Without question, the suffering that plagued the Captain most was the thirst. It was like a dry rock desert cutting through his throat. And as he sat, huddled and hidden amongst the rocks at the back of the cave, the Captain was reminded of a line from a poem he'd read many times, one that seemed fitting, especially now.

> Day after day, day after day,
> We stuck, nor breath nor motion;
> As idle as a painted ship
> Upon a painted ocean.
> Water, water, everywhere,
> And all the boards did shrink;

Water, water, everywhere,

Nor any drop to drink

On the rocks, close to where the Captain lay, the rising tide pushed the briny water, its gentle lapping motion lifting over the ragged stones and then ebbing back toward the deeper portions of the cave, making soft trickling sounds that forced the Captain to lick his cracked and bleeding lips. So many times he wanted to bend down and drink from the pools, to quench the nagging thirst that was driving him to madness, but his thinking self, his logical self, scolded him, warning him that to do so would kill him. The salt would turn his blood angry, he knew this, and instead of saving him, would plunge him into a lunacy even more desperate.

The Captain had no idea how long he had been there. Minutes and hours seemed to drift into one another making time seem indifferent and uncaring. The irksome pain in his back and shoulders, and most especially the one at the side of his head throbbed. Hunger called to him, and the chill of the dark cave threatened to overwhelm him. Nevertheless, he continued to hold on, even managing to stay awake, remembering that sleep, too, would bring death.

As the Captain lay there, listening to the occasional shouts and angry taunts that emanated from beyond the rock precipice that he hid behind, he suddenly heard an indistinct shuffling sound coming from behind him. He craned his neck in the direction of the noise, supposing it was some poor, lost varmint that had lost its way, crawling into the depths of the cave looking for food. What the Captain saw, however, wasn't far from his initial guess. Behind him, slithering amongst the jagged rocks, was a boy. His tattered clothing and bruised face identified him as the one who had been slapped, beaten, and dragged into the ancient Viking ship, Naglfar, the infamous ship of mystery that lay at anchor only a few hundred yards away.

The Captain was startled by the boy's presence and jerked around quickly, putting himself into a defensive pose. He groaned with pain as he did so, but found the anguish to be nothing compared to the sudden shock he felt at seeing the boy. At first he thought that the marred and beaten youth had been sent to finish him off, that Loki had sent a mere lad on the errand of murder. But then he noticed the boy's own surprise as the youth's face became pale with fright and his eyes lit up with terror. The Captain let his defensive posture relax for just a moment as he sized up the poor trampled teenager who cowered in front of him.

"What's yer name, lad?" he said, his voice a low, sharp whisper.

The boy, his shock of black hair drooping over into his eyes, stared dumbfounded at the Captain. He inched himself backward as if he expected the Captain to pounce on him, but his movements, too, were slow and obviously painful.

"It's all right, boy. I'm not goin' to hurt ya," the Captain said. "Just tell me yer name and yer purpose."

The boy continued to stare, but his eyes narrowed and his head cocked lazily to one side as if he had suddenly understood something important or as if he had unexpectedly found something of value that had previously been lost.

"I... I," he began to say as he raised himself from the jagged rocks and crouched low on his haunches. "I'm Chaz," he finally muttered, as a flood of tears began glazing over his eyes. "I want to go home now. This isn't fun anymore."

Surprised by the boy's last statement, the Captain wondered to himself what kind of treachery the evil Loki had used to entice the youth to this dank, foreboding atmosphere in the first place.

Easing forward, his movements slow and gentle, the Captain stretched forth his hand, his palm down, his fingers extended slightly, and reached toward the boy, almost as if he were attempting to pet a volatile dog. Chaz drew back, afraid the bloodied and battered man in front of him would strike him.

"Don't worry, son. I need ya to help me up. Can ya do that? Can ya help me stand?"

Chaz regarded the Captain curiously, his head tilting, his eyes narrowing.

"You... you want me to help you?"

"Yes, lad. I'm badly hurt, just like you. And you want to get out of here don't ya?" Chaz nodded, but his movements were reluctant and untrusting.

"Good," the Captain said. "Then we'll need to help each other. I don't want to be here either. Together maybe the two of us can get out. But I need ya to trust me, boy."

Chaz' face showed the mental conflict that was raging in his mind. His eyes shifted back and forth, his hands trembled, and he bounced nervously on his haunches. When he finally spoke again, his voice was a soft whisper, like a distant call for help.

"This isn't fun for you anymore, either?"

The Captain hesitated only a moment, knowing he had succeeded in gaining the boy's attention and trust, but realizing that maintaining it might be like holding on to a frightened bird, its fragile wings eager to escape the grasp of a predator.

"No, lad. There's nothin fun about this place. Never was."

A moment later, the Captain was surprised to feel a sudden, strong grasp on his hand as Chaz took hold of him, his leg extending to a nearby rock as he pulled him to an awkward standing position. The Captain teetered for just a moment as he tried to regain his balance, feeling a rush of dizziness overcome him, his face turning a sharp pale and his knees threatening to buckle under his weight. Chaz advanced quickly, wrapping his arms around the Captain, the sudden embrace sending a surge of comfort into each of them. Loneliness and pain had taken its toll, the unexpected warmth of friendship provided an outpouring of strength that was desperately needed.

Chaz, his left arm still wrapped around the Captain's waist, continued to steady his wounded companion, and together they began to make their way slowly out of the narrow rocky cleft, Chaz leading the way. Together they skirted the tumble of rocks that made up the floor of the cave, edging in and out of other constricted passages that threatened to bar their way. Eventually they stumbled to the far end of the cave where the mouth opened to the windy outside and the narrow cove that the Captain had first entered. The Captain turned, once again, to glance back at their progress, always mindful of the shouting from the far end of the cave where some unknown work and preparations continued; where the group of captive youth was subject to the unyielding physical and mental tortures of the wicked Loki.

The Captain caught a glimpse of his boat that was still moored in the calm, deep waters of the cave and longed to be on it, sailing away from this place, wishing he had never set foot here. Chaz tugged on his arm, pulling his attention back to the present.

"Let's keep moving, old man," Chaz said. "We've got to hurry before Mr. Loden notices that we're gone. Otherwise it's back to the bottom of the fingernail boat," he continued with a grimace. "And trust me, we really don't want that."

"I'm Bart," the Captain said, allowing Chaz to lead him out of the cave toward the sharp cliffs that rose some three hundred feet straight up.

Chaz stopped and turned to look at the Captain. "What?" he said, his face a mixture of pain, exhaustion, and curiosity.

"I'm Bart," the Captain repeated. "I don't want you to call me 'old man'. I may look old, but up here," the Captain pointed toward his head, "up here I'm young. I've still got a lot of livin to do. So call me Bart, Chaz," he said, emphasizing the boy's name, "and help me get out of here alive."

Chaz regarded the Captain with a serious expression, and then, slowly, a small smile began to appear on his bruised face. "Okay, Bart, I'll get you out of here," he said, turning to survey the cliff that loomed before them. "But it isn't going to be easy. This place is well protected, and that," he said, pointing at the cliff, "is the only way out."

The Captain followed the direction the pointing finger

indicated and stared at the intimidating precipice that stood before them, its sharp loftiness taunting him. He sighed in painful resignation and nodded slowly.

"Lead on, McDuff."

"What?" Chaz asked.

"Never mind," the Captain said. "Let's just get this over with."

The two fugitives sidled unsteadily along the bottom of the cliff, keeping themselves low and hidden from view. They stumbled among lose rocks, the Captain occasionally emitting a suppressed moan of pain. Eventually they reached a worn section of ground, some two hundred yards from the cave's opening where a path led to a coarse route that would take them upward, a scattered array of handholds dotting the natural vertical trail. They marched toward it, focused determination filling both of them, and they began to climb.

ᛣ

Five hundred yards away, standing tall on a rock that jutted up from the cave floor higher than all the rest, stood Loki, a look of perfect satisfaction on his face as a gust of wind entered the cave's mouth and tossed a thin line of his long, blonde hair over his chiseled jaw line. He smiled, and a shallow wrinkle creased his cheek.

"Careful, boys," he said, as he watched the Captain and Chaz begin their long, dangerous climb up and out of La Cueva del Diablo. "I can't have you falling and killing yourselves, you see. Not just yet." And he chuckled lightly under his breath. "Do your job, and bring them all here. Let's get this done all at once."

CHAPTER TWENTY-TWO
The Pied Piper

The climb took well over three hours, and when Chaz and the Captain finally reached the top, they were exhausted to the point of near unconsciousness. As they pulled themselves over the last ledge and found themselves on firm, level earth, the two wounded and beaten companions fell heavily to the ground, their breath coming in short gasps, and their bruised and swollen faces dripping with sweat.

After twenty minutes of lying on the near frozen ground, Chaz became aware of the swirling wind about him, the taste of dirt in his mouth, and the nagging, throbbing pain that encompassed his entire body. He rose slowly, bringing himself up to an awkward sitting position and looked at the Captain who was lying just a few yards from him, his breathing still labored, his broken body painful to look at.

"We've got to keep moving, Bart. It's getting cold and I think it's gonna start to rain soon." Chaz tried to stand, bringing himself up on all fours, and then gently, as a nagging cramp began to rise in his leg, climbed to his feet, staggering slightly with dizziness and the forceful push of the wind.

"I ...I can't," the Captain moaned, his eyes closed, his breath huffing against the ground, sending volleys of dirt toward Chaz' feet.

"You've got to..." Chaz paused, thinking for just a moment. A smirk creased his black-and-blue face. "...Old man."

The Captain's eyes opened quickly and he stared up at Chaz. At first a flash of anger flushed across his face, but then he smiled, painfully, as a new trickle of blood emerged from his head wound. "I told ya not to call me that, lad." The Captain responded, knowing that Chaz had just pushed the right button.

Chaz bent low, easing his arms underneath the Captain's, and pulled while the Captain pushed. Together, after a long succession of painful gasps and quaking groans, they succeeded in getting the Captain to his feet. He wobbled for only a moment, but then a look of determination filled him and he stood firm.

"There's a road about a half mile from here," Chaz said, pointing westward. "It's a tough walk, but if we go slow and keep moving steadily we should be able to make it in about thirty minutes."

The Captain nodded. He knew the lay of the land well, in fact, he probably knew it far better than Chaz could ever imagine, but he allowed Chaz to resume the lead, realizing that the boy had been through a lot. A little boost for his crushed self-esteem couldn't hurt.

The two started off, trudging along the uneven, rocky ground with their shoulders hunched against the wind. As they walked, their eyes scanning the distance for some sign of a road, the rain began to fall.

ᚷ

Vivian Proper handed Marjorie Anders a steaming cup of hot tea, her hands shaking slightly with the effort and the mounting stress of recent events, while Zeke and Devon struggled with the small teepee of kindling they had assembled in an attempt to build a fire in the fireplace.

The two women sat on the couch sipping their tea while they watched the brothers' feeble efforts at starting a fire. Marjorie sat to the far side of the couch and avoided making any eye contact with Vivian, her comfort level in the Proper home still remaining tense and awkward. Marjorie knew that Percy, shortly after the incident with the Korrigan, had disclosed everything about Marjorie's past, about her involvement with David Vernon and Peter Roberts, and her terrible blunders with regard to her own brother's death. Her feelings of guilt for her actions had never subsided, and she realized they probably never would. Nevertheless, she felt her guilt was her punishment. How could she be brought to proper justice through the courts of the land? Who in their right mind would believe the tale of a mythical creature and a vengeful god? And yet, who would be silly enough to think that Marjorie Anders was really getting off scot-free. Her painful internal conflicts were a daily reminder of her mistakes. She needed no other punishment.

"Perhaps if you cut the wood a little thinner and placed a little paper underneath it'd help the wood catch fire," Vivian Proper said as she watched her boys continue to struggle with the lighting of the fire, the white smoke continuing to rise, but the flicker of flames noticeably absent.

"Mom," Zeke whined, "I've built a fire before. I know what I'm doing."

Devon looked back at his mother, his eyes rolling and his shoulders shrugging. He had suggested the same thing to Zeke just a moment before with the same result. He turned back to the project and offered Zeke another piece of crumpled paper. Zeke once again pushed it aside. "Nope, don't need it. I've almost got this," Zeke said, his determination becoming more solidified.

Marjorie was watching the exchange between the two boys when she suddenly felt the gaze of Vivian Proper upon her. She turned to look at her late nephew's wife and noted the softened look of concern written across her face.

"What's going on, Marjorie?" Vivian asked. "What's happened to Taylre?"

Marjorie sighed heavily and placed her teacup gently on the small antique table next to the couch.

"She's been acting very strangely. Very un-Taylre like. She's normally a very 'up' person, but she's been extremely sullen lately. She stays in her room with the door locked. She won't talk to me anymore. She leaves for school much earlier than she ever did before and comes home much later. When I try to ask her about it, she gets angry. She tells me to mind my own business, which is so different from the Taylre that I know. And her clothes," Marjorie continued, "they're so dark. Taylre always used to wear such bright colors, almost a little too much at times. But the stuff she's wearing now..." Marjorie trailed off, a look of exasperation crossing her features.

Vivian turned to look at the boys who had turned their attention away from building a fire to the present conversation.

"Zeke," she said, beckoning him to sit beside her. "You mentioned earlier that you noticed something was strange about Taylre, too. What do you think is going on? And where do you think she might be?"

Zeke sat down beside his mom, sinking heavily into the soft couch, the springs issuing a strained sigh. "The Ferocious Fenrirs," Zeke began. "It's a new club at school. And just take a guess as to who the club's advisor is."

Vivian shook her head slightly, a look of confusion creasing her face. Then her expression suddenly changed. "Loden," she said, her head now nodding with comprehension, her face becoming pale.

Marjorie Anders noted the change.

"What?" she said, her eyes shifting quickly from Vivian to Zeke. "What's this about? Who...Who's Loden? Wh...What's a Fenrir?"

Vivian reached over and rested a calming hand on Marjorie's arm.

"There are some things that we need to tell you," she said, turning to look back at Zeke. "And I think a few more things that haven't been mentioned yet, isn't that right, Zeke."

Zeke nodded slowly.

"There is," he began. "I'll tell you what I know about the Ferocious Fenrirs, the rest you'll have to explain. I don't think I can go over it again."

"Fair enough," Vivian said, nodding her head. "But I'll leave the retelling up to Devon. He seems to have a pretty good handle on things."

"Okay, here it goes," Zeke began, and he related the events that took place when he ventured, unknowingly, into the trap Loden laid for him in his classroom with the Ferocious Fenrirs. Marjorie and Vivian sat in stunned silence as they listened. Their faces revealed their disbelief as Zeke recounted how Taylre had turned her back on him, how she had recited the haunting, repetitive mantra, and how she had even been involved in beating him along with the rest of the misguided youth in the room that day.

When Zeke concluded with the condition he found Devon in when he finally returned home, he ended his narrative abruptly, the memory of the event causing him to shudder inside.

Marjorie Anders was sitting on the edge of the couch, her back stiff, her lips pursed together, and her eyes reflecting an angry glare.

"That's impossible," she said. "We can't be talking about Taylre here. She could never do a thing like that. She could never be so cold, so treacherous as that. Never."

For a moment, there was silence, and then Marjorie spoke again, her back slouching, her shoulders hunched over in defeat. "But it was her, wasn't it?" she admitted reluctantly. "It's as if she's been taken over by some sort of a spell, like a scene from some horrid fairy tale." She eased back into the softness of the couch, letting the air out of her lungs in a slow push, echoing the sound of the springs under the cushions as they settled beneath her.

"But there's more, Aunt Marjorie," Devon said, sliding himself over closer to the couch, his knees resting uncomfortably on the cold wooden floor. "We know that Loden is behind all this. He's the one causing all of the problems."

"Loden?" Marjorie questioned. "The teacher?"

"Yeah," Devon responded. "Except he isn't really a teacher. And his name isn't really Loden. It's Loki."

Marjorie quickly sat back up, perching herself again on the edge of the couch. "Loki," she said, a kind of knowing pitch in her voice. "Of course he is." She stood and began pacing around the room. "He's here because of the Korrigan, isn't he?" she questioned, even though it was clear that she knew the answer before she even asked it.

She suddenly stopped her pacing and whirled around to face the three Propers who sat watching her frantic movements.

"Oh, this is bad," she suddenly exclaimed, her hands rising quickly to cover her mouth. "This is really bad."

Zeke leaned forward in his seat. "What's the matter, Aunt Marjorie?" he asked, his own frantic movements mirroring hers. "What's going to happen?"

"Happen?" she said, her voice taking on a far-away tone. "I don't know. What I do know is that Taylre is with him. All of them are. He's the Pied Piper. He won't bring them back until he gets what he wants. Until he gets what he feels he is due."

ᛉ

The rain came down in torrents, a deluge of cold, enormous drops. When the Captain and Chaz finally reached the road, they found it a sludgy, muddy mess. The road was an old, un-maintained, un-named logging road that snaked its way down from Mt. Sif and rarely had vehicles driving on it. So it was pure luck that, as the Captain and Chaz stood on the side of the trail, their feet sinking into the mire, that an ancient, rusted out version of a four-wheel drive Jeep came plodding along the path. The vehicle's fat tires came splashing through the potholes, sending showers of brown water in all directions. In the driver's seat sat a lanky young man, his dirty, long blond hair tucked haphazardly behind his ears while a faded green baseball cap kept the rest in place. He wore a thick flannel shirt that had holes in the elbows but, oddly, seemed to match the faded blue jeans he wore that also exhibited a well worn past, the material thin, peppered with holes, revealing his knobby knees.

As the vehicle neared the two weary travelers, the driver slammed on the brakes causing the Jeep to come to a sliding stop beside them.

"Wha's up dudes?" the driver said, his skinny body leaning awkwardly out of the open door. "Crazy day for a walk, huh? You guys need a ride or somethin', or are you just out enjoyin' this weather?"

The Captain turned to look at Chaz, who had a surprised look on his face that mirrored the Captain's. Neither of them had expected anyone to be passing by so their shock at seeing this unexpected gift seemed to leave them both mute.

"Well?" the young man said, as the rumbling un-tuned engine of his jeep spewed blue exhaust into the cool air.

"Aye, lad," the Captain finally managed to say. "We could surely use a ride. Back into town if ya don't mind."

"Hop on in, old man. And watch ya don't get too much mud on the floor, I'm tryin' to keep this baby lookin good."

Chaz laughed. He couldn't help it. Even though his body ached with pain, the young man's comment penetrated the agony. What made the comment even funnier, Chaz thought, was that the driver was serious.

"Alright boys, hang on, it's going to be a bumpy ride."

The three took off over the uneven road. And even though the Captain had spent years on the open sea battling some of the most severe weather imaginable, he could not remember a time when he had experienced a rougher, more dangerous journey.

§

A fire blazed in the hearth and Zeke sat beside its warming glow feeling a pleasant sense of satisfaction at finally getting it going. He turned to look proudly at his mom and Devon, who had now inched themselves closer to the warming flames leaving the comfort of the soft couch for the solace of heat that radiated from the flickering light.

Marjorie Anders remained on the couch, her shoulders wrapped with a soft thick blanket while she watched with sadness the fatherless family huddled together for warmth. Her thoughts were distant, drifting into despair as she considered the horrible possibilities of Taylre's presence in the company of an evil, vengeful god. Her many years of dabbling in the dark arts had educated her with regard to the ways of iniquity. She understood all too well the penalties of disobedience to any kind of deity, whether they be righteous or wicked.

Suddenly her thoughts were interrupted by the reverberating, rolling sounds of an engine outside the house, its echo contrasting with the swirl of the buffeting wind. She looked up from her reverie to see Zeke stand and move to the window. He pulled the curtains aside and peered out, parting the drapes slightly in his attempt to see more clearly.

"There's an old Jeep outside," he reported. "It's sitting in our driveway."

The small group rose quickly and gathered around Zeke, their heads all pushed together as they peeked out the window just in time to see the Jeep back up into the street and pull away. As they watched the vehicle drive off, a soft knock rattled the door. Vivian went to the door, but she once again moved tentatively, her fear of an evil intruder foremost in her mind. The others followed as she reached for the door, their curiosity overshadowing any fear they might have. The door opened easily helped by the push of wind and the pelting rain.

"Hello, Vivian. May we come in?" the Captain said, his posture strained and his lilt more pronounced as he leaned upon Chaz for support.

CHAPTER TWENTY-THREE
Table Talk

The X-rays confirmed that the Captain had suffered a mild concussion and that both he and Chaz were suffering from extreme dehydration. Thankfully there were no broken bones, although both of the weary travelers left the emergency room heavily laden with bandages wrapped around festering wounds and enough antibiotics to keep them going for at least two weeks, just in case some form of infection were to set in. The hospital contacted Chaz's parents, but they said they had work that was keeping them busy. The Nelson's asked if Vivian could keep Chaz at her house until they could find time to pick him up. Vivian Proper, having never met Chaz's parents, pondered the situation, wondering how any parent could care so little for their own son.

"It's pretty typical," Chaz said, shrugging his shoulders and passing off the question as unimportant. "My parents never ask about where I am. They leave on vacations without me and pretty much let me fend for myself. It's been like that for years."

When the group returned to the Proper house, Vivian and Marjorie set about fixing a large pot of hot vegetable and beef soup with plenty of toasted bread to go along with it. Zeke and Devon helped set places at the table, while the Captain and Chaz sat glumly next to each other, both of them pouring out a third and fourth glass of cold, clear water and drinking it down eagerly.

When they finally sat down to eat, Zeke eyed Chaz suspiciously from the opposite side of the table. He remembered all too well that it was Chaz and Teddy Walford who had attempted to lead him out to the woods to do him more harm. To kill him. He wondered if Chaz's presence here in the house was somehow another Loki trick, and he couldn't help but feel that he must maintain a very careful watch over him; Zeke simply didn't trust him.

Then a thought began to ring in Zeke's ear, a chime from some distant place: *Be vigilant, Zeke. There are those that are close to you that will betray you, but make no mistake; they are deceived. Trust no one...*

Both the Captain and Chaz dug at their food like starving men, their approach to their meals both forceful and determined. Devon, as he watched them eat, chuckled lightly to himself as he noted an errant noodle that clung precariously to the Captain's chin. It was apparent that, at least for the time being, all attempts at proper table etiquette had been thrown out the window. Vivian tried hard to ignore the bad manners, realizing that this particular occasion did not warrant the usual behavior she had come to expect around her kitchen table.

As the Captain finished off his second full bowl of soup by tilting the bowl's remaining contents into his mouth, he wiped away the excess from his face with the back of his hand then slammed the bowl on the table causing the small group huddled around their meals to look up in surprise.

"There are things that need to be discussed here," the Captain barked. "This silence is too much. We're avoidin' what needs to be said and the questions that need to be asked."

The clinking of bowls and the sounds of eating stopped. Zeke was the first to speak, his eyes still on Chaz. "I think the questions would have been easier to ask if *he* weren't here," Zeke said, his head nodding in Chaz's direction.

"Him?" the Captain questioned, his hand rising to rest on Chaz's shoulder. "What's wrong with him? This boy brought me back from the brink of death."

"That *boy*," Zeke said, a touch of scorn edging his voice, "almost *brought* me to my death. He has no business being here; especially when we have things to discuss that just might involve him." Zeke stood, pushing his chair back with his legs and tipping it over onto the hard linoleum floor. He ignored the crack it made when it struck but could not ignore the astonished stares that looked up at him from those still seated around the table.

Vivian Proper rose to her feet, a touch of anger marking her features.

"Zeke, you apologize to our guest. You have no right to be so unkind."

Zeke began shaking his head in protest. "You don't understand," he told his mother, his hands extended in a pleading gesture. "Chaz here was one of the two boys that pulled me out of the meeting with the Ferocious Fenrirs."

Devon stood abruptly, his hands leaning on the table like a lawyer reproaching a witness as he also recognized Chaz.

"That's right," he said, his arm lifting and his finger pointing accusingly at Chaz. "You were at the bookstore, too. You and that other big kid."

All eyes turned to look at Chaz.

"I...I don't know what you're talking about," Chaz pleaded, his position amongst the small group suddenly feeling very awkward. "I've only met you a few times at cross country practice at the beginning of the year," he said to Zeke. Then turning to Devon said, "And I've never even met you. I honestly don't know what you're talking about."

"What a load of crap that is," Devon blurted out.

"Devon!" his mother yelled.

"Sorry, mom, but what he just said isn't true. Not one word of it. He and that other dork nearly ripped my head off. And you should have seen what they did to my backpack."

The Captain suddenly stood, his big frame pushing against the table sending dishes flying and glasses crashing to the floor.

"Whoa, whoa, now!" he hollered. "Everyone jus' be still. Thar be no need to go on like this. Everyone here's a friend. We jus' need to do a little explainin' is all. Now sit down and calm yerselves."

Devon sat immediately, his fear of the Captain's booming voice overshadowing any sense of courage he may have had, but Zeke remained standing, his penetrating, angry glare focused on Chaz.

"Master Zeke," the Captain said sternly "I'll not be telling ya again. Sit down and do it quickly."

Zeke blinked once, as if he had just heard the Captain for the first time. He looked toward him, gave a reluctant nod, and then sat, the look of anger still etched across his face.

"Good," the Captain sighed. "Now, like I said, thar be some explainin to do. But ya've got to let me speak before ya go spoutin off again." He turned to look at Chaz, once again placing a light hand upon his shoulder. "This young lad here speaks the truth. I have no doubt about that. I don't believe that thar be any way he could've known what he was doing. That he hasn't been under his own thoughts for quite some time now, that I have no doubt. Nope," the Captain continued, "this boy has been under the influence of somethin' evil. Somethin' powerful and wicked. So he can't be blamed for what he's done."

Zeke's angry glare softened quickly, realization striking him, and he began thinking about Taylre. He knew that she, just like Chaz, had been under the influence of something evil when he went to see her that day in Loden's classroom and that wherever she was right now, she was probably still under that influence. He looked up once again at Chaz and then back at the Captain.

"It's Loki, isn't it?"

The Captain took in a short, quick breath, as his eyes grew wide with surprise. "How do ya know such things, boy?" he whispered sharply.

"Dreams," he answered quickly. "Careful observation, research, and gut feeling. Devon and I have been hashing it out. We've been thinking about the Korrigan and all of the events surrounding that night." Then he dropped his eyes as tears began to overflow. "My dad's death, too."

"What?" the Captain said, his face dropping in astonishment, his eyes reflecting sadness and sympathy. "What's happened here? What terrible things have befallen this family?" The Captain looked around the table, his eyes resting on each member of the remaining Proper family.

"Vivian," the Captain continued. "I had no idea. Tell me what's happened."

"Oh, Bartholomew," Vivian Proper answered. "I can't talk about it. I'd fall apart before I even began."

"I'll tell him," Devon volunteered. "We've got to get everything out into the open anyway. Obviously the Captain knows something. If we somehow put all of our stories together then maybe we can reach some sort of solution."

"A truly worthy plan, lad," the Captain added, a somber tone reflected in his voice. "You begin, and then Chaz and I will tell our tale. I'm quite certain that we'll find the two accounts are somehow connected."

Devon turned to Zeke. "You okay with that? Do you want me to tell the story?"

Zeke shrugged. "Go ahead. Retelling it is starting to grate on me. My nerves can't take it anymore. I'll help out if you forget something, but for the rest, you're on your own."

"Fair enough," Devon responded. He looked at his mother and she nodded simply, a brief movement that was almost imperceptible.

"It started with a dream," Devon began. "I've had them before, if you remember, right around the time that the Korrigan was snaking its way up the Stick River. This one was very similar, simply because it felt so real. In fact, I believe it actually was real. It was as if I'd been transported somehow. As if I'd actually left my bed and been somehow relocated into another space, similar to the space we're in now, and yet somehow different." Devon shuffled uncomfortably in his seat, his fingers working together nervously.

"I know that sounds strange. It doesn't even make sense to me as I say it, but there it is." The Captain watched Devon as he spoke and nodded his head knowingly. He opened his mouth to speak, to say something of significance regarding Devon's dream, but he held his tongue, recognizing the need to let Devon have his say. There would be time, he thought, time to say all that needed to be said.

"In this dream I walked through the vacant, dark streets of Alder Cove. It felt like someone was there, watching me, someone who hated me and wanted to kill me. Eventually I made my way to the marina. When I arrived, there was a ship. It was like an old Viking ship. On the front was the giant head of a dragon or a snake of some kind. When I saw it, it scared the crap out of me and I fell. That was one of the many things that made me think that the dream was not really a dream; I actually felt the pain in my butt when I hit the ground. In fact, I had a bruise on my thigh the next day." Devon began rubbing absently at his right leg, as if the phantom memory of tenderness from over a month ago was still there.

"I sat up and that's when I saw him. It was Loki. I have no doubt about that now. He was ... I don't know...just dark. A thick darkness that I could feel all around me. A darkness that I could even taste. It was like eating a handful of mud scooped from the bottom of a polluted river.

"When I woke up I had dirt on my feet. My pajamas were wet, too. I tried to tell Zeke, but of course he wouldn't listen," Devon said, turning a quick eye toward Zeke. "He was so wound up in his running, and school, and whatever else he had going on."

Zeke quickly interrupted. "I *was* busy. If you weren't always such a goober I might have listened to you right then and there."

"Zeke, don't interrupt your brother," Vivian Proper said, almost as if the response were automatic. "Go on, Devon. Finish your story."

But here the Captain interjected. "Devon, what did he look like, lad? I mean, besides the darkness. Did he actually have a form in yer dream, or was it just some sort of vague image that ya saw?"

"A little of both, I suppose. He was tall and very strong looking and he had long hair, but his face was indistinct. There were no noticeable features except for the fact that his eyes were missing. Just big black empty spaces."

The Captain grunted again. "And did he speak to ya? Did he say anything familiar or significant?"

"He did speak to me," Devon said. "But his mouth didn't move. It was in my head, as if the sound were all around me..."

"And what did he say?" the Captain asked, twirling his hand in an anxious manner.

"Bring them to me." Devon stated matter-of-factly.

The Captain shook his head, confused. By now everyone was leaning in close to hear Devon's story.

"Bring who?" the Captain begged, the tension rising in his voice.

"I don't know," Devon said. "Maybe my dad. Maybe that's what he meant. I don't really know for sure."

"Yer dad," the Captain said. "What happened to Percy?"

"Dad bought a boat. A nice sailboat. He was really proud of it and he was anxious to take us out so that he could teach us how to sail. But there was a girl..."

The Captain gasped. "A girl ya say? A wee girl was she?"

"No," Devon answered. "She was--"

Zeke interrupted. "Alicia," he said, his voice rising in despair. "It was Alicia Edda. At least that's what we were led to believe."

"But it wasn't a girl at all was it?" the Captain stated.

Devon and Zeke both looked intently at the Captain, their curiosity growing.

"No, it wasn't," Zeke answered. "How did you know?"

"The same thing happened to me, lad. The very same thing." The Captain stood, pushing away the chair gently, his movements slow as the aches and pains in his body still pierced his senses. He began pacing the room, his hand coming up occasionally to scratch at his whiskery chin. He turned then to Vivian Proper. "Vivian, would ya mind so much if I were to have a wee puff on my pipe? It eases my mind and helps me to think."

Vivian shook her head kindly. "No, Bartholomew. You do what you need to do. I won't mind at all."

"Ya really don't mind?" he asked again, sure that he would be told to take his smoking habit outside. "Because ya know the smell it might make."

"Really, Bartholomew. I don't mind," she answered, giving a little wave of her hand, urging him to continue.

The Captain reached into the breast pocket of the tattered

jacket he wore and pulled out a pipe. From his other pocket, he brought out a pouch of tobacco. He filled the bowl of the pipe expertly. He brought the pipe to his lips and produced a match, almost as if it came from out of nowhere, lighting it and setting the flame to the top of the bowl, puffing gently, letting the smoke fill his mouth, some of it escaping from the corners of his lips, some drifting from his nostrils. A sweet aroma filled the air and the others who sat at the table breathed the tobacco-filled scent as they watched the Captain's ritual. The Captain took up his pacing again, resuming the scratching of his face. Suddenly he stopped and looked at the two boys.

"Whar did this happen? Whar did ya see this girl?"

"She was in the water," Zeke answered. "We all thought she was drowning. She even called to us for help. That's when Dad jumped in to try and save her..." Zeke stopped, shuddering slightly at the memory of what happened next.

"But where were ya, lad? I mean, what location? Was it near the docks? Was it far out to the south?"

"No," Devon piped in. "We were north. Near some cliffs."

"Aha," the Captain exclaimed. "Just as I thought. You were right near La Cueva del Diablo."

Everyone seated around the table appeared puzzled, all except Marjorie who shifted uncomfortably in her chair.

"I've heard of the place," she said. "I've never been there, but when I was young it was said to be haunted. Only the brave and stupid went there. Many teenagers lost their lives trying to get there by boat. Walking there, I've heard, up over the mountain and along unmarked paths, is almost impossible."

"Aye, Marjorie. That it is. Almost. But that is exactly where the lad here and I have come from. La Cueva del Diablo."

"Where?" Vivian Proper asked, her curiosity getting the better of her.

Marjorie turned to her, a look of grief in her eyes.

"The Cave of the Devil," she said. She turned back to the Captain, "How did you get there?"

"On my boat," the Captain answered. "But it's not easy. Ya have to know what you're doing. Otherwise ya'd crash on the rocks."

"But why?" Devon asked. "Why were *you* there?"

"Because of a girl, a wee lass that I saw standing in the cave. However, it turns out she wasn't a girl. No," the Captain repeated. "Not a girl at all. Turns out, she was he. Loki. The evil shape shifter himself."

"I read that," Devon said, looking to Zeke for confirmation. "We both did. Loki can turn into whatever he wants. Even a girl if he wants to."

"Aye, lad, that he can."

"What about a wolf?" Zeke asked, his eyes narrowed to fine slits.

"Aye. A wolf, a fish, a bird. Whatever suits his purposes."

Zeke sat back in his chair, understanding filling his mind. He turned back to the Captain.

"What do you know about the Ferocious Fenrirs?"

At the mention of the school club overseen by Loden, Chaz sat up, suddenly taking a keener interest in the conversation.

"I know nothing about ferocious anything," the Captain stated. "I do know about Fenrir though, he being another offspring of the evil Loki."

"Like the Korrigan," Devon declared.

"Aye, very much the same. However, Fenrir was the first and most powerful of Loki's children, he being among the same brood as came the great serpent and Hel herself."

"But what is Fenrir?" Zeke asked. "What does it look like?"

"Why it's a wolf, lad. The biggest, most vile creature you've ever set eyes on. At least so I've been told."

A silence took over the kitchen as each member of the group seemed to be lost in their own thoughts. Smoke continued to rise from the Captain's pipe and the soup, still sitting full in some of the bowls on the table, sat cooling. Finally, Marjorie Anders broke the quiet.

"Bartholomew, when you were in the cave, what did you

see? Was Loki there? Were there other things there as well?"

"Aye, Marjorie, there was. And I know what ya be askin about. There was an entire host of younguns' there, all of them under the same spell that poor Chaz here was under. And yes, she was there. Taylre was there under the spell of that monster, too."

"Oh my God!" Marjorie exclaimed, bringing her hands to the sides of her face, pulling haphazardly at the curls of hair that hung down. "We've got to go to her. We've got to go now!" Marjorie rose from her seat, a panic beginning to take hold of her. Suddenly everyone jumped to their feet, a sense of alarm spreading through the room like a malicious contagion. Vivian reached for Marjorie and tried to hold her by the shoulders, to calm the dread that had set in, but she wriggled free, wrenching herself away and setting off toward the hallway and the front door. But the Captain, moving faster than his large body would seem to allow, stepped in front of Marjorie, blocking her way. He placed his strong hands firmly on her shoulders.

"Still yerself, Marjorie!" the Captain shouted, his booming voice echoing in the hollow hallway like a foghorn, its bass a penetrating call for composure. Marjorie stood still, as if the voice were a slap in the face that forced her to return to reality. The Captain slid his hands down the length of Marjorie's arms, then taking her hands in his own brought his voice to a quiet hush, a reassuring, measured tone that drew everyone in to a sense of normalcy. The Captain stared at Marjorie for a long time, and there seemed to pass between them an unspoken understanding. Marjorie's shoulders relaxed and finally the Captain looked up, taking a moment to stare at each member of the small group that had assembled near the front door.

"This is exactly what he wants us to do. He wants us to panic. He wants us to rush out there and try to be the rescuers. But if we do, we fall into his trap. He's a deceiver. The greatest liar of them all. We can't let him win."

"What do we do?" Zeke asked. "I feel like time is running out. If we don't do something quickly something awful is going to happen to all those kids."

"Aye," the Captain grunted, moving away from the group slowly, pacing his way into the living room, his hand reaching up to scratch once again at his whiskery chin. "But we need to understand some things first. If ya don't know yer enemy, things can go wrong very quickly. I think it's time that I give ya's a quick lesson on the Northerner's gods."

CHAPTER TWENTY-FOUR
The Legends

"Since I were a wee lad," the Captain began, "my mother taught me all of the old stories. She swore they were all true, but I passed them off as mere fairy tales, like anyone would've. But now, now things are different. I've seen things for myself. Now I know the stories she told are true, and we have much to fear."

The solemn group huddled together under the hopeful protection of thick blankets in the living room, while a fire, one that the Captain had restarted, blazed in the hearth. Outside, the windstorm continued to thrash the sides of the house. The Captain stood in front of the small group, pacing back and forth like a general laying out a battle plan for his soldiers. The others watched his every move, their eager minds taking in all of his words.

Devon quietly interjected, though he was reluctant to break the spell that the Captain cast with his instructive words. "We've been doing some studying," he said, handing the Captain a piece of folded paper, one that he'd gathered from his room before the group took their seats on the couch.

The Captain unfolded and then scanned the paper quickly. "You've got nice hand writing, lad," he said, almost as an afterthought. Devon looked over at Zeke when the Captain said this, the sharp, annoying grin that Zeke hated marking his features. The Captain paused for a moment, as if considering something beyond his comprehension.

"This is good work, Devon, but let me speak. I'll put it all together for ya." He folded the paper and handed it back to Devon, a proud smile creasing his face. Devon looked again at Zeke, who was shaking his head, suppressing a smile.

"Before I start," he said. "You've got to put aside all of your current thoughts of God and religion. On the other hand, a better way of saying it might be to take what I say and try to combine it with what ya already think ya believe. That, I suppose, will be the best way to comprehend what I have to say." Marjorie looked up at the Captain with a knowing gaze; her understanding of things beyond the normal world of western civilization had been stretched to its limit. Vivian, however, simply stared at the Captain with a confused expression. Her upbringing had been strictly Christian, and any thoughts of multiple gods competing and fighting amongst each other was far beyond her comprehension. She, at least for now, would be much harder to convince.

Chaz sat on the floor, set apart from the others, as his comfort level with the rest of the group still remained tentative, his mannerism aloof and his bearing like that of a lost soul. He said little during the exchange between the family, though he did draw sympathy as he related his apparent loss of memory. His last recollections, he said, were of reading a poster in the hallway at school, and then, standing before the Captain in the damp cave. He remembered virtually nothing of his experience with Loden. The Captain considered this a true blessing in disguise.

The Captain pulled over a stiff, oversized chair from the corner of the room, dragging it roughly over the thinly carpeted floor, setting it in place, and sitting heavily, creaks and groans emanating from both him and the chair. He looked up slowly and began to speak.

"At first there was Odin. Well," he said, correcting himself. "Technically he wasn't the very first, but he was the first born of the Frost Giants. But I won't go into that. We'd be here forever if I do. Odin was the main god, the one who guided and led the rest. He is known by many names: Father of Thor, the first and foremost of the Aesir, the most powerful of the gods. He is god of poetry, battle and death. He is known also as All Father, the Terrible One, One-Eyed, and the Leader of Souls. But none of that really matters. What matters is that he was the one in charge. It was his job to protect humankind and to keep evil, like Loki, from infecting man. However, there came a time when his son, Balder, also known as the Beautiful, a peaceful god loved by all, was killed by a blind god named Hod. His death was brought about by trickery. Hod didn't know what he was doing. Loki tricked him into throwing a poison dart at Balder taking his life and sending his soul down to Hel."

Zeke suddenly sat up quickly, his eyes widening with understanding.

"Wait," he said, holding his hands in front of him as he considered his next words. "Are you saying that Loki killed Balder and that Balder was known as 'The Beautiful'?"

"Aye, lad. Balder was the most peaceful god there was. All of the other gods loved him. That's why there was so much anger toward Loki for his betrayal."

Again, a distant whisper seemed to echo in Zeke's mind as he recalled his visit with the old man of his dreams. *He is being punished, for he is a fallen god. He has destroyed that which was beautiful. His own treachery has caused his downfall and he has become darkness.*

"He was captured and punished, wasn't he?" Zeke declared.

"Aye, he was," the Captain said slowly, astonished at the knowledge of his young pupil. "Punished horribly. Bound to jagged rocks, he was, and by thick chains that were supposed to make him stay put, at least until the beginning of Ragnarok. But the chains, it appears, have been broken. What that may mean I fear to even think about.

"Ragnarok," he repeated. "The beginning of the end; the destruction of the powers. A time when the world will come to an end. A time when the gods of the Aesir will battle the giants. It is said that Loki will lead the Giants against Odin and his son, Thor. It will be his desire to destroy Odin and replace him as the head of the gods. Loki will break free and sail on his evil ship, Naglfar - the ship made from dead men's nails."

As the Captain spoke, Zeke kept nodding his head; a full remembrance of his dream was forcing itself to the forefront of his memory. He realized that he saw Loki escape when he was pulled into his dream with the old man; that he had indeed broken his bonds. The true meaning of this hit Zeke like a sledgehammer; he suddenly understood that the end of this world as he knew it was at hand. That the battle between the gods would soon begin and that Loki was here, preparing his motley crew to go to war. Zeke looked up at the Captain, his face pale with fear.

"What else did you see when you were in the cave, Captain?" he said, his voice quivering, as if a sudden rush of cold had entered the room.

The Captain breathed a deep sigh and shook his head. "It was there, too, lad. The ship, Naglfar. It was moored in the back of the cave while men of enormous size milled about, pushing the children and making them do what kind of evil work I know not. It seems to me that he's getting ready to leave. That he's preparing for the battle to come."

Marjorie took a quick intake of breath that drew the attention of the others. She raised her hand to her mouth as fresh tears began to flow from the corners of her eyes. Vivian placed a reassuring arm around her shoulders and tried to calm her, consoling her like a mother with a child. Vivian turned to the Captain.

"Do we need to be concerned that he'll take the children as well?" she said, voicing the thoughts of everyone who sat about the Captain. "Will he leave and take Taylre, too?"

Devon sat forward quickly as the others turned to look at him expectantly.

"He's not going anywhere. Not yet, anyway. He won't leave until he's settled his score with us. This is about revenge. He wants revenge for the Korrigan, and I don't think he's going anywhere until he's finished what he's started."

The Captain cleared his throat and nodded his head.

"Aye, lad. I think this much is true. And if it is, then we need to act quickly and get Taylre and the rest of them out of that god-forsaken cave before it's too late. We've got to come up with some kind of plan of attack, a distraction, some way to liberate those poor hostages." The Captain stood and began to pace the floor again, his movements reflecting agitation and a sense of helplessness.

Devon spoke again, his voice hurried, as if he were trying to keep up with the Captain's pacing.

"We've got an obvious disadvantage, though. Any attempt at rescue would most likely end in disaster considering the fact that Loki is an ex-god who just happens to have the ability to change shapes at will and move from place to place any time he wants."

The Captain suddenly stopped his pacing and turned to look at Devon, a sudden expression of understanding crossing his features.

"Wait a minute," he said, his eyes shifting back and forth between Devon and Zeke. "Both of ya have mentioned the fact that you've been in dreams that have seemed particularly real. Almost as if the dreams themselves weren't dreams at all, but actual life." The Boys nodded slowly but bewilderment etched itself across their young faces as they tried to determine where the Captain was going with his thinking. Then the Captain spoke again, his words penetrating the small group of listeners like a sharpened blade, his voice echoing like a piercing whisper.

"You've been in the Mist," he said, his words hissed, causing shivers to rise up the listener's backs.

"The Mist?" Zeke questioned. "What's the Mist? What are you talking about?"

The Captain began to move again, this time slowly with his hands raised to the sides of his head, as if he were pressing it for more information.

"Why didn't I think of this before?" he said, turning once more to face the baffled group.

The Captain suddenly recognized the confusion that stared back at him, and he smiled to himself, realizing that his words probably sounded like pure nonsense. He stood for a moment longer as he tried to determine the best way to explain himself.

"Listen," he finally said. "There's more that ya got to understand about the Northerners and their gods. There's more to know about the way they see the universe put together and how everything connects. When I explain that you'll understand about the Mist."

The Captain reached into his jacket pocket and once again removed his pipe. Zeke smiled to himself, picturing Taylre, once upon a time, mouthing the words: *This is going to be a long story*. Her clue always came from the appearance of the

Captain's pipe, his way of relaxing and focusing his mind.

And so, the group settled themselves once again into the comfort of the blankets and the couch, eager to hear about the Mist and the possibility of saving the imprisoned youth who struggled under the burden of Loki and his giant henchmen.

CHAPTER TWENTY-FIVE
The Mist

Sweet smoke rose from the end of the Captain's pipe as he puffed at its tattered end, letting a curl of blue haze drift lazily from the corners of his mouth. He squinted against the smoke that drifted past his eyes. The look made him appear thoughtful and somewhat scholarly. He turned at the sound of Devon's feet descending the stairs returning from his errand of retrieving a pad of paper. Devon held the pad firmly in his hand, the other held a stubby yellow pencil with teeth marks on the end where Devon had gnawed away part of the wood and what was left of the eraser.

The Captain took the pad of paper, folding over the pages until he found one Devon hadn't already marked up with his drawings and unfinished sketches. The Captain laid the paper down on a coffee table that sat between him and the others, scooting himself forward on his seat so that he could write and talk at the same time. Everyone leaned forward to get a better look at the vacant page. Even Chaz, who pushed past his shy awkwardness, leaned in to have a better look at what the Captain was about to write and explain.

"There are several realms," he began, taking a moment to jot down an unfamiliar word on the top of the paper, "that the Northern People believe exists. Here," he said, pointing and circling the word he'd written, "above all else, is the realm of the gods themselves. Asgard is its name. It is here that the twelve divine gods and the twelve divine goddesses live. They control all, at least for now.

"Down here," he said, writing a new word at the bottom of the page, "is Niflheim, the world of the dead. Hel, another daughter of the evil Loki, oversees it. It is her job to look after the dead, all those of the nine worlds who die of illness or old age. It is place of darkness and despair.

"Over here is Jotunheim." Again, he wrote out the strange word on one side of the page. "It is home to the giants, a hostile group of ruffians who have now joined with Loki and will continue with him throughout Ragnarok. More will join him, I fear, as the ship that sits in the cave continues its preparations. But here," he said, writing out another word in bold block letters in the very center of the page, "is Midgard. It is home to man. In other words, Earth, where we live now.

"There are other worlds as well - nine in all, as I've mentioned - but the ones that I've written here are the most important," he said, a slight sweep of his hand emphasizing the words he'd carefully written on the page. "The key to all of this, and the reason why I've been talking about the Mist, is that all of the worlds are connected. There is a way to travel from one world to the next, but that can only take place by first entering the Mist. However, it takes a special person to do that. One must be endowed with a special gift in order to enter the Mist and live to tell about it.

"The gods, of course, can come and go through the Mist at will, but it is another thing for a mere mortal, like us, to be able to do it. Loki, having once been a god, can do it whenever he wants. That's how he's able to travel quickly from place to place. One moment he can be floating in the ocean, for instance, and the next moment be sitting on the deck of your boat."

Vivian Proper, who hadn't spoken in a long time, slid the page the Captain had written on toward her and began to examine it more closely.

"These worlds," she said, dragging her finger from one unusual name to the next, "how exactly are they connected? Because it would seem to me a mist would be pretty unsubstantial. I mean, even gods have to walk on something, wouldn't you think?"

"You're right," the Captain explained. "But keep in mind that the name Mist is simply a reference to a hidden place, one that is just out of sight from the world of the living, almost as if it were shrouded in a thick fog, hidden from view. The substantial part of it, the thing that truly connects all of the worlds together is Yggdrasill, also known as The World Tree. It is a giant ash that links and shelters all of the worlds."

"Bartholomew," Vivian said, her voice revealing a touch of scorn, "do you really expect us to believe that our universe is just one big tree with branches sticking out everywhere? This just sounds like some fairy tale nonsense. And this thing about the Mist. The boys have just had dreams, that's all. There can't be anything more to it than that."

The Captain sighed, leaning back in his chair, as everyone seated around the coffee table watched and waited for his response.

"I knew you'd be a tough nut to break, Vivian, but you have to understand that before the events of the last two days, I, too, thought that these stories my mother used to tell me were just a bunch of nonsense. But now I've seen things, Vivian, things that have convinced me that these myths are not just myths. They're real."

"Okay," Vivian said, easing back into the softness of the couch, her arms crossed in subtle defiance. "Let's suppose these gods do exist. Suppose there is a universally giant tree and a Mist where one could theoretically move from world to world. How is knowing this going to help us in this situation? The boys are not gods. They can't just magically jump into this Mist and start walking around at will."

"A fair question, Vivian." The Captain said. "But first let me say that the boys have already been in the Mist. We just have to figure out how to make them go back into it. They've got something special about them. Something you and I don't have that allows them to go to the Mist and then come back again. How exactly it can help us?" he sighed. "Well, of that I'm not sure of yet. I only know - and I feel it here," the Captain said, drawing his hand up to his chest and resting it over his heart, "that they've been granted this gift for a purpose. And when the time comes, they'll both know how to use it."

All eyes turned to look at Zeke and Devon who sat with bewildered looks on their faces, fear and foreboding reflected in their eyes.

Marjorie Anders, who had also remained quiet throughout the brief lesson spoke up, her patience drawing thinner by the moment.

"So what do we do, Bartholomew? How and when do we go and get Taylre?"

"We split up," the Captain announced. "Some of us will go by sea, the rest overland. We'll come at the cave in two directions. Those of us who enter from the ocean will act as a diversion for the others who will need to scale the cliffs down to the cave. Somehow, the ones on the boat will draw the attention of Loki away from Taylre and the rest of the children. Then, hopefully, we can gather the hostages on my boat, the one that's already moored there, and get away before Loki has time to react."

"That," Vivian Proper said, her head shaking with the alarming doubt that she felt, "sounds like an absolute suicide mission."

"Aye," the Captain replied. "But if you know of a better way, any of you, then please let me know. Because I'm listening."

The only sound was the wind that continued to buffet the outside of the house. No one spoke or looked at each other as an awkward shifting of feet and a steady wringing of the hands began. Finally, the Captain grunted and pushed himself forward standing above the rest and looking down on them. "So it is decided then. We follow my plan."

Vivian nodded a reluctant agreement and Marjorie stood quickly, eager to start the task of rescuing her granddaughter from the clutches of the evil Loki. Zeke remained seated alongside Devon, both of their thoughts swirling in a mist of their own, wondering how this would all end and if any of them would live to see a new day.

CHAPTER TWENTY-SIX
Approach from the Sea

Taylre found that she had to cover her face constantly in an attempt to protect herself from the heat of the fiery forge, its extraordinary temperature scratching against her face like overgrown thorns in a sweltering jungle. The sweat rolled from her forehead in torrents, and the moisture mixed heavily with the dampness of the cave, making her feel completely filthy. Loud shouts and the continual snapping of a whip forced her to move, as did the persistent nipping of a large wolf that wandered about the cave barking and howling at the terrified workers as if he, and not Loden, was their leader. Taylre's legs felt heavy with fatigue and she wept often, feeling a pervasive lack of humanity and a chilling loss of self. Added to her burden was the weight of the steel weapons that she was forced to carry, delivered from the hands of a giant blacksmith. Lifting the bulky, sharpened

swords and shields, she was expected to plod awkwardly to a
narrow plank that led up to the deck of an enormous ship.
Upon reaching the plank, with the cumbersome load constantly
threatening to make her lose her balance, Taylre transferred the
weapons to another beleaguered member of the Ferocious
Fenrirs who, in turn, carried the metal trappings of war up the
steep wooden plank and then deposited the load into the hands
of another captured youth.

And so it went, hour after hour. A makeshift assembly line
that began in the bowels of the great ship, where raw material
was carried out to the giant blacksmith who formed the weapons
in the blistery heat of the forge. Then came the constant
pounding of a heavy hammer shaping the metal into instruments
of destruction. Afterward, the newly formed weapons were
loaded back onto the ship and once again placed into the
deepest recesses of the boat to be stored. To Taylre, the
purpose for the deadly cargo meant nothing. Her life had simply
become a drudgery of monotonous routine, an existence
wherein she and her fellow captors were given only a couple of
hours of rest each day, where the little bit of food they were
forced to eat was bland and tasteless, and where the only thrill in
life came from the daily pep talks provided by Mr. Loden.

Taylre looked to the brief meetings with Loden with quiet
but determined anticipation. Loden was her beacon, her light at

the end of a very dark tunnel that was shrouded in despair.

When his call came to gather, the group of child workers and giants alike would stream into a narrow fissure of rock, its steep sides providing excellent acoustics for his melodious voice, and listen with rapt attention to his words of motivation, encouragement, and love for those who served him so faithfully. As Loden finished each point, his fist slamming against the palm of his open hand, the crowd would obediently recite their mantra: It is the way. It is the law. Then the besieged group of listeners would sway back and forth, ignoring the pains that racked their bodies, accepting each vile word that spilled from Loden's mouth as if they were tiny pieces of gold to be scooped up and treasured.

Nevertheless, always, somewhere, in the back of her mind, Taylre would catch glimpses of some long forgotten memory, a distant recollection of color and warmth that overshadowed Loden's words, filling her heart with a different kind of peace. She would try desperately to cling to these thoughts, to embrace the tender feelings that would tug on her mind, pulling her, urging her to another place and another time. But the memory was buried deep. Whenever she tried to examine it closer and begin to uncover the thoughts that tugged at her, another arduous task was added by Loden or one of the giants to the already burdensome chores that afflicted her. Thus, the feelings would flee, like a startled bird fluttering out of sight, its identity remaining a mystery.

ጰ

The tempestuous winds of the previous two days had finally died down to a stiff breeze, though the open water beyond the marina remained turbulent, its waves building then cresting over, exposing foamy whitecaps. Devon, his ginger hair tossing in the mild gusts, stood on the gently rocking pier, swaying with the soothing movement as small, errant waves, ones that had managed to escape the open water, lapped against the wooden floats. Beside him, fastened firmly to the pier, was a rusted metal cleat that held a rope securely connected to the bow of the Skipper Jack. The Captain stood on its deck, his hands extended, waiting for Devon to untie the rope and toss him the end. Devon worked quickly, unwinding the tie from the cleat. Then, with deft hands, he tossed the rope into the waiting arms of the Captain. Devon leaped from the pier onto the deck, joining the Captain and beginning their perilous journey northward toward La Cueva del Diablo.

"Keep the sails tied, Lad," the Captain said as he moved quickly and efficiently toward the tiller. "We'll unfurl them later, as soon as we've had a chance to get out of this marina. Then, if

God be willin, we'll test 'em in the wind and see what we can do."

Devon sidled up to the tiller, and saw that the Captain was looking at him.

"What?" Devon asked, wondering if he had done something wrong.

"Nothin, boy. Thar's no need to be so sensitive. I've just been markin how well you be handlin' yerself on a ship. I do believe you're a natural." The Captain smiled and reached over to ruffle Devon's hair.

Devon grinned to himself, playfully pushing away the Captain's hand, but feeling proud that the Captain had noticed his adeptness at sailing even though he had hardly spent anytime at all around boats.

The Captain started the small inboard engine and slowly eased the Skipper Jack away from the pier. The keel sliced smoothly through the water as the boat easily made its way into the open ocean. Behind them, a taut line towed the Captain's old twelve foot fishing boat, its bow slapping against the waves as if attempting to defy its involvement in the journey. When the sailboat reached the freedom of the ocean, the Captain, still holding firmly to the tiller, ordered Devon to begin unfurling the sails. The thick canvas opened quickly, immediately catching the wind and pushing the boat northward. The Captain cut the engine and an eerie silence took over as the two sailors sat upon the swaying deck of the boat, their thoughts mixed with concern and foreboding.

"Captain," Devon said, finally breaking the silence of the moment, "the last time I was out here, when my dad was with us, we came in sight of the entrance to the cave. It looked pretty scary. There were rocks everywhere. I'm worried that we won't be able to sail in there without crashing against those rocks and doing some real damage."

"Aye. You're right there, Lad," the Captain said, reaching into his breast pocket to extract his pipe and a small pouch of tobacco. "That's why we've brought ol' Nellie with us," he said, indicating the fishing boat that followed closely behind, its faded wooden hull bobbing up and down with the swell.

"You mean that you're going to jump into *that* boat to move through those rocks?" Devon questioned.

The Captain chuckled slightly under his breath. "I *mean,* that we're *both* going to get on that boat and cross over the rocks. This isn't a one-man job, Devon. Confronting and distracting Loki is going to take both of us, along with our cunning and our patience. But mostly our courage. Loki will try to cast his fear into you. If he does that and you succumb to it, you're finished. We've got to be vigilant together." The Captain paused a moment to light his pipe. "And yes, *we're* going to take *that* boat through those rocks. I can do it. Have no fear of that.

I've done it plenty of times in my own boat, the big fishing one I shared with your grandad. If I can do it in that, I can do it in anything."

Silence once again took over as the two sailors looked out over the incredible vastness of the ocean and the towering cliffs that marked their approach to the entrance of the cave.

Devon was the first to see the ragged opening, its entrance distinctly identifiable from the rocks that struck up from the shoreline like the razor sharp teeth of the Korrigan.

"There," he said, standing and pointing.

The Captain turned from his own silent reverie, his mind wandering with thoughts of the open sea, and looked toward the direction Devon had indicated.

"That's it, lad. You've a good eye." Then, holding firmly to the tiller, the Captain directed Devon's attention to the sails. "Take 'em down, lad. We'll run the engine from here. We've got to get in close enough so we can set the anchor but not so close that we bump up against the rocks or cause the boat to toss too much in the waves."

Devon steadied himself on the deck, balancing like a tight-rope walker, and approached the main boom. He pulled on the tight ropes, releasing the sails, then the Captain started the engine and the Skipper Jack continued on its perilous trek.

As they drew near the looming cliffs, the sea seemed to calm. The Captain, becoming more sensitive to the will of the gods that had been instilled in him by his mother, seemed to sense that Odin or perhaps one of his many servants was watching from the guarded walls of Asgard and guiding them in their task.

With the anchor dropped and the Skipper Jack floating securely within sight of the entrance to the small cove that hid La Cueva del Diablo, the Captain and Devon began to pull on the rope that secured 'ol Nellie, bringing it up next to the sailboat. The Captain held the rope steady while Devon inched his way onto the aged fishing boat.

"Careful when you sit down, boy. Thar's splinters in those old seats that'll pierce yer behind quicker than you can say Davy Jones." Devon looked up into the Captain's face expecting to see his usual grim smile. But the Captain's expression was serious, as if the painful remembrance of extracting tiny slivers of wood from his own buttocks was still a close recollection.

After Devon was seated, he held firmly to the side of the Skipper Jack in an attempt to keep it from rocking. The Captain, a length of coiled rope slung over his left shoulder and his trusty shot gun suspended over his right, swung his bulky body over the side, teetering slightly as he plunked himself down on the wooden bench. The frame bent a little as his weight settled on the paint chipped lumber. The Captain motioned toward the outboard motor at the boat's stern, right next to Devon.

"Let's see what you can do, lad. Give it a pull and let's get on our way. And," he said, chuckling lightly under his breath, "if ya can start it on the first pull I'll give ya a hundred dollars." The old engine never started on the first pull, and if Devon did get it started, it would only be after he'd reached the point of complete and utter exhaustion.

Devon turned to look at the ancient Evinrude motor as if he were facing an opponent in a boxing ring. He took hold of the rubber grip that was tied over the mottled piece of nylon rope, and tilted his head slightly, noting a silver toggle. He flipped it upward into the "on" position, pulled out the choke, just like he had done a hundred or more times with the lawn mower at home, took in a deep breath, and pulled the rope with all his might.

The engine roared to life.

Devon turned to look at the Captain, a cheesy grin covering his face. The Captain just stared, his mouth open in awe.

"I guess I'll be headin to the bank when we get back," the Captain muttered.

When Devon turned the throttle on the antique motor, a small gust of black smoke issued from its underside. Nellie pulled away from the side of the Skipper Jack, its bow pointed toward a jagged gap between two enormous cliffs. The Captain rode in the front, letting Devon tend to the motor in the rear. His trust in the boy's abilities mounting with each display of skill.

As he held firmly to the curved wooden edge of the boat with his left hand, the Captain took a deep breath and gripped the handle of his shotgun with his right, bringing it in closer to his chest, as if its mere presence brought a measure of comfort.

CHAPTER TWENTY-SEVEN
Land Approach

Vivian Proper was convinced that the axles on the mini-van would snap in two at any moment. The gravel logging road they were driving on was so covered in potholes, rocks, and narrow, deep cut ruts, that the journey up Mt. Sif was feeling more like a roller coaster ride than an excursion up a so-called county maintained road. Her grip on the steering wheel was so firm that her knuckles were turning white. The others riding in the van clearly shared the same worries, their grips tight on the arm rests and dashboard.

Zeke gripped a handle above the window he sat beside, his eyes scanning the passing landscape with a kind of deep reverie. His imagination, mixed with that of the blurred scenery, took him to the past where ancient Northerners settled the land in incredible numbers. Here small villages were scattered amongst the tree line where innocent people lived amid malicious forces, and the will of the gods, both the evil and the just, tried to control the will of man, just like they did on this particular day. He tried to imagine what depth of terror the cave held for him and his companions. Like his encounter with the Korrigan however, Zeke had no idea what to expect. He considered how nice it would be to have a bag full of white stones he could throw at Loki, but even that was a distant memory, almost like the faded past of the Northerners who were the first to occupy this land so many years ago.

Zeke turned from his view of the passing foliage and rough rocks to the scene before him where the gravel road seemed to extend onward and upward for miles and miles.

"How will we know when we're there?" he asked, his question hanging in the air for anyone to answer.

Marjorie Anders, who sat in the passenger seat next to Vivian, turned to face Zeke in the back seat.

"It's been years since I've been up this way, but I think I'll know the trail when I see it. Plus, Chaz just came from the trail with the Captain. Maybe he'll recognize the path when we get near it."

Zeke looked at Chaz sitting next to him. Chaz shifted uncomfortably in his seat, his hands holding tightly to the armrest and the seat in front of him.

"Yeah, I guess," he said, feeling as if the eyes of those around him were boring holes into his skull. "But when Bart and I came along here we were pretty messed up. I've gotta admit, I wasn't really paying attention to the path."

Marjorie nodded her head in understanding. "Well, we'll just have to keep our eyes open and hope for some good luck."

"My fear," Vivian said, glancing over at Marjorie, "is that we'll miss Bartholomew. Seems to me this crazy plan of his all depends on the right timing."

"That's what the Captain said," Zeke responded. "If we're not there and ready to go when he arrives, then the plan won't work. We've got to locate the trail, and soon," he said, a touch of anxiety edging his voice.

The others nodded, turning their eyes toward to the road ahead. Vivian slowed the van trying to avoid yet another deep pothole when Chaz suddenly sat forward, his eyes fixed on a small opening in the dense forest.

"There!" he shouted, directing the gaze of the others in the same direction. "That's where we came out. I'm sure of it. The guy that picked us up was coming from the road beyond, just where it makes that sharp turn. And there," he said, pointing to another spot in the road, "is where he hit that big pool of water, sending all of that mud over me and Bart. I'll never forget that."

Vivian brought the van to an abrupt halt next to the nearly invisible path, slamming the transmission into park. The small group exited the vehicle, a slight breeze raising goose bumps on their skin. Vivian Proper stepped back and reopened her door, taking out a heavy sweater that she quickly wrapped around herself.

"It's a little cooler than I thought it would be up here," she said, crossing her arms and patting her shoulders for added warmth. "Are you sure you three will be alright?" A look of motherly concern passing between her and Zeke.

"We'll be fine, mom," Zeke replied, as he, Chaz, and Marjorie donned their own light jackets. "If what Chaz and the Captain said about this trail is right, then we'll be warm soon enough. Nothin' like a good hard walk to bring up the 'ol body temperature," he said, giving his mother a gentle, sad smile.

Vivian stepped forward, taking her son firmly in her arms and hugging him tightly.

"Please don't do anything foolish. Come back to me safely. Both you and Devon," she whispered in his ear. "I love you both so much. Don't leave me alone." Then she kissed him hard on the cheek, leaving a faded lipstick imprint. She stepped away, tears beginning to well up in her eyes. "And Marjorie," she said, staring at the aging woman through her blurred vision, "watch over my boys. I can't lose any more. I don't think I'd survive that."

Marjorie nodded, tears now beginning to fill her eyes. "I will Vivian. And don't worry, we'll be back before you know it. Everything will be fine, you'll see."

Marjorie, Zeke, and Chaz turned to leave, pushing their way through the undergrowth and the thick pine bows that blocked their way. As Zeke pushed past the thickest branch, he turned to look at his mother one last time, his hand lifting in a solemn wave. Then he disappeared behind a curtain of green.

Vivian took her place behind the steering wheel, gripping it firmly with both hands. She leaned forward, rested her forehead on the wheel, closed her eyes, and began to cry uncontrollably.

ᛣ

The trail, though heavily overgrown, was easy to follow. Zeke, however, was having a tough time keeping up with Marjorie, who, though well into her sixties, was setting an exhausting pace. He now understood where Taylre got her stamina. Majorie led Zeke and Chaz through a maze of tall trees, small ground cover, and rocks and boulders of various sizes and shapes. The path followed a steady incline, eventually cresting on a flat rock precipice that offered an incredible view of the churning blue ocean that sat far below. From here the trail took a sharp descent amongst scattered rocks and low, sharp weeds, a place where tall trees no longer grew, where the forces of the torturous winds swept away anything that the dry ground tried to produce.

Zeke's legs were aching with the effort of the hike. He recognized, with a pang of disappointment, that he still had not fully recovered from his lengthy convalescence. His breathing was difficult, sweat flowed freely and abundantly from his forehead, and he felt dizzy. The combination of the symptoms made him feel old beyond his years.

As he wiped his hand across his face to clear the perspiration, a sudden wave of nausea struck him, forcing him to stop walking and bend over at the waist, his hands resting heavily on his knees. He looked up once to see Chaz and Marjorie continue on, their minds focused on the perils of the path in front of them. Zeke tried to shout out a plea for them to stop, but his voice became lost in his throat as his breakfast threatened to introduce itself once more to the world. He tried to stand, but the dizziness hit him again, this time in a swirling mass of darkness that was so thick Zeke thought he could actually taste it.

Then he fell. Hard. As he did, he struck the front of his

head against a rock. A sudden darkness enveloped him and a mist covered him like a winding sheet.

ꙅ

"Zeke," a voice called gently, its sound familiar and pleasant. "Open your eyes and discover the Mist. It waits for you."

Zeke's eyelids felt like lead and he struggled to open them, almost as if he were waking from a potent dose of anesthesia. With the palms of his hands he could feel solid ground beneath him. He tried to push against the firm surface, but his arms felt weighty too, like a dream that refused to end.

"I can't," Zeke whispered weakly. "I can't wake up."

"You must, son. I can't help you with this part. You've got to do this one on your own. Fight against the seam. It seeks to keep you from slipping through."

Zeke fought against the heaviness again, bringing his hands to his eyes to help pry them open. With this final effort, Zeke began to see some light, but only a fragment, like a soft illumination emanating from under a closed door in a darkened room. Then, shading his eyes from the brightness, Zeke was able to open them fully. The brilliance of the light made him squint. He sat up quickly, almost as if he had received a poultice of new strength and saw standing before him the old man who once before visited him in his dream.

"Grandpa John," Zeke said, an awkward smile draped across his face. He stood confidently now, holding out his arms, pulling his grandfather toward him in a full embrace.

Zeke stood for what seemed like a very long time holding on to his grandfather. John Proper returned the embrace with enthusiasm as he wrapped his arms around his grandson's narrow waist. Zeke, his eyes closed against the tears that began to force their way through his lids, breathed in the old man's scent. As he did, Zeke began to see images form in his mind. Images of freshly turned gardens with rich black dirt, the calm of the open ocean, the smoke of autumn leaves burning in an old barrel, and of toiling in the backyard and on the sea. He saw the sowing of seeds, the netting of fish, the harvest of fresh vegetables, helping a neighbor rake the fall leaves, and nights beside a soft fire with a book, a loving companion, and calloused hands entwined. This, Zeke realized, was the true scent of his grandfather. The genuine essence of John Proper.

Slowly and reluctantly Zeke pulled away and looked into his grandfather's sparkling green eyes, Zeke's mind continuing to swirl with images that to him represented peace, warmth, and unconditional love. But then a numbing ache entered Zeke's mind, one that reminded him of something valuable that had been lost.

"Where's my dad?" he asked, all previous thoughts of the trek to the cave forgotten.

"Your father is not here, Zeke. Only a few can enter the Mist. The Seam will not open for him. There are very few, in fact, that are allowed to be here. Nevertheless, your father is safe and very happy and to you he sends his love. Unfortunately, these are things that we cannot afford to linger on. You must return to your friends quickly. It is enough for you to know that you can enter the Mist when your need is great, that the Seam will see you through. Moreover, you must know that your greatest battles have to be fought here. You cannot win any other way. Face the Entity and relinquish your fear. Know that your courage will light your way.

ᚱ

Zeke felt a sharp pinch in the middle of his back where the edge of a jagged piece of rock jutted out, poking him through his light jacket and the t-shirt he wore underneath. He opened his eyes quickly, at the same time pulling himself away from the source of pain. Immediately he saw Chaz standing in the middle of the path, his back turned to Zeke, staring off into the distance toward the road they had come from. On his other side, standing just off to the side of the path in a small tangle to dried weeds, stood Marjorie Anders, her back also turned to Zeke, her hand raised to her forehead shading wind and sunlight from her vision. She appeared to be scanning the horizon for something of interest, her attention completely absorbed in her examination of the landscape.

"What are you guys looking for?" Zeke asked.

Both Chaz and Marjorie, startled out of their intense perusal, jumped at the sound of Zeke's voice. Marjorie shrieked, a small squeaking noise issuing from the back of her throat. Chaz said nothing; his wide-open eyes and stunned expression did all of the talking.

"Wh... where did you come from?" Marjorie managed to stutter.

"Where did I come from?" Zeke questioned. "What do you mean?"

"I mean," Marjorie said, stepping closer to Zeke but slowly, almost as if she feared he might be a ghost, "that we've been wandering around here looking for you for the last half hour. We have literally scoured this area calling your name as loudly as we could. And I know you weren't sitting there a moment ago." Chaz was stepping closer too, quietly nodding his head in amazed agreement.

"Well I've been..." Zeke began to say, brushing dirt off the front of his pants. "I've been..." he muttered again, his mind quickly mulling over his latest encounter with his grandfather. "I've... been... in the Mist," he finally said, an expression of wonder and bewilderment lighting up his features.

"The Mist," Marjorie said, turning to look around her, almost as if she expected to see some residue of smoke or fog that would prove what Zeke said was true. "How?"

Zeke shook his head.

"I don't know exactly. I started feeling sick. Then I got really dizzy and fell. The next thing I knew I was hugging my grandfather."

"John?" Marjorie said. "You spoke with John? What did he tell you?"

"He said I could enter the Mist when my need was great, and that I would have to fight all of my battles there."

"There?" Marjorie questioned. "You mean there, in the Mist?"

Zeke shrugged his shoulders.

"I guess," he answered simply. "Oh yeah. He also said that I can't be afraid. Now that I think about it, he said something like that before. I'm not quite sure why, but it must be important."

"I'm sure it is, Zeke. You'll have to keep that bit of advice in the forefront of your thoughts. How are you feeling now? Do you still feel dizzy?"

"No," Zeke said as he jumped up and down and shook his arms and legs, as if that alone would prove that he was now in perfect health. "I feel great. In fact, never better."

"Alright," Marjorie said, looking from Zeke to Chaz. "Shall we continue then?"

The two boys nodded, Chaz allowing Zeke to walk in front of him while they continued to follow Marjorie along the trail that continued its downward slope.

They quickly came to the end of the path. Soon, all three stood upon a windy sea cliff looking out at a breathtaking view of the cold ocean some three hundred feet below. Zeke looked down the face of the cliff reluctantly, another intense rush of dizziness suddenly sweeping over him as he felt the swirling sensation of vertigo invade his mind. He stepped back from the edge quickly, grabbing on to Chaz for support.

"Holy crap," he said, taking a deep breath to clear his mind. "You and the Captain really climbed up *that?*"

Chaz nodded, also looking over the edge a bit fearfully. "We did," he confirmed. "But if you'll notice, there're handholds and a path of sorts down the side. So it's not as bad as you might think."

"Yeah, right," Zeke retorted, looking over at Marjorie who seemed to be frozen to her small spot on what was left of the path, her wide eyes taking in the immense height of the precipice before her.

"I don't think I can do this," Marjorie said, wringing her hands fitfully as if she were battling some great inner turmoil. "I *want* to help save Taylre, but I'm not going to be able climb down there."

Chaz marched over to Marjorie and grabbed hold of her arm, startling her for a moment and taking her mind away from her near paralysis of fear. "Miss Anders," Chaz said forcefully, an action that, up until now, seemed very un-Chaz like. "You can do this. You've got to. I've seen how quickly you can walk. You're in good shape. You're strong. I know you can make it. You *have* to."

Marjorie stood back for a moment looking at Chaz with a deep expression of confusion.

"Why? Why do I have to? You two can do this on your own. You don't need an old woman like me slowing you down. What possible good can come from me tagging along?"

Chaz, taken back for a moment, a jumble of thoughts racing through his mind, looked back and forth between Zeke and Marjorie.

"Well...Taylre will need you," he stuttered. "She'll need to see your face to... give her confidence. She'll need to see you to help her remember who she is."

Marjorie continued staring at Chaz, but the confusion on her face began to soften. She turned again to the cliff, managing to step closer to its edge and peer over the side. She took a deep breath and then turned back to Chaz and Zeke.

"I'll try," she whispered softly.

CHAPTER TWENTY-EIGHT
An Inside Connection

The wolf stared at Taylre, watching her from the shadows of a boulder. Her skin prickled with fear when she looked at it. She could have sworn that it was smiling at her, its eyes hooded and yellow, but she had never heard of a dog smiling before, and she wondered for the umpteenth time who owned it and why it was there. She walked past the small niche that the wolf stood in and continued to plod her way back to the giant blacksmith who seemed to labor unendingly in his task of forging weapons over the intense heat of the fire that blazed in the middle of the cave. The pounding and shaping of metal sent a continual tremor throughout the immense hollow of the open rock, causing an unending ring to echo in Taylre's ears.

She climbed a small rise that brought her within a few yards of the giant and noted again how incredibly huge the man was.

If, she thought, she could actually call him a man. His skin, bronzed from the fire, was hairless, though the long blond hair on his head hung down like a waterfall; the muscles in his massive arms rippled and shimmered with sweat in the heat's glowing light. He never looked at Taylre when she approached, nor did he speak to her. He just continued to swing his hammer. A machine with no apparent off button.

Taylre reached toward the pile of swords that lay in a glimmering stack beside the forge. She managed to pick up two of the weapons though their weight bit into her flesh, causing slowly mending sores to open anew. She swung around with the swords in her arms, and in doing so accidentally grazed the leg of the giant with the sharpened tip of one of the blades. A trickle of blood began to flow from the small wound.

The giant suddenly stopped his work.

Taylre looked up at the giant with a sudden, sharp intake of breath.

The giant turned to Taylre, looking at her for the first time, and dropped his massive hammer. With his hand free, he swung at Taylre, striking her in the face and sending her flying from the rocky platform onto the sandy floor of the cave.

A wave of blackness mingled with tiny sparkles of light moved its way across Taylre's vision. Her mouth filled with sand and her glasses, which had been flung toward the water's edge, lay twisted and broken, a star-like crack piercing the center of each lens. She rose slowly from the ground, pushing her way upward, her arms aching with the effort, and began coughing the sand out of her mouth while dirty tears flowed down her now bruised and swollen face. Taylre scrambled about on her hands and knees searching for her glasses, feeling through the sand in an anxious attempt to find her sight. Bumping her head against the small boulders that were scattered amongst the open spaces of sand, Taylre finally reached the water's edge and found her glasses partially wedged in the wet sand, their frames half in and half out of the cool water. She placed the twisted spectacles on her face, relishing the small victory.

When she opened her eyes and saw the crack that folded itself in tiny kaleidoscopic layers across her vision, she once again began to cry.

ᚷ

The Captain leaned forward, perching himself over the sharp bow of the fishing boat, while Devon, sitting at the stern, controlling the small outboard engine, watched and listened with intensity to the Captain's directions. Looking into the green waves ahead, the Captain scrutinized the shallow sea bottom for obstructions - sharp rocks jutting up from the ocean floor - that could possibly puncture a hole in the bottom of their small craft, effectively ending their mission.

As the boat and its small crew approached the narrow opening that would bring them within the bay that was home to La Cueva del Diablo, Devon kept the motor running at a slow idle, allowing the craft to creep up on the cave like a lion stalking its prey. The Captain looked back over his shoulder giving Devon a thumbs up sign, a gentle indication that they had slipped past the worst of the obstacles and that their way was now clear to enter the bay. With the silent wave of his hand, the Captain indicated that Devon was to point the bow of the boat toward a large outcropping of rocks and boulders. There, the Captain felt, would be a perfect place to hide from view and stage their final attack on the unsuspecting Loki.

When they reached the tiny beach, its location obscured by towers of stone, Devon cut the engine, allowing the boat to drift into the sand, its hull coming to an abrupt halt.

"Should we tie it up?" Devon whispered to the Captain as he reached for the coil of thick rope that lay at the bottom of the boat.

"No, lad," the Captain said, his own whisper echoing amongst the surrounding boulders. "We'll need that rope for other purposes. Besides, thar hardly be any current here anyway, nothing that'll take ol' Nellie away." The Captain clamored over the side of the boat, sinking slightly into the soft sand. He clutched the shotgun tightly under his arm and motioned for Devon to throw him the rope. Devon made the toss easily and then followed the Captain out of Nellie and onto the beach.

"Now what?" Devon asked, scanning their surroundings as a sense of dread crested over him.

"We wait," responded the Captain. "Look there," he continued, pointing to the jagged cliffs that towered before them just to the left of the large opening of the cave.

Devon looked up, taking in the monolithic precipice of stone with its eroded façade and stark appearance, and wondered how anyone could have scaled its surface.

"Is that where they'll be coming from? Down the side of that?"

"Aye," the Captain answered simply, sitting heavily on a smooth stone. He took his pipe and a small pouch of tobacco from his pocket and began to smoke, this action marking the beginning of a long, patient wait.

ᛉ

Taylre found, to her delight, that if she tilted her head just slightly to one side and shifted her eyes to the corners she could still see. And though the effort was awkward, the result was ultimately pleasing.

She stood slowly discovering that her legs felt a bit wobbly, but mostly she worried about the swelling on the side of her face. She rubbed at it tenderly, wincing with pain as she did so. When she looked up, she was startled to find Mr. Loden standing in front of her, his head shaking from side to side with a sort of sad smile confronting her.

"Tsk, tsk, tsk, Taylre," he said slowly, clearly annoyed. "You are such a stupid girl. You must learn to be more careful around Surt. He has very little patience for idiocy such as yours, you see. Next time watch what you are doing." He turned for a moment as if to leave, then stopped and glanced back at Taylre. "Well, get back to work. There is much to be done, you see." Then he departed, his stride confident and strong.

Taylre stood for a moment, disappointment filling her thoughts. She had expected Mr. Loden to be kinder. She felt that he, of all people in this godforsaken place, would show some pity toward her, to comfort her and show some understanding, especially considering how hard she had been working and the constant loyalty she had shown toward him.

She turned slowly to make her way back to the blacksmith's forge and once again continue her arduous task when she caught sight of something moving just beyond the entrance to the cave.

A small boat perhaps, floating between some rocks and then disappearing behind another set of large boulders. She tilted her head, focusing on the tiny bit of unblemished lens that would allow her to see clearly, but could only make out what she believed was the fading image of a small outboard motor, its gentle, almost inaudible rumble vanishing as fast as the swarthy vision of the boat.

Taylre turned frantically to look for Mr. Loden. She had to tell him. It was the way, it was the law. Incredibly, when she finally saw him, he was already at the far end of the cave ascending the plank toward the deck of the large serpent ship. She thought to call to him, to warn him of possible intruders, because wasn't that what Mr. Loden had said in all of their meetings? That each member of the Ferocious Fenrirs should always be on the look out for intruders, their important work here could not afford to be disrupted by anything or anyone.

She cupped her hands around her mouth, filling her lungs with air so that everyone in the cave would hear her shout. As she brought her hands near her face, however, she brushed up against her cheek, tender, swollen, and now bleeding. She stopped, her hands shaking.

A switch seemed to flicker in Taylre's mind, like a dark room suddenly bathed in a wash of light, and she remembered with absolute clarity who she was and who and what was truly

important to her. She felt a sense of deep shame as she recalled
a vision of Zeke curled up in a tight ball, lying on the floor of
Loden's classroom, his hands and arms covering his head as he
bore the onslaught of kicking feet, driving fists, and dark words.
She shuddered as a sob escaped her throat, and she turned back
to look at the water where she had seen the boat hide behind the
rocks.

And then she understood.

Taylre and the rest of the so-called Ferocious Fenrirs were
just a group of captives, young and inexperienced, who had been
brought under the influence of something very evil. They were
all under the misguided impression that they were here under
their own will. However, this was obviously not true. In addition,
Taylre, normally a happy, optimistic individual, was becoming
angry. Very Angry. She hated Loden for his tricks, and though
she had no idea who or what he really was, she understood that,
like the Korrigan, impossible evils really did exist. The supposed
order that she imagined the world held onto was fragile at best.

All sense of time had fled from Taylre's mind long ago; she
really had no idea how long she had been in the cave.
Nevertheless, she recognized the small boat that was now hidden
from view as the Captain's. She knew, deep within her, that help
was on its way. She also knew that there were some demonic
forces to be reckoned with. Saving all of the Fenrirs and taking

them away from this place would be an almost impossible task. But then, she thought, so was destroying a hideous monster that lived beneath the dark waters of a river. The Captain would need her help to pull this off. Moreover, she was in the perfect position to offer that help.

CHAPTER TWENTY-NINE
Father and Son Connection

"Looking down will only make it worse, Mrs. Anders. Just try to keep your eyes on the rocks in front of you. Let your feet find the steps. They're all there; trust me. You can do this." Chaz continued to speak words of encouragement throughout the terrifying climb down the side of the cliff. He led the way, carefully searching the gnarled pathway for footholds and resting places to ease the arduous journey. But Marjorie, her arms and legs shaking with fear at every step, made the slow trek seem like a never-ending torture. She whined and sobbed constantly and would often stare up at Zeke with tear-filled eyes, her trembling lips asking an unspoken question: what, in the name of all the gods, am I doing here? Zeke, discovering that he had his own sense of dread over this particular journey, remained silent. He tried his best to smile and nod, offering what he felt was his best attempt at encouragement, but his aunt's complaining only made things worse for him. He wanted the climb to end just as much as she did.

Finally, after what seemed like hours, Chaz looked up at Marjorie and gently grasped her by the ankle, his other hand holding firmly to the rock in front of him. "Mrs. Anders," he said calmly. "I want you to slowly look down now. Don't be afraid."

Marjorie, a trickle of sweat beading down the center of her forehead, reluctantly took her eyes off the rock face before her and peered down between her feet. To her delight she saw that they had nearly reached the bottom, that with just a few more steps she would be off this cliff and once again on solid ground. A sigh of relief passed her lips. The end, at least of this part of the journey, was finally in sight.

ᚱ

Taylre felt that her best course of action would be to follow her routine, to just appear as if she were still in the grip of Loden's spell and carry on with her normal chores. In doing so she recognized that she would have to be more vigilant and become more aware of her surroundings. Helping the Captain would require her to clear the way to provide an opportunity for rescue and escape. Her powers of observation would have to become sharpened, and since she was not aware of the Captain's plans, she would have to apply a little ingenuity of her own.

There were a vast number of people milling about the cave, people that Taylre had ignored before, but now - having broken herself from Loden's enchantment - had suddenly become very noticeable. The giants, of course, remained an obvious focal point since their incredible stature and immense proportions were difficult to miss. Taylre vowed to remain as distant from them as possible, especially considering her most recent run in with Surt. Among the giants were the remaining Ferocious Fenrirs. As she thought about the day she walked into Loden's classroom, the sign on the wall almost beckoning her to enter, she realized that the spell Loden weaved upon her began there. She shuddered to think that she had been such an easy target. She had always thought she held a stronger will than that.

As Taylre made her way back up the marred, rocky path that led to the forge where Surt continued to bang his hammer, she grabbed a newly completed sword, intent on giving the impression that she was dutifully continuing her task. She edged as far away from the giant as she could, taking a good look around the cave, watching the monotonous routine of movement as raw material moved from one hand to another. She found it difficult to catch all of the activity because of her shattered glasses but managed to pick out a few familiar faces - other students who had succumbed to Loden's will. She suddenly took in a quick, surprised gasp as her perusal of the cave exposed one very familiar face, one that she never expected to see again.

Acting as a kind of director ensuring that material was moving consistently, was Chief Teddy Walford, the same bumbling police officer who Taylre first saw standing in the backyard where Terrance - a former classmate - crouched animal-like among some scattered bushes. She also recalled seeing him at the site of the battle with the Korrigan. Taylre remembered watching Walford and his three goony friends waddle into a boat after the Korrigan's destruction and escape down the river, adding to the mystery that still marred the reputation of the town and its missing city officials. The event had created quite a stir around Alder Cove, its aftermath still affecting the lives of some individuals in and around town. One of those individuals, a person that Taylre was at that moment watching muddle about on the deck of the mysterious ship, was Teddy Walford, Jr. He was affected most by his father's sudden disappearance, as Taylre had come to understand through rumor and personal observation. The embarrassment to both him and his mother had caused Teddy to turn from a relatively kind person into a bully intent on making everyone else's lives miserable like his own.

Taylre's kaleidoscopic vision shifted back and forth between the father and the son. The father was at one end of the cave constantly yanking up his uniform pants as they continually sagged beneath his big belly. He called out to members of the Ferocious Fenrirs in an angry voice, urging them to move faster, step lively, quit mulling about; there was work to be done. The son seemed to be intent on keeping close to Loden, always standing on his right hand side. He would nod approvingly whenever Loden barked an order at someone and would sometimes push people around who appeared to be moving too slowly. When he did that, Loden would pat him on the back and give him an approving smile. Taylre, moving slowly toward the ship with her metallic load, continued to observe the father and son, finding it strange that they didn't even acknowledge one another. It was almost as if they were completely unaware that the other was there.

Then it dawned on her. They didn't know.

The spell that was cast on Taylre, attracting her to the meeting of the Ferocious Fenrirs, was probably cast on the Walfords as well. They, like Taylre, had forgotten everything. Their allegiance to Loden, or whoever he was, was all-encompassing. With that realization, Taylre had an idea, one that would involve another slap in the face. But first, she had to get the Captain's attention.

ᚷ

With Zeke now in the lead, the small group balanced their way among scattered rocks, eventually approaching the entrance to the cave, their movements slow and as stealthy as possible. They hid themselves behind a large boulder and were able to see an immense plume of black smoke issue out of the cave's mouth. The sight reminded Zeke that they were indeed entering the Devil's domain, the smoke prompting him to consider what the actual doorway to hell might truly be like.

Marjorie was eager to see into the cave; her desire to find Taylre was overwhelming her. Pushing Chaz aside, she inched herself between Zeke and the rock, managing to take a quick peek into the cave itself. All at once, she gasped, bringing her hand to her mouth. She pulled herself back behind the rock and quickly crouched down.

"What is it?" Zeke hissed.

"She's there. I saw her. Near the big fire where the smoke is coming from," she stuttered.

"Taylre? You saw Taylre?" Zeke said, crouching down

beside Marjorie, trying hard to keep his voice to an even whisper. He waited for more, but Marjorie was silent. He would have to look for himself.

Zeke edged himself around the rock, just as Marjorie had done, and glanced about the semi-darkened cave, quickly taking in what at first appeared to be a chaotic rush of smoke and frenzied movement. However, as he continued to stare, Zeke could see that the movement was anything but chaotic. It was in fact quite organized, like a machine set on high, issuing its product quickly and efficiently. A shudder of fear raced through Zeke's mind. He imagined Loki to be nothing but an evil bumbler, an enemy whose intentions were single-minded. This operation, however, appeared to well planned and rehearsed, reflecting a mind that was quick and highly intelligent, capable of many evils at once. Finally, he caught sight of Taylre. She was standing with her back turned to him, but her tall, lanky form was difficult to miss. He would have recognized her anywhere. She was standing on a small rise, a glimmering, heavy sword clutched in her arms. Her head, tilted awkwardly to one side, seemed to be gazing intently toward the bay, where a narrow gap allowed limited entrance into the cove. Zeke followed the direction of her gaze and glimpsed a slight movement washed in gray, like the rocks that shrouded the rugged inlet and the overcast sky that continually threatened to rain. From where he stood, he knew that the Captain and Devon had succeeded in entering the cove safely without being seen. He was confused, then, as to why Taylre was looking so keenly at the spot where the Captain had chosen to hide, realizing that from where Taylre stood there was no way she could see them. All Zeke could do was presume that she had seen something to arouse her suspicion, perhaps when they were pulling in. This worried Zeke. Stealth and secrecy were vital to the success of this mission; the Captain had said so. If Taylre had in fact seen the Captain and Devon enter the cove, then that vital facet of secrecy may have just been blown.

Zeke turned back to Marjorie and Chaz, keeping his movements slow.

"Did you see her?" Marjorie questioned.

"I did," Zeke said. "But we may have a big problem." He looked at Chaz. "Is there another way that we can get in closer? Some way that we can actually enter the cave without being seen?"

"We could retrace the path that Bart and I came out. There are some parts that are pretty tricky, though." Chaz said, looking toward Marjorie as he spoke. "It'll edge us around the back of the cave which should give us a good view of Bart's boat, the ship, and Loden. If we go slowly and keep ourselves low, we should be okay."

"Alright," Zeke breathed. "I guess it's the closest thing to a plan that we have. We'll follow you, but we've got to hurry; I don't think we've got a lot of time left."

ᛉ

Taylre was getting nervous. She knew she should be moving toward the ship with the sword, giving the impression that nothing had changed, but she had to find a way to signal the Captain. She felt the eyes of the other Ferocious Fenrirs watching her, the giants, too. But then again, she may have just been imagining it, allowing her anxiety to get the best of her.

She turned and continued along the well worn path that led from the forge to the narrow plank running up to the ship. Once again she took a furtive glance over her shoulder, hoping, as the Captain would say, that Odin, or one of the other gods, would lend a helpful hand. She felt a rush of excitement as she noticed Devon, his ginger hair poking up from the top of his head like a tuft of unruly grass, peering around the side of the boulder. He was looking directly at her. She quickly looked around to see if anyone else had noticed, but finding she was the only one looking toward the cove, felt safe in assuming all was well. Then, still holding the heavy sword close to her chest, she did the only thing she felt she could: she closed her fist and raised her right thumb in the air, hoping Devon would catch the sign and know what to do.

CHAPTER THIRTY
Convergence

Devon stepped back quickly from the shelter of the boulder, his eyes wide with surprise as he trudged through the shallow cold water, his pant legs rolled up to his knees. He stumbled in the soft sand as he hurried toward the Captain, using the edge of the beached boat to steady himself. "She just gave me the thumbs up sign!" he whispered sharply.

The Captain looked up calmly from his close examination of a fiddler crab as it attempted to make its way across a small patch of sand and hide itself among the shelter of the rocks. The Captain's eyes squinted against the smoke that continued to rise from his pipe, shrouding his stubbly face in a haze of blue smoke.

"Thumbs what?" the Captain asked, pulling the pipe from his mouth and tapping out the ashy contents on a nearby stone.

"Taylre," Devon said. "She just looked at me and gave me the 'thumbs up' sign." He looked at the Captain with his thumb sticking awkwardly in the air as he tried to imitate Taylre's action.

The Captain stood abruptly, a concerned, confused look creasing his brow. He stomped noisily into the shallow water, indifferent to the fact that he still wore his boots, and pressed himself up against the boulder, edging up to the end where he could easily peer around the side and steal a quick look into the cave's mouth.

And there she was, just as Devon had said. Taylre looked up and smiled at the Captain, once again bringing her thumb up.

The Captain slunk back behind the boulder and turned to look at Devon, a surprised expression now covering his face.

"What does it mean, do ya think?"

Devon shrugged, his goofy grin revealed once again.

"I think she's back," he said simply.

ᚱ

Taylre was satisfied, sure that her brief message had been interpreted correctly. She smiled to herself, but not too much; any misplaced attention now could ruin her plan. She turned from the cove where the Captain and Devon lay hidden, making her way toward the former Chief of Police

Teddy Walford, Sr. stood proudly next to a tall, bearded giant who sat at a grindstone, sharpening a huge axe. The giant seemed completely unaware of Walford's presence, though the way Walford stood, one would think that he and the giant were the best of friends. Walford had his hands on his hips. His pudgy chin was stuck out, and his chest filled with air as he tried to draw the attention of the onlookers away from his enormous belly. Occasionally he would point at one of the youth and yell something about moving faster, but most often he was completely ignored as the parade of weapons and metal kept pushing forward despite his efforts. Suddenly, he became aware of someone standing next to him. He turned quickly to find a tall, lanky, red headed girl with broken lenses in her glasses staring directly at him.

"Good day, Officer," Taylre said, her smile broad and pleasant. "You are certainly doing a fine job here. Has anyone ever told you that?"

Walford, too confused for the moment to say anything, simply stared. He opened his mouth to say something, but then closed it again, as if the sound was pulled completely out of him.

Taylre continued. "And did I mention what a fine job you did with the mayor and Mr. Roberts? I am quite certain they were both very proud of the service you rendered that day when the monster came out of the water. Do you remember that, Officer? Do you remember that day?"

Walford Sr. opened his mouth again, this time followed by a painful disconnection of words. "You... must... get... back...it's... the way...it's the...what? What did? Roberts... he and the... died... I saw them." Then he began to shake and his knees began to buckle beneath him causing him to teeter, his pear-like shape bending and twisting, threatening to fall at any moment.

Taylre pressed on, hoping that this particular kind of "slap in the face" was exactly what the former police chief needed to bring him back to reality.

"And did you know, Officer Walford, that your son," she said, stepping closer to the man and pointing to the deck of the ship, drawing Walford's attention away from the confused stares that were beginning to form about him, "is standing right over there. I'm sure he misses you. Wouldn't you like to see him again?"

Walford's eyes followed Taylre's pointing finger, and suddenly he recognized - for the first time in many months - the figure of his one and only son, who was at that moment standing next to Loden.

His shaking stopped, and his eyes grew wide as a soft reflection of joy radiated from his face.

"Teddy," he whispered, trying to call across the shadowed distance of the cave. "Teddy," he said again, his voice growing stronger. "Teddy," he called louder still, as those who began to huddle around him, stopped their work. "Teddy!" he finally managed to yell, his voice expanding like his understanding.

All movement stopped.

Teddy Senior's voice echoed over the now stilled hammers and the hushed clinking of metal. All eyes turned to look at him, including his son, Teddy Jr., and, most frightening of all, those of Almar Loden.

ᛣ

The air seemed to change and the direction of the wind shifted. The Captain could sense it immediately, as could Devon. The smell was different. There was no longer the scent of ocean, tides, and drifting seaweed. Instead, there was the odor of burnt flesh, like anger that has become too hot. There was a palpable weight, too, almost as if the humidity had suddenly risen, pressing down on them so that they could feel it in their shoulders, a burden that seemed impossible to bear.

The Captain and Devon looked at each other as the shadow of the receding sun drifted behind their rock.

"What just happened?" Devon wondered aloud.

The Captain shrugged his shoulders slightly, as if he was trying to pass off the phenomenon as unimportant, but Devon could see the worry on his face.

"I think there's a storm comin', lad," the Captain said as he waded out to the edge of the boulder, peering around the corner once more to gaze into the cave.

The smoke from the forger's furnace continued to billow forth in black clouds. The Captain watched it rise in a rolling torrent, reaching the cave's roof. At its apex, it curled around itself and pushed into the open air, its black weight now pressing down on the small cove, dimming the gray light and causing the chaos in the cave to become hidden, as if a thick curtain suddenly fell over the actors in a gruesome play.

CHAPTER THIRTY-ONE
Indelible Images

When Teddy Jr. turned and saw his father standing below him in the darkened cave, the spell that was upon him broke, but its hold on him was reluctant to leave. To Teddy it felt like he had been struck in the face with an enormous tree branch, and it caused him to rear back a step or two. For just a brief moment he felt lost, like a man who has suddenly woken from a very deep sleep. But then things began to clear. Looking about him, taking in all of the faces that stared up at him, a full recollection of what had brought him to this place suddenly filled his mind. He looked again at his father, expecting to feel compassion toward this man who lived, once upon a time, in the same house as he and his mother, but instead he felt a deep sense of loathing, hatred so thick that his face turned red and his eyes bulged, their whites creased with tiny rivulets of bloodshot crimson.

"YOU!" he yelled. "You ruined my life!"

Teddy Sr., standing several yards away on a small plateau, his hands outstretched as if pleading for forgiveness, suddenly looked crushed and defeated. He tried to speak, but the words became caught in his throat, and he began to gag on them.

Loden, who remained at Teddy Jr's side, clapped Teddy on the shoulder, his eyes alive with fire, his smile dangerous and penetrating.

"You've done well, Teddy. I knew you would." He turned and stepped near the railing of the ship, resting his hands on the cold, jagged surface. Then, raising his arm and pointing his finger directly at Teddy Sr., he began to shout. "Take him! Take him and destroy him. He is no good to me now!"

Like a swarm of angry fire ants, the giants and the remaining members of the Ferocious Fenrirs fell upon the former Chief of Police, taking him from his perch and dragging him toward the blazing fires of the forge.

His screams seemed to pierce the very rock itself, and the smoke, which instantly turned black from the former policeman's burning fat, curled up and filled the cave with its acrid odor.

ᚴ

It was too much for Taylre. Her mind simply could not process what had just happened. Instead of running and ducking for cover among the rocks, using the smoke as a camouflage to escape and join up with the Captain and Devon, she found herself crouched near the edge of the cool, lapping water, her feet sinking in the soft, wet sand. Her arms were pulled up over her head in a vain attempt to protect herself from any other atrocious, falling images that might come her way. She sobbed, choking on the uncontrollable tears that fell freely from her stinging eyes. Pushing away her glasses, she tried several times to wipe away the image of Teddy Walford - his screams and his terrible shivers of pain. Nevertheless, the impression was indelible, and she knew that this would be the source of many nightmares.

"You really are a stupid little girl, aren't you," Loki said, his tall, muscular form casting a ghostly shadow across Taylre's battered form. "But I suppose Surt's smack across your face shook out a little more than I assumed it would. Nevertheless, now I'm going to have to also deal with you, you see."

Taylre, shaken out of her grief, looked up to see Loki standing over her. Behind him stood Teddy Jr. He was smiling.

Taylre could not comprehend how a son could watch his own father die and then feel nothing. Teddy had changed. Loki had changed him, his wickedness penetrating deep into Teddy's very soul.

Taylre's fear began to overwhelm her, but she managed to quiet her crying enough to speak to Loki.

"Wha...what are you going to do to me?" she asked, the horrible vision of Teddy Sr. once again at the forefront of her mind.

Loki laughed, deep and raucous, and those around him, including Teddy, joined in.

"That, I haven't decided yet, you see. Perhaps for now I will simply place you in the bottom of my ship. I am planning a very long voyage, you see. You will come along. It will give me time to consider what kind of punishment will best suit you." Loki snapped his fingers and all at once Taylre was surrounded by a throng of Ferocious Fenrirs and giants. Together they lifted her from the soft sand, her squirming and fighting useless against the mob.

They carried her screaming up the narrow plank that led to the deck of the enormous ship. Other giants were there, waiting. They took her from the enraged horde, carrying her below into the darkest recesses of the ship where her shouts and screams faded, drifting away like a memory in the mist.

CHAPTER THIRTY-TWO
It Is the Way. It Is the Law.

Zeke felt the change, too. He began to cough as the acrid smoke filled his nostrils and caused tears to well up in his eyes. He turned to Marjorie and Chaz, and through his blurred vision saw that they too were struggling with the tainted air. He crouched as low as he could, crawling among the scattered stones, and reached toward Marjorie, touching her gently on the arm.

"Keep low, Aunt Marjorie. The smoke's not so bad if you stay below it." He turned to Chaz who was listening to Zeke's instructions and trying to remain as low as possible.

"Something's happened, Chaz. I wonder if the Captain found a way in? Maybe we should make our move now."

Chaz nodded. "I think you're right," he said, coughing

quietly into his fist. "Whatever Bart's done has created a perfect diversion. No one will be able to see us if we go in now. Plus, there seems to be a lot of activity going on in there. If we don't go now, we may never get another chance."

Indeed there was a lot of commotion coming from the cave. Zeke could hear angry shouts and screaming. He could only imagine what kind of horrible things were happening just beyond the rocks.

He tried looking across the small bay to catch a glimpse of the Captain and Devon, but the smoke was too thick. He realized that he would have to go on instinct.

Zeke took the lead as Marjorie and Chaz followed. They kept themselves crouched low to the ground, using the protection of the rocks and the smoke to conceal their advance. Zeke followed a makeshift trail that led, he hoped, to the last place he saw Taylre standing. His plan was to confront her, to somehow draw her out of her trance and enlist her help. The strategy, he knew, was full of holes; nevertheless, he was aware that the Captain and Devon were probably - at that very moment - working their way into the cave from the other side. With that thought in mind, he felt a small measure of comfort. Knowing he was not in the mess all by himself somehow lifted his spirits and gave him the push to move on.

As they moved farther on into the darkness, the yelling intensified. Zeke recognized the loudest voice as none other than Loki himself. Fear began to creep into Zeke's mind as the prospect of running into Loki again filled his thoughts with a deep foreboding. His spirits suddenly plummeted.

"Why are you stopping?" Chaz said, his forehead ramming into the middle of Zeke's back.

Zeke turned and sat on a soft patch of sand, his back pushed up against the edge of a flat stone. Marjorie and Chaz huddled around him.

"He's there. Loki. He's there just beyond this rock, and that scares the hell out of me," Zeke said. "I knew he was going to be here, but now that we're this close...I don't know. I'm not sure I can do this."

Marjorie rested a comforting hand on Zeke's shoulder, attempting to induce a measure of courage into him with her touch, realizing that she had none to give.

Chaz pushed aside Marjorie's hand, startling both Marjorie and Zeke. His eagerness as he stepped in front of Zeke, pushing up on Zeke's chin so that Zeke was looking him straight in the eye, seemed very un-Chaz-like.

"You'll be fine." Chaz stated forcefully. "We've got to keep moving. People need help. Are you just going to sit here in fear?

Are you a coward? Let's get moving before we lose the distraction of the smoke."

Zeke was dumbfounded and a bit surprised at Chaz' zeal and turned to Marjorie, wondering if she, too, had noted his odd behavior. Looking back at Chaz, Zeke nodded.

"Okay. I just need to catch my nerve, that's all. Why are you so eager to get in there?"

"Why?" Chaz questioned. "Because...because those are my friends. I've got to help them. It's the least I can do since I'm the only one to have escaped. So, let's get a move on."

"Okay. Okay. Don't rush me," Zeke said, pulling his arm out of Chaz' grasp.

Zeke stood, slowly, remembering to keep his head low, and once again began to take the lead.

"Hang on," Chaz said, stepping in front of Zeke. "I'll go first, maybe now we'll be able to move a bit quicker. I don't think you're as fast as you used to be."

Zeke frowned at the dig.

"Fine," he said, gesturing curtly toward the jagged path they were following, his movements revealing the anger he could feel rise in his chest "You lead. Just make sure you get us to Taylre."

Chaz said nothing as he began shifting through the scattered rocks, his form melting into the thick smoke.

Zeke tried to keep up as he towed Marjorie along behind

him, her hand gripped tightly around his shirttail. Soon, however, Zeke lost sight of Chaz as he desperately scanned the makeshift path in front of him. He tried to clear his eyes of tears that blurred his vision as the thick smoke continued to drift throughout the cave, scratching at the back of his throat like sharpened claws. He stopped, letting Marjorie catch up to him.

"Do you see him?" Zeke whispered.

Marjorie shook her head as she squinted into the swirling mass before them.

"I think he might have gone that way," she said, indicating with the slight movement of her head an opening that seemed to magically appear just beyond a large rock. Zeke hesitated for only a moment before he trudged on, seeing that their options were limited.

When they reached the rock and then stepped into the open space, the air seemed to clear a little, and Zeke thought he could make out some hazy movement. Then, as if out of nowhere, Chaz once again appeared out of the smoke, an odd expression reflected in his stare.

"I really think he's going to be happy to see you," Chaz whispered.

Zeke squinted, partly because of the smoke, and partly because of the confusion he felt.

"What? Who? What are talking about? Is it the Captain? Did you find the Captain and Devon?"

"No, Zeke. The Captain will be dealt with soon enough. First, though, he wants to see you."

"I don't understand, Chaz. Who's going to be happy to see us?" Zeke could feel Marjorie pinching the back of his arm, her panic and fear transferring itself into his own mind.

Chaz' expression finally changed, as a small grin appeared across his lips.

"Why, Loden of course. Why else do you think I brought you here? It is the way. It is the law."

CHAPTER THIRTY-THREE
Supplication

Both the Captain and Devon had no idea what had happened in the cave. From the time they left their haven near the cove, they were forced to edge far off to the north and then slowly skirt their way back by means of a rocky, uneven trail. The way proved to be tricky and often painful, as the Captain found himself falling on and between the rocks on several occasions. The wounds he received the last time he was in the cave were now re-opened, and he had new bruises to add to them. Devon remained close behind the Captain, always lending a helping hand whenever he fell.

The two carried very little with them as they traveled. The Captain held tightly to his shotgun, and Devon clung to the length of rope that the Captain insisted he carry, wrapping it uncomfortably over his head and shoulder.

As they approached the cave's opening from the north, striving to keep themselves hidden among the large stones, they were disappointed to find that the smoke that once filled the cave and the surrounding area had dissipated into a gray, wintry haze. There would no longer be refuge in the black smoke. Their chance at stealth had passed, and they were compelled to stop and reconsider their options.

The Captain found a smooth patch of ground where soft sand, slightly warmed from the timid sun, remained dry and free of debris. He placed his gun on the ground beside him and knelt on the sand. Devon stood a few paces off to the Captain's left, a look of concern on his face. He feared that the Captain had once again fallen and that his strength had finally given out. He stepped toward the Captain, his arms extended in an attempt to help him once again to his feet. The Captain looked up, his eyes hooded behind a darkened, determined expression.

"No, lad, I'm fine. Just bring me the rope," he said, bowing his head and raising his arm toward Devon.

"You want the rope? Now?"

"Aye, lad, place one end in my outstretched hand. When you've done that, wrap the rope around my body; not too tight, just enough so that it covers my upper torso."

Devon was even more bewildered, but he knew enough not to question the Captain, especially now; his tone was very serious. And so, he began walking around the Captain, binding him like a prisoner, the cords of rope layering over one another until he had reached the end.

Devon held on to the final length of rope, giving the Captain a silent, questioning glance.

"Drop it, lad, but stand close; I may need yer help."

Devon dropped the rope and stepped back a short pace, still unsure of the Captain's motives. He watched reverently as the Captain, his head still bowed, closed his eyes and searched his memory for some distant words once taught to him by his mother. The ones that he hoped would reach the gates of Asgard and enter the realm of Odin, the greatest of gods.

Finally, a calm expression spread across the Captain's face, and he raised his head, his eyes focused on the heavens. His voice stirred the air about them, elevated in humble supplication.

"Whitebeard, the Terrible One, Bringer of Wisdom,
Binder of Loki are you, Lover of Feasting,
Father of freedom, fighter most brave,
Bewilderer and Bringer of Sleep. Defender, dearly we need thee,
Hear us, Odin; hasten to help us,
Gifts thy great ravens fly to bring.

I fight to release myself from the fetters that bind me,

For here, we are bound by shackles we cannot fight.

Release us, oh Father, great Leader of Souls.

Send thy gifts upon us."

After the Captain had spoken his pleading words, he began to pull free of the rope that encircled him, slowly and methodically he let the restraints fall harmlessly to the ground. Then, almost as an after thought, he uttered a final word. "Amen." He looked up at Devon, who was staring in silent wonder.

"I've just called upon Odin for his help, lad. We're goin' to need it more than ever now. I hoped we'd be able to cross the threshold of the cave in darkness, bein' covered by the smoke. But alas, that is not to be. I don't know where else to turn."

"It's okay, Captain," Devon answered apologetically. "Zeke's still out there somewhere. I'm sure he'll figure out a way."

The Captain chuckled as he bent down to pick up the rope from the ground, winding it as he went. "Ya've got to have more faith in the gods than that, boy. My mother certainly did. If she were here, she'd be telling me to be patient, to wait for the answer to come, because it always does. But only when the need is greatest."

"So what do we do in the meantime?" Devon asked. "Just wait and hope that something happens? Wait and see if there really is an Odin who's listening when you ask him for help?"

"Nope," the Captain answered simply. "We trudge on, Devon; sometimes faith requires action. If we don't get movin', Odin might not think we're serious. Grab hold of the rope, wrap it around yer head and shoulder again. I'll pick up my shotgun and we'll be on our way."

"But what if no help comes?" Devon asked, a sense of alarm rising in his voice.

"Ya mean what if we die?"

Devon nodded his head almost imperceptibly. "I suppose."

"Then it was meant to be," the Captain said. "Go ahead and hide under a rock if ya like, but you'll not live one moment more. Your story's been told, lad. Yer moment to die was set a long time ago. You'll either die in the cave with me, if it's meant to be, or you'll die here. It's up to you."

Devon thought for only a moment before he took a deep breath, took hold of the rope to place it once again over his head, and faced the Captain.

"Let's do this," he said, flashing the Captain one of his cheesy grins.

The Captain smiled back. "Good choice, lad. Good choice."

Devon followed the Captain, and the two of them continued to the cave's opening which now stood less than a hundred yards away.

When they Finally reached the border of the cave, the Captain came to a stop, edging himself along the rock face so he could peer inside. He held up a warning hand for Devon, urging him to stop and wait. Devon, his curiosity getting the better of him, crouched down and tried to squeeze himself in between the rock and the Captain so that he could also get a look inside the cave. The Captain flashed an angry glare, motioning Devon to stay behind him.

"What do you see?" Devon asked, his curiosity mounting.

The Captain stood for a moment longer looking into the cave, his eyes moving about the immense cavern, taking in all of the sights. "All of the movement from before has stopped," he said, still scanning the inside of the cave. "The fires from the forge have almost completely died down and thar's no more parade of youth carrying weapons on board the ship. Thar seems to be a large group gathered at the far end of the cave, but it's too far, and I can't make out what's going on."

"Are they anywhere near your boat?" Devon asked.

"No," the Captain responded. "That's been left unguarded." He turned to Devon. "Do ya think we should try to get to the boat?"

Devon nodded. "Absolutely; this may be our only chance."

The Captain brought his hand across his face, wiping the sweat that had begun to accumulate on his brow, wishing that he had his pipe and could sit and reflect on the best course of action. However, time was not on their side. A decision was needed quickly.

"Fair enough, lad. Follow me and keep low. We'll keep to the water's edge. If anyone sees us, stay behind me. I'm taking the safety off of my gun and won't hesitate a moment to use it."

Devon nodded his head and squared his shoulders. When the Captain began to move, Devon followed, mirroring his every step.

Reaching the Captain's boat was easy. In fact, the Captain thought, it was too easy. There is no way they should have been able to find their way so quickly without anyone stopping them or sounding an alarm. Neither the Captain nor Devon let down their guard. If anything, they were more vigilant. Their nerves tightened like coiled springs and their senses noticed even the slightest movement or sound. When they came to the side of the boat, the Captain motioned for Devon to climb on board. While Devon entered the boat, the Captain continued to survey the surrounding cave, his shotgun at the ready, noting that a large group of the captive students and menacing giants remained gathered, their attention focused on something other than the work of hauling weapons to and from the infamous ship, Naglfar.

"I'm not likin' this, lad. No, not one bit," the Captain said nervously. "Thar's something wickedly portentous about that gatherin' over thar."

Devon, who was quietly releasing the ropes that held the boat to its temporary mooring, looked up and over at the direction the captain was indicating.

"I know," he said, coiling a short length of rope onto the deck. "I saw that crowd when we first came around those boulders over there. I can't help but wonder where Zeke and the others have gotten to. And where's Taylre? When I saw her give me the thumbs up, it sure did seem like she was back to her old self. You think she might be over there too?"

"Chances are," the Captain retorted. "But we won't know until we venture over there and have a look see. Are ya done yet?"

"Just one more rope left," Devon answered.

"Leave that one, boy. We've got to keep her moored. That one'll be the last one we untie before we set off. And hopefully, if all goes well, we'll have a boat load of youngin's like yerself to bring along."

CHAPTER THIRTY-FOUR
Huginn and Munnin

Loki stood on a smooth, black rock. His arms were folded, and his long blond hair hung down over his shoulders. His smile was wicked as he looked about his motley group of followers, feeling a silent loathing for each of them. Nevertheless, they were all he had, at least for now. He would have to make do.

"My children," he began, artificial benevolence dripping from his mouth like venom. "You see that I am above all; that I am supreme. Nothing can stop me. I have led you to greatness, and soon, very soon, I will take you, my warriors, to the gates of the gods, and we will prevail!

"You know that I can do it, don't you? For you see before you a menace. A bane of cruelty whom I said would walk, voluntarily, into my home. Now he is ours to deal, you see. What shall his punishment be?"

The gathered host of Ferocious Fenrirs and giants turned their adoring eyes away from Loki and stared menacingly at the rope bound figures of Zeke Proper and Marjorie Anders, their semi-conscious bodies laid out like carrion on the coarse sand.

Zeke tried lifting his head, but the cords that held him were tight and their ends seemed to be anchored to the ground, pinning him to the earth like Gulliver among the Lilliputians. Speaking, too, was out of the question. His mouth was gagged with some kind of filthy rag that tasted like a mixture of rotting eggs and sour milk. He struggled with the ropes that held his hands and arms, but they, too, were tied so tightly that Zeke was forced to accept the fact that he was trapped. There was no possible way out of this predicament.

He shot a quick glance over at Marjorie, and saw that she, too, was bound to the earth. The absolute fear in her eyes let Zeke know that they were in a completely hopeless situation.

Zeke's stare returned to the ceiling of the cave when Loki's face suddenly blocked his view, yellow tinted eyes glaring down at Zeke. Loki knelt in the sand, bringing his mouth close to Zeke's ear.

"You and I, Zeke, we're so much alike, you see." Zeke began shaking his head forcefully from side to side, a mixture of overwhelming pain and fear seizing his mind. "Oh yes, yes. We really are, Zeke. We both want things. And we will both stop at nothing to get them. The difference is that I always get what I want. I always win. You, on the other hand, fail. You are an idiot. You are an empty-headed dwarf-scum whose purpose is relegated to the depths of Dark Home. You are nothing but a dweller of potholes and caves. There is simply no more use for you and your pathetic followers, you see," he said, glancing quickly over at Marjorie. "And so, your doom is sealed, your end is at hand, and the fires of the forge await you. *My* followers have decided your fate. Apparently they liked the way our last victim sizzled in the heat. They want to see it again."

Zeke began struggling against the ropes, his fear becoming total as he considered the idea of being tossed in a furnace while he was still alive and kicking. Loki stood up once more, looming over Zeke, and waved his hand toward the crowd of onlookers.

"Take them," he called. "The others will be along soon enough, I'm sure. When they come, we will take care of them. For now, this is the prize we've waited for."

The large circle of hypnotized onlookers began edging forward, arms outstretched, fire and blood lust reflected in their eyes.

Then, a single shot rang out.

Reverberating off the walls of the cavern, the sound of the Captain's shotgun brought the riotous mob to a confused halt. Everyone began looking around for the source of the shot. Even

Loki appeared slightly startled, though his concern was tempered behind his dark, clouded expression. He spun himself around, his gaze searching the shadowed alcoves. Finally, his eyes rested on the silhouetted form of Bartholomew Gunner as he stood on the edge of a flattened boulder, its precipice slightly elevated above the surrounding rocks. Behind him stood Devon. In the crook of Bartholomew's arm, steadied firmly against his shoulder, was the shotgun, its barrel pointed directly at Loki.

"I think we've seen enough damage done here today!" the Captain shouted. Then lowering his voice, authority and control marking its tone, he continued. "You'll be letting these youngin's go now," he ordered.

Loki smiled and shook his head sadly. "So nice of you to come, coward. Have you brought along your yellow stench of fear, too?" Loki mocked with a slight chuckle.

"You're finished, Bart. There is nothing you can do; it will take much more than a little toy like that to stop me. For you, it will take a miracle." Loki nodded toward one of the giants who stood on the outer edge of the throng. The giant nodded back at Loki and then started forward, trudging his way up the path toward the Captain and Devon, his left hand clenched in a tight fist while his right held a large, glistening sword.

As the giant approached, the Captain did feel fear. The sound of his confident voice was only a ruse, a desperate act to save Zeke and Marjorie's lives. Nevertheless, the Captain kept his finger on the trigger and lifted the gun, his right eye squinted shut while the left peered down the smooth, metal barrel at the looming giant.

"Keep yer distance, ya brute, or I'll send ya back to hell whar ya come from!" he hollered.

The giant kept coming, heedless of the Captain's warning, his muscled arm raising the sword above his head.

The Captain's hands began to shake. He was not a violent man, despite the rumors spread about him. Shooting another person, regardless of the fact that that person was some kind of other-worldly beast, was despicable to him. He was not a killer. Yet the giant pushed on, and it was evident that he would undoubtedly swing the sword he held and probably succeed in decapitating both Devon and Bartholomew in one fluid sweep.

Devon held on to the back of the Captain's shirt while he peered around his husky frame.

"Um...Captain?" Devon managed to whisper. "I think now might be a good time to pull the trigger."

The Captain felt a bead of sweat roll down the middle of his forehead and trickle forward, clinging precariously to the end of his nose. It hung there for just a moment while he continued to watch the giant step closer, the loud stomping of his feet on the padded earth sounding in the Captain's ears like the warning roar of thunder.

Then, just for a moment, there was silence, but for the sound of the Captain's heart beat and rapid breathing.

The drop of perspiration fell from the tip of the Captain's nose.

He pulled the trigger.

For some reason this shot seemed much louder than the first. Zeke, whose view of the Captain was blocked by the giant, never saw the pull of the trigger or the resulting recoil of the gun. On the other hand, he did see the back of the giant and the gush of smoke and blood that emptied from the hole that suddenly appeared between his shoulder blades. He also saw the giant drop his sword as he jerked backward, landing with a solid thump upon the ground. When the giant hit the earth, Zeke could feel the vibration of the impact as it reverberated through the sand. He watched as the massive form heaved once as though fighting to take in one last breath. Then, as if time suddenly stopped, the giant lay still, a dead heap of flesh staring wide eyed up at the ceiling.

The Captain winced with pain. He could never remember a time when the recoil of his gun had been so powerful.

Something about the shell he used, perhaps; he wasn't sure. What he did know, however, was that the attacking giant was no longer a threat. And for some reason he felt good about it. He was no longer a coward who stood in reluctant indecision. No. This time he acted.

He could feel Devon still clinging to the back of his shirt.

"Stay whar ya are, lad. This isn't over yet. Not by a long shot." He rubbed at his shoulder where the butt of the gun jolted into him after he fired. Then as quickly as he could he reached into his vest pocket and retrieved two more shotgun shells that he deftly inserted into the gun's chamber, pumping the handle on the barrel once before setting the stock back into the crook of his shoulder and taking aim, once again, at Loki.

It took a moment for Loki to realize what had just happened. His mouth hung open in obvious shock at the giant's defeat. But then, his mind clearing, he began to clap, slowly and theatrically.

"Bravo, Bart. I really didn't think you had it in you," he said, stepping away from the crowd of amazed onlookers and walking up the path the giant had just taken toward the Captain and Devon. "I honestly thought you'd had it there, that Sokkmimir was going to slice you to pieces. But I guess I was wrong." He continued to clap as he walked slowly on.

"Stop right there, ya filthy beast," the Captain said, adjusting the tip of his finger on the edge of the trigger. "One more step and I'll send ya flyin across the cave just like I did to yer rotten friend ."

Loki stopped and placed his hands out in front of him in a pleading gesture. "Now, Bart. There is no need to get violent. Think of the children. You don't want them seeing all that death and carnage, do you?" Loki spoke almost sweetly, though Zeke, who was still lying on the ground behind him, could hear the anger begin to rise in his voice.

"You heard me, ya devil. Back away and let these poor kids go. Thar's been enough brutality here to last a lifetime. Let's be done with it."

Loki paused, and the Captain could see his face begin to change as a shadow fell across his features. "I agree, Bart. Let's be done with it."

In a flash, like a streak in an over exposed film, the Captain saw Loki rush toward him so swiftly that he barely had time to blink. The gun was forcefully pulled from his hands and thrown, its metal clinking amongst the distant rocks at the far end of the cave. The Captain, his mind racing to catch up to what had just happened, found himself looking up into the smiling, yellow eyes of Loki. Like a vision from a sordid nightmare, Loki growled, his features changing into a snarling wolf.

The animal pounced on the Captain, pushing him back and sending Devon sailing, his body slamming into a nearby rock while the Captain lay on his back with the grizzled form of Loki standing over him.

Zeke watched in horror at Loki's sudden movement and incredible transformation. And then suddenly he realized where he'd seen the animal before, recalling a time not too long ago when he ventured along a sodden path in the early morning hours and saw a wolf standing among the foliage. He understood that Loki had been waiting for him all along. Teasing him. Taunting him. Hurting him physically and emotionally, taking his father away from him. And now, as he looked on from his helpless position on the sandy earth, he saw that Loki was about to take away his friend and his brother, too; there was nothing he could do about it.

The wolf inched forward, jaws agape, saliva dripping from its jowls. The Captain fought to catch his breath, but shuddered with fear as the beast's mouth inched closer to his throat. Devon, too, watched in terror but could do nothing. He teetered on the edge of unconsciousness, as the death of the Captain appeared imminent.

ᛟ

A shadow crept across the mouth of the cave, blocking the gray light that tried to filter in from the late afternoon. The air in the deep cavern seemed to flutter, like small ripples on the surface of a pond. Loki, still a wolf, the altered form of the fallen god, stopped, his dripping, glistening teeth just a fraction of an inch away from the Captain's bare throat.

His yellow eyes looked up. And Bartholomew Gunner, though caught in the grip of fear himself, saw terror fill the eyes of his enemy.

The beast reared back, edging away from the Captain, and the wolf began to scream.

Bartholomew looked again to see the monster change back to his Loki form, but reluctantly, as if someone or something were tearing the soul of the wolf out of his body.

All movement stopped. The giants' faces seemed to reflect the same kind of dread that was in Loki's. The youth, the involuntary members of the Ferocious Fenrirs, looked about them in complete bewilderment, their minds now reeling in confusion; Loki's scream appeared to have peeled away the tiny scales of dark magic that held each one of them bound.

Everyone looked toward the sky.

Two ravens appeared, their sleek bodies as black as the waters of the Stick River. Their wings were spread wide, extended much further than would seem possible as their forms drifted between mist and reality. Loki stared up at the sudden

onslaught of wings and beaks as the two birds flew into the cave,

swooping at the giants, scratching their heads and flailing arms

with their talons as they soared past. The resulting dissonance

sent a shudder of pain through the ears and minds of those who

stood below.

Loki turned an angry stare at the Captain.

"What have you done, Bartholomew Gunner?" he shouted,

his voice barely cresting over the loud screeching, his arms

covering his head against the birds' assault.

Devon, having recovered slightly, crawled over to the

Captain.

"What is it? What's going on?" he said, trying hard to

project his own voice above the clamor.

"They're an answer to prayer, lad. That's what they are. An

answer to prayer." A confident smile formed on the Captain's

lips as he looked from the swooping birds to the terrified Loki.

"I don't understand!" Devon hollered. "Are we in danger?"

"No, Devon, not us. But they are," the Captain said,

pointing at Loki and the scattering giants. "They're birds sent

from the very presence of Odin himself. They're Huginn and

Muninn. Thought and Memory. They perch themselves on the

shoulders of Odin and carry out his will, servin' him when he

has need. Allfather has heard our plea, Devon. He's sent his ravens to aid us."

The Captain was slow to get up, but with Devon's help he managed to regain his feet. Then, as they watched the riot of feathers and screams below them, they saw Loki was running as if in fear for his life; the ravens seemed to be paying particular attention to him.

"Look!" Devon hollered.

The Captain followed Devon's pointing finger and saw Loki begin to diminish, his body taking on an ethereal appearance until he finally faded into nothingness, like a wisp of smoke among dying embers.

"The Mist, lad. He's gone to the Mist."

ᛦ

Zeke, still bound in tight ropes, watched Loki and the rest of the giants pass by. His mind was awhirl with thoughts of escape, of the sudden appearance of the mysterious giant birds, and the whereabouts of Taylre. So far, he had not seen her, although he looked with care among the crowd of youth when he and Marjorie were captured. He worried, among other things, that she had been hurt during all of the confusion. Or, that she had become so deeply entrenched in the will of Loki that her mind was now irretrievable.

He struggled with the knots on the rope but found his strength ebbing. He looked toward Marjorie, hoping that she had somehow made progress on the knots that bound her, but she appeared far too terrified to even move as her eyes widened with panic, paralyzing her among the rocks and sand.

Zeke looked toward the Captain and Devon for help but saw that they too remained fixed to their position on the small rise. He and Marjorie desperately needed help to escape the ropes, but Zeke also understood that if either the Captain or Devon tried to move from their current location they would be caught in the ruckus and panic that stirred about them. Nevertheless, he knew he had to do something. He feared that Loki would leave, and he needed to know that Taylre was safe.

Lying there, on the cool sand in the semi-darkness of the cavern, Zeke suddenly felt a familiar wave of nausea assail him. Sweat began to form on his forehead, but he felt cold; his muscles were tightening, cramping. He turned quickly on his side, fearing that he would vomit. But then, as if his mind were being gently pulled from his body, he felt a smooth, comforting release as the Mist once again enveloped him, taking him past the seam that divides the worlds.

He found himself standing next to the ship, Naglfar, free of the bonds that held him, free of the madness and bedlam of Midgard.

CHAPTER THIRTY-FIVE
Shaker

Here, in the Mist, all was quiet. The struggle for life and death among the giants felt distant. Zeke could sense it, though he had no idea where that other place was or how to get back there.

Reflected light caught Zeke's attention, and he turned to look closer at the sides of the ship. Its hull glistened and an iridescent cascade of colors shimmered along its entire length. His first impression was how beautiful it looked. The colors seemed to dance, their melody expressed like the gentle, lapping waves of the sea. Upon closer inspection, Zeke realized what the small, scale-like material was, and he reared back in horror and revulsion. The Captain had told him that the ship was evil, its course destined toward the gates of Asgard where the final battle with the gods would commence, marking the beginning of

Ragnarok. He had also mentioned that the ship was built from the painfully extracted fingernails of the dead. The beautiful, glimmering shape of the hull was the product of that torture. Zeke had to turn away; its implications were too much to bear.

Zeke stepped away from the ship, surprised to find that it was not sitting in the water. Instead, it seemed to be resting on a thin film of vapor, like steam from a boiling kettle. In fact, there was no water anywhere. No water, no rocks, and no sand. The only thing that appeared even remotely the same was the ship.

Keeping his distance from the ship, Zeke walked on soft ground toward a sturdy, equally colorful gangplank that led up to the deck of the boat. He hesitated, dreading the prospect of walking on the surface now that he realized its true nature. Nevertheless, he sensed that he had been allowed to enter the Mist once again only because there was a reason to do so. He had to discover what that purpose was.

He walked quickly, stepping lithely onto the deck, noting that the shimmer of the fingernails continued along the deck's immense surface and even extended up the three tall masts that towered overhead. He tried hard to keep his eyes off the surface, once again feeling a wave of repugnance attempt to overpower him. Just ahead, near the center of the ship, Zeke saw that there was a large enclosure. On its side was an ornate door, its façade emboldened with colorful carvings. When he looked closer, Zeke saw that the vibrant carvings were nothing more than gruesome depictions of horrible, painful deaths in some past or perhaps future battle. As he continued to search the surface of the door, he found amongst the engravings a small knob that appeared to be made entirely of solid gold. He turned it tentatively, feeling the latch give allowing the door to swing inward.

Zeke's eyes were met with darkness, though the scant light that seeped in from the outside did illuminate the beginnings of a set of stairs leading into the vast underbelly of the ship. A fresh gust of fear swept over Zeke as he considered the idea of entering the darkness and exploring the depths of Naglfar. Nevertheless, he felt compelled to continue; someone, or something was in that gloominess and he had to face it.

The stairs were steep and continued downward in a tight spiral. There were no railings, so Zeke found himself stretching his arms to the sides, feeling for the cool walls and using them as guides. Eventually Zeke reached the bottom, his feet finding security on a flat, solid surface. Darkness, however, continued to pervade his surroundings. He felt its touch on his skin, almost as if it had a life of its own. Standing in the dark, Zeke felt exposed. He imagined all sorts of chilling entities that could be dancing around in the shadows, and he shuddered again with fear. His mind began reeling with dread-filled thoughts. He wondered again why he was here in the Mist and what possible good he could do while he stood helpless in the dark.

Then a quiet thought entered his mind, reminding him that somewhere out there in the vast incomprehensible Mist, others were watching over him with hope and expectation.

Know that your courage will light your way.

Finding courage would be a difficult task, Zeke thought. But perhaps, if he were to put one foot in front of the other, that, in itself, would be enough.

Zeke extended his arms, groping the darkness for some unseen danger. As he walked, a cloud seemed to lift from his eyes, little by little, until his surroundings were exposed by a kind of dim morning light. Zeke found himself walking a long corridor, its sides crammed with row upon row of weaponry. Glimmering swords, sharpened lances, and heavy battle-axes, along with shields and thick armor, stared out at Zeke like sinister foes, the toys of the devil himself.

Turning his eyes and his thoughts away from the brutal implements of war, Zeke's gaze was attracted by a narrow beam of light that almost seemed to resonate from the far end of the passage. He immediately began marching toward it, sure that his purpose in the Mist was somehow connected to that light.

As he approached, the light shone brighter and larger, its

radiance now filling the corridor. Then, he stopped abruptly, disbelief and alarm filling his mind.

Inside the light, floating on a bed of air, was Taylre. To Zeke, she looked almost angelic, though her tattered clothing, tangled hair, and broken glasses seemed to mock that impression. Nevertheless, the light surrounding her made her glow, like a treasure on display at a museum. He tried to step in closer and touch Taylre's sleeping form, but something prevented him from approaching. As if some unseen force was reflecting his progress.

"There are things, it seems, that can even surprise me," a voice said, startling Zeke out of his shock. He turned around quickly to see Loki standing in the darkness, his manner relaxed as he leaned against the heavy shelves of the narrow corridor. "How did you, Zeke Proper, manage to cross the seam into the Mist?"

At the unexpected sight of Loki, Zeke began to feel an overwhelming fear begin creep back into his mind. He tried to speak, but the words would not come. The dread of facing Loki, the beast that killed his father, made it even difficult to breath.

"Never mind, you stupid, pathetic dwarf. It doesn't really matter, you see," Loki scoffed. "In a moment this will all be over. You will die. Your friends will die. And the little distractions that your supposed benefactor sent will simply get bored and fly away."

Zeke, though encumbered with fright, was watching Loki as he spoke, his words spilling out like poison. When he mentioned the birds and the existence of a "supposed benefactor", his look became shaded, almost fearful, as if the appearance of the ravens in the real world brought a measure of dread to Loki as well.

"Wha...who..." Zeke tried to say.

"Wha...who..." Loki mimicked, a kind of childish inflection in his voice. "Oh, do speak up, simpleton. I don't have time for your babbling, you see. Nevertheless, I do see that you've found my prize." His eyes shifted from Zeke and gazed intently, almost hungrily, at Taylre. "She will indeed make a splendid hostage, don't you think?" Loki smiled, but Zeke noted that it seemed forced, as if things weren't going quite the way he had planned.

Zeke turned to look at Taylre once again, and saw the faint shimmer surrounding her body, a faded appearance of a mirage that diffused the yellow light. Suddenly, Zeke realized why he could not touch her: she was not in the Mist. She was still in her own world, Midgard. Zeke couldn't touch her because the seam was preventing him from slipping through, back to his own world. He realized that the Mist was a confusing place, that its make up was a complicated maze of doors and windows that would only open and close for those who truly knew the way and *understood its passages. Right now, Zeke was just a guest.*

You must let go of your fear.

Zeke looked back at Loki. His smile was still there, but worry was evident in his eyes. "You...you've got to let her go," Zeke stuttered.

"Oh, do I? I think not," Loki answered.

"Then I'll just take her," Zeke said boldly, though his voice continued to quaver.

Loki laughed, his tone bitter and belittling. "You can try. However, I think you will discover that it is easier said than done. You can see her, but that is only because she is stowed deep in the bowels of my ship, you see. It has the special ability to be in two places at the same time. Unfortunately, she does not," he said pointing at Taylre.

"So what are you going to do then?" Zeke asked, his voice gaining confidence. "You obviously wanted us all here in La Cueva del Diablo to kill us. So why not do it? I'm here. Taylre is there. The Captain and Devon are in the cave. Kill us. Just get it over with." Zeke could hear himself talking, but couldn't believe what he was saying. It was as if someone else were giving him the words.

At that moment, two things suddenly occurred to Zeke. One, Loki seemed to be stalling. Why wasn't he attacking Zeke? If he was so intent on killing him and the others, why not do it now? Zeke was defenseless and would fall easily to Loki's power. Why not end it now?

Two, Loki had the ability to move at will into and out of the Mist. But instead of facing the giant ravens that menaced him on the other side, he chose to come here, to escape.

Loki was afraid.

A voice echoed again in Zeke's mind.

Your greatest battles have to be fought here. You cannot win any other way. Face the Entity and relinquish your fear.

Fear was the key. Loki fed off of it. Fear in the presence of Loki made him stronger. But here, within the Mist, Loki was powerless, at least he hoped he was. Zeke would be safe as long as he relinquished the terror that Loki's very existence caused.

"You...you are... a coward," Zeke said firmly.

Loki's eyes squinted as the smile disappeared from his face. "What did you say, scum?"

"You heard me. You are a coward. A nothing. You once had it all. You were a god. Now you are nothing, and you are afraid. I can see it in your eyes." Zeke stepped forward and Loki actually stepped back.

Zeke paused for a moment, caught his breath, and tried to maintain control.

"We're going to leave here now. We're going to take all of

the children you stole. The Captain, Marjorie, Devon, and I, we are all leaving. We are taking Taylre too. You," Zeke said, his voice rising in controlled anger, "will leave and never come back. Your time here is done."

"No!" Loki screamed, his shout penetrating the air causing the receding fear to once again creep up Zeke's spine. "My time here has just begun, a fact that you're going to have to get used to! I will leave when I'm good and ready, not when some inferior dwarf like yourself tells me to."

Loki turned quickly, groping toward the darkened passage, its long shelves lined with the deadly implements of war, and pulled down a sharpened spear. With the speed of a trapped animal and the deftness of a seasoned athlete, he whirled around, throwing the missile at Zeke, its sharpened tip finding the flesh of his thigh.

Zeke shrieked as an explosion of white-hot pain erupted from his leg. He fell backward, his head striking the shelves behind him, but managed to reach for the lance, its driving length still protruding from his pierced muscle. He pulled at the spear, feeling and hearing the sucking squish of wounded flesh as the muscle surrounding the lance molded itself, cramping in a spasm of agony. Helmets and swords fell from the shelves, dropping on his head and chest. The sounds of clanging metal striking the floor beside him echoed Zeke's own cries of anguish. Then, with a final, quick jerk, he pulled the spear free, its painful extraction followed by a gush of hot blood.

Zeke screamed again, rolling over on his side and grabbing hold of his pant leg, the denim material darkening with the flow of red.

Encumbered by the weapons that had fallen, Zeke pushed them aside, his mind whirling with panic as the heat of the wound enveloped him. In his agony, Zeke also felt the overwhelming need to move, to prepare himself for another onslaught from his enemy before it was too late.

"Now you'll get your wish, Zeke Proper! Prepare yourself for a most painful death." Loki laughed, the raspy, deep-throated, raucous sound filling the bowels of the ship with a kind of insane mirth.

He bent down, retrieving a heavy battle-ax from the floor, a remnant of the weaponry that had fallen on Zeke when his body struck the shelving.

"This," Loki said, holding the arched blade high above his head, "will take you apart one swipe at a time. I really do think I'm going to enjoy this, you see."

Zeke rolled quickly and painfully to his left, but not before catching a glimpse of light reflecting off the blade, its downward thrust moving rapidly. Without thinking, as if the impulse were sent from somewhere within the Mist, Zeke grabbed a shield *that lay within reach, pulling it over his body.*

The sudden impact of the axe head on the shield sent a shudder through Zeke, accentuating the ferocious pain that had seized him. He shrieked as the bleeding wound in his leg contracted, pouring more blood through its gaping hole. And yet somewhere, deep within the secret recesses of his mind, there echoed a call, a voice that pleaded.

Anger will be your motivation. Let it guide you.

Pulling free of the paralyzing agony that tore at his leg, Zeke reached for the discarded lance, its tip still dripping with his own blood. He gripped it firmly, the weight and balance extending the length of his arm. Loki stood over him, his frustration emphasized in grunts and screams as he tried to extract the battle-axe's blade from the shield. As he pulled it free with one final groan of effort, Loki once again raised the weapon, his determination hardened; his will to slay his enemy inflexible.

A shadow of darkness passed over Zeke's mind. He recognized that he would soon black out; the pain's grip was too strong. He struggled to hold the lance as his strength ebbed, knowing the end was near. Despite his anger, despite his will to thrust the spear into Loki's black heart, he could not hold on. He quickly whispered a silent prayer to any god that would listen, his lips moving in quiet petition.

Suddenly, the darkness passed, and a warmth as pleasant

and fresh as a spring morning enveloped Zeke. The pain in his leg faded, and his eyes seemed to brighten. Indeed, the very air surrounding him appeared to sparkle with a charge of electricity. Loki's mouth fell open, and he dropped the ax, its metal clanging to the floor behind him. He began to back up, his face turning pale, his lips trembling.

Zeke watched in amazement as Loki inched away, his hands raised defensively, his eyes no longer glaring down at him. Instead, Loki seemed to be looking around in panic, as if he were suddenly faced with his own deceitfulness. Finally, Zeke, gaining a measure of courage, took his eyes off Loki, feeling the presence of another person nearby.

The woman who appeared to Zeke's right was beautiful. He stared at her in complete amazement as her still, tall, and slender form, commanded instant authority. Zeke felt an immediate desire to obey whatever command she put forth; her power and strength was at once recognizable.

Her hair was long and blond, braided down the length of her back, and held fast with a solid gold clasp. Her features were sharp with high cheekbones and her skin was completely unblemished, as if she were Galatea herself, a polished sculpture that would soon take on a life of its own. Her eyes were a striking aqua blue, the color of a warm tropical sea, and from them there seemed to radiate an intensity that held power and confidence. In her left hand, she held a shield bejeweled with what appeared to be rubies and diamonds. In her right, she held a sword that glimmered with a light that shone from the woman herself. Her frame was covered with sparkling armor that extended to her knees, and her feet were shod with sandals, leather straps wrapped crisscross up the length of her calves.

"Come to collect some souls, Shaker? Or Are you just interested in witnessing the demise of my young friend here?" Loki spoke from the shadows of the long hallway. He was attempting to make his voice sound confident, but it was quite obvious to Zeke that the woman who stood staring at Loki was terrifying him. His voice shook when he spoke and he fidgeted compulsively: rocking from side to side, repeatedly wiping his hands down the sides of his pants as the sweat on his palms accumulated.

"You know why I've come, Loki. The Allfather has sent me." The woman's voice was as smooth as her complexion, and yet the air seemed to reverberate with the certainty of its conveyance.

"Ah," Loki said. "So the great benefactor has chosen to save yet another worthless grub worm from destruction. So typical of his cowardice."

"Shut your mouth, Loki! Odin is given only respect. You will not profane his name in such a way while I stand." The woman moved forward, her shield raised, her sword at the ready.

Loki took another step backward, this time striking his head against the shelves and knocking down more of the weaponry. "Keep your distance, Shaker," Loki murmured. "This is not my time, and you know it."

"Perhaps not your time, Loki, however, new chains have been fashioned, ones that are stronger, and ones that will not yield to your strength. I've come to take you. To once again bind you before you cause anymore mischief."

Loki took a quick intake of breath. Zeke, still sitting on the floor, could almost taste the fear Loki had at the mention of chains.

"I'll not be threatened, Shaker. It would take you and all of your sisters to bind me again. Even then the task will be difficult."

"Then leave, Loki. You've caused enough trouble here." The woman named Shaker lowered her shield, but kept her sword at the ready. "I will call upon my sisters if necessary, but there's no need to start a war now. Just leave. Take the Frost Giants with you if you choose, but leave this place in peace. There has already been enough death and pain."

Loki looked from Shaker to Zeke, his eyes closing to narrow

slits of loathing as a reluctant sense of resignation came over him.

"This is not over, Zeke Proper. I'll leave. However, I will be taking Taylre. She is mine, you see. There is nothing you can do. If you want her, come and get her, if you can."

Loki stepped back farther into the darkness of the corridor and then vanished, leaving Zeke alone with the woman, the glowing, unconscious form of Taylre still stretched across a floating wisp of air.

Shaker, the woman, the stalwart figure who stood beside Zeke, shifted her eyes and stared at him. "You must leave the Mist now," she ordered, her lack of emotion unsettling.

"First tell me who are you," Zeke said. "Where did you come from?"

The woman seemed to pause, and though Zeke wasn't completely sure, because her expressions were subtle, he could have sworn that she was troubled by the direct question. As if it had never happened before.

"I am Shaker," she finally answered. "I am one of the twelve sisters who serve Odin. We are the Valkyries. It is our charge to watch over the warriors and bring them home to Vahalla." She stopped speaking, and her eyes softened. She turned and looked directly at Zeke.

"Are you a warrior, Zeke Proper?"

Zeke was flustered by the sound of his own name being uttered by this valiant beauty, but not surprised. He'd seen so much lately, the fact that she knew his name was of little consequence.

"No," he answered quietly. "No, I am certainly no warrior." He looked at Taylre, a sense of deep sadness filling his mind.

"But Taylre," he said pleadingly. "Can he really take her? Can't you stop him?"

Shaker shook her head sadly. "No. She is without the Mist. I cannot interfere in Midgard. It is not my place. But you," she continued, her expression neutral, "must try harder. You have strengths that you know not of. Work with them. Practice them. If you don't, you will remain weak, and your friend will perish. It is up to you."

Then, as quickly as she appeared, she left, the air shimmering around her vacant form like heat rising from the arid desert sand.

CHAPTER THIRTY-SIX
Return

Zeke opened his eyes to an onslaught of movement sweeping past him. Dirt, rock, and sand seemed to be flying everywhere as it was kicked up from the heels of those who rushed by. Among the scattering throng were giants and members of the Ferocious Fenrirs. Most of the Fenrirs were directionless. They, like Taylre and Teddy Walford Sr., had awoken from their spell to find themselves in an unusual and unfamiliar location. The giants, however, had their sights fixed on Naglfar and the safety of its underbelly.

The ravens, Huginn and Muninn, continued to circle the cave, swooping and diving, biting flesh and pecking at the eyes of the giants. Their determination to inflict as much discomfort on them seemed relentless.

Zeke's attention was drawn to a slight movement beside him. He turned his head as much as possible - his body still encumbered by the ropes - and saw the Captain and Devon, their backs turned to Zeke, trying to untie the complicated knots that held Marjorie Anders.

"I'm...I'm here," Zeke managed to say.

Both the Captain and Devon whirled around, shock and confusion across both of their faces.

"Where have ya been, lad?" the Captain questioned. "Ya weren't thar a moment ago."

"The...the Mist," Zeke said painfully, as he tried to push his voice past the incredible thirst that tightened his throat and the throbbing ache that pulsed in his upper thigh.

The Captain paused for a moment, considering the implications of Zeke's words. Then he nodded. A simple, knowing movement coupled with a smile of understanding.

Released from their restraints, both Zeke and Marjorie Anders moved into an awkward sitting position. Their tired and battered bodies felt the affects of their earlier rough handling. Zeke had the added pain of a now unseen wound, but one that could certainly be felt. He looked about him. The riot of fleeing bodies was beginning to calm. The giants had all gathered on the ship, pulling in the gangplank and unfurling the sails as if their intentions were to make a swift departure. The remaining

Fenrirs were huddled on the wet sand near the water's edge, most hidden behind boulders and rocks of various sizes. Marjorie, her face tear streaked, looked about the cave wildly.

"She's not here, Aunt Marjorie." Zeke spoke earnestly, his voice revealing anger.

"What do ya mean, lad?" The Captain said, a shared sense of doom emanating from him to Devon and Marjorie. "Is it Taylre that yer speaking of?"

"Yes. Taylre. She's not with the group of kids over there. She's in the ship. Loki has her. There is nothing we can do about it, at least not now."

The Captain stood quickly, anger and hate clouding his features. "I'll be damned if thar isn't som'thin to be done!" the Captain said, hefting his shotgun over his shoulder and heading toward Naglfar.

"Stop!" Devon shouted, his arm reaching out to grab hold of the Captain's pant leg. "You'll lose if you go over there. Zeke is right. There's nothing we can do. I have a feeling we need to let this go for now. Our time will come. We've got to be patient."

"But we've got to help her!" Marjorie yelled, standing uneasily, pushing the Captain as though urging him to battle.

The Captain held Marjorie's arms as frantic tears coursed down her cheeks, her panic and irrationality stopping him in his tracks. He turned back and looked from Zeke to Devon, his mind swirling with a myriad of emotion.

"Stop, Marjorie. Stop. The boys are right. This isn't the way."

Marjorie crumpled to her knees, her loose, gray hair falling over her face, covering her red, swollen eyes and muffling the shuddering cries of pain that choked past her throat.

"You...you've got to stop him, Bartholomew. He...he'll take her. Then we'll never see her again."

The Captain bent to his knees, taking Marjorie in a full embrace, pushing back her tangled hair and brushing the tears from her face.

"Marjorie. We'll get her. I know it." Then he turned and looked again at the faces of Zeke and Devon, whose own stares reflected a kind of hopelessness.

Suddenly a loud crack issued from behind them, reverberating off the walls of the cavern. The noise sent the ravens scattering out of the cave, their wings beating frantically as they sailed up higher into the sky, their black bodies fading into the gray heavens until they finally disappeared. Another crack sounded as a second thick rope, one that held the giant ship fast, snapped.

Naglfar rose out of the shallow water of La Cueva del Diablo.

The four onlookers stared in wonder as the ship lifted higher and higher, as if on invisible wires, its masts nearly brushing the ceiling of the immense cave. It started forward, the sails filling magically with some unseen wind. It moved slowly, maneuvering expertly through the boulders, passing the smoldering forge, and soaring quietly over the heads of the Fenrirs. Giants stood on its deck, jeering at the confused onlookers below as the ship finally passed out of the cave and into the open cove. It lifted even higher, marking its way through the narrow inlet, hovering over the open ocean, casting its shadow over the bow of the Skipper Jack that still lay at anchor in the rolling waves.

Zeke, Devon, Marjorie, and the Captain joined the rest of the youth who stood on the soft, wet sand watching the amazing spectacle. Some stared open mouthed while others kept wiping their eyes and then opening them again to see if what they were looking at was real. Finally, Devon gasped and pointed at the flying ship as the macabre figure of Loki appeared, his long blond hair tossing in the wind, his form bent casually over the gunwale. Beside him, held tightly in his grasp, was Taylre. To the onlookers she appeared to be in a trance, her eyes unfocused, her body limp, and her features blank. Loki stroked her coarse hair almost lovingly, his wicked glare with its twisted smile penetrating the gray light and focusing on Marjorie Anders.

Marjorie let out one last shudder of pain and then fell to the ground as the ship continued to drift, once again, through the air, its ghostly form melding into the fog.

ᛦ

There were over twenty passengers on the Captain's boat, but virtually no conversation, as they made their way through the turbulent afternoon waves back to Alder Cove. Behind them sailed the Skipper Jack with Devon at the helm and Zeke, who was moving slowly with an obvious limp, pulling and fastening the halyards. Ol' Nessie was in tow behind the Skipper Jack.

The Captain held a stoic pose as he guided his boat into the marina, his thoughts bombarded with the competing control of emotion and logic. Beside him, sitting on the musty floor of the cabin, was Marjorie Anders, her face blank and unreadable as she stared off into nothingness. On the deck, huddled in an attempt to stay warm, were the remnants of the Ferocious Fenrirs, a group of outcast youth who involuntarily succumbed to the whisperings of another outcast. Their minds were muddled with the mumblings of confusion as they tried to sort out the sordid events of the last few days. Most of them were too confused to put words to their experience.

Notably absent on the deck were Teddy Walford, Jr. and Chaz Nelson. Their lives had obviously taken on a new and deadly direction as the influence of evil became too much to resist.

The Captain pulled his boat in easily next to the floating pier. The stranded youth watched as he shut down the engine and climbed over the sides, tying the craft securely to the wooden dock. The youth exited quietly and orderly, making their way sullenly up the boarded pathway to the marina gate. Vivian Proper stood at the threshold of the gate and watched as each former member of the Ferocious Fenrirs walked past her into the barren streets of Alder Cove where no parents waited, or, for that matter, cared. She could tell from their passing faces, however, that something had changed inside each of them. Their brush with true evil had forever altered their perceptions of themselves; that sharing this experience with others would be useless, perceived only as another lie. Nevertheless, they knew better.

Vivian passed through the gates and walked toward the Captain and Marjorie who stood next to the slip where Devon was easing in the Skipper Jack. When it, too, had been tied off, the small group silently huddled together in a comforting embrace, saying nothing, but together shedding silent tears.

"Where's Taylre?" asked Vivian.

The Captain looked into her eyes and shook his head, his mouth unable to speak the words. Then he turned to Zeke who was looking out toward the horizon, past the white capped waves, and into the fog.

"Did ya see the way they went, lad?"

Zeke nodded almost imperceptibly.

"Aye, Captain," he said, pointing toward the northeast. "That way. Toward the mist."

Read on for a special preview

Gates of Asgard

The Zeke Proper Chronicles: Book Three

...coming Summer 2013!

An odd diffusion of light and movement, reflected through the broken lenses of her glasses, caught Taylre's attention, making her believe that the thing that was crawling out of the small hole was a cat, one that had encountered a brutal life of near starvation and the mange. Then she saw the tail, the long, skinny appendage that dragged itself behind the animal like a dead snake. In horror, Taylre realized that the pitiable small cat was in fact a hideously large rat. As she reared back on her tiny cot next to the cold, bare, stone wall, drawing her knees up to her chest and wrapping her arms around her legs, she wondered how the creature had managed to squirm its fat body through such a small opening.

The rodent, perching itself on its haunches near the barred, wooden door, looked up at Taylre and appeared to be smiling, its jagged, sharp teeth reflecting a dull light that managed to penetrate the minute cracks in the granite walls. Taylre felt her heart sprinting as a shiver parted the middle of her back, both from fear and from the coldness that surrounded her in the tiny cell.

Taylre had woken from a fitful sleep about an hour before and found herself curled up in a fetal position on a filthy cot. A thin mattress that covered the rotting wooden slates displayed a myriad of stains and exuded an odor that she couldn't quite identify, but tried hard to ignore. When she woke she found her mind still raced with nightmarish visions of burning flesh, snarling wolves, and the vile, contemptible grin of Almar Loden, whose face seemed to be peering down at her from some faraway place, a place shrouded in mist and memory. She struggled to shake the cobwebs from her thoughts and push away the mental pictures that haunted her, hoping she could make some sense of her present surroundings.

As she stared through the broken lenses of her glasses, occasionally sobbing with an inescapable sense of loneliness and dread, she had a vague recollection of someone entering the stone enclosed cell at some point during her captivity, but the memory seemed to be shrouded in in a hazy fog, like a hard, cold mist that settles amongst a forest of thick trees. The person who entered brought in a plate of food that still sat on the dirt floor beside Taylre's cot. The rat was eyeing the platter and appeared to be weighing the possibility of making a run for it but couldn't seem to decide what kind of threat Taylre might be. Taylre looked again at the food and saw that a thin layer of green fuzz had begun to grow on its surface. Her appetite, meager though it was, instantly left. She reached down slowly from her tucked position, careful not to startle the creature, and grabbed the plate of food, throwing it hard. The mangy rodent barely moved as the fuzz covered meal hit the wall above its head, the metal plate clattering against the stone. Immediately the rat raced to the largest piece of moldy food, grabbed it in its jagged teeth, and dragged it into the narrow hole it crawled out of. Taylre shuddered with relief as she watched the creature disappear into the narrow fissure between the granite.

With the food now gone, Taylre discovered her hunger again. She thought of her grandmother; how she used to hum quietly to herself as she baked cookies in the kitchen, the thick aroma of molasses and ginger wafting through the air. She thought of her own bed with its cozy down comforter, the one she would sometimes grab and drag into the family room, wrapping it around her shoulders as she and her grandma sat on the couch watching old movies together. She reflected, with a brief smile, how they would share a big bowl of hot buttered popcorn, savoring each crisp bite.

Her stomach began to growl.

Suddenly, the thick wooden door that kept her prisoner, shook. Taylre assumed a fearsome wind had begun to blow, but then quickly realized that someone was trying to enter. She began to panic. Once again she brought her knees up to her chest, drawing them in tightly with her long, skinny arms. Her breath came out in bursts of terror, and she imagined with horror that her worst fears had come true: her life would now come to a violent end in this godforsaken place, and she would never have the chance to ask her grandmother for forgiveness.

Brad Cameron

is a high school English teacher who has been inspired to write Young Adult Fantasy through his countless hours of teaching and reading to students. He is an avid follower of all things mythological. When not writing, Brad spends his time in the outdoors either on his bicycle or motorcycle touring the stunning countryside near his home. Brad is currently working on book three in the *Zeke Proper Chronicles, The Gates of Asgard.* Due out in the Summer of 2013.

To learn more about the Korrigan and Loki, the trickster god who spawned her, and Ragnarok visit www.bradcameron.net.

Made in the USA
San Bernardino, CA
17 February 2018